EAGLE AND THE FLAME

ADAM LOFTHOUSE

B

Boldwood

First published in Great Britain in 2025 by Boldwood Books Ltd.

Copyright © Adam Lofthouse, 2025

Cover Design by Colin Thomas

Cover Images: Colin Thomas

A CIP catalogue record for this book is available from the British Library.

Paperback ISBN 978-1-83678-522-4

Large Print ISBN 978-1-83678-521-7

Hardback ISBN 978-1-83678-520-0

Ebook ISBN 978-1-83678-523-1

Kindle ISBN 978-1-83678-524-8

Audio CD ISBN 978-1-83678-515-6

MP3 CD ISBN 978-1-83678-516-3

Digital audio download ISBN 978-1-83678-518-7

This book is printed on certified sustainable paper. Boldwood Books is dedicated to putting sustainability at the heart of our business. For more information please visit https://www. boldwoodbooks.com/about-us/sustainability/

Boldwood Books Ltd, 23 Bowerdean Street, London, SW6 3TN

www.boldwoodbooks.com

In loving memory of Jo Randall-Kattner.

1

JUNE, AD 367

Summer in the far north always was a bit of a non-event. Something southerners talked of; something people of the north could never quite comprehend. That day was a reminder why.

It was a grey day. Low banking cloud swept across a desolate landscape, and a hint of rain hung in the air, threatening to unleash the gods' wrath on them at any moment.

A grey day, not that Tribune Sixtus Victorinus seemed to care. He was a man built for grey days. For howling rainstorms and the crack of thunder, for over-sized coats of fur and wide-brimmed hats to keep the rain from his face.

He wore such a hat today. As dark as the rain

clouds, as miserable as the scowl he wore on his bearded face.

'What do you see, Halfhand?' he called to one of his men, who had dismounted and was on all fours, studying the pattern of footprints on the grass, as at home as a smith at the forge.

'Footprints going south,' Halfhand said in that rasping voice of his, as if he had swallowed the smithy's flames and was choking on the coals.

'How many?'

'Too many to count. Thousands, for sure.'

'When?'

'Yesterday? Maybe the night before.' Halfhand moved forwards on his knees, prodding a pile of excrement before leaning down and giving it a sniff. All about the glamour, this one.

The wind kicked up a stir, rolling off the distant hills to the east, rippling through the long grass.

'How could we have missed them?' Victorinus mused, nudging his horse around so he faced the north.

Ask anyone in the south, even the south of this desolated island, and they'll tell you there's nothing north of the Wall. Nothing of note, anyway. And they'd be right about that, in a sense, Victorinus supposed. But there was a lot of land. A lot of space, a lot of hills and mountains. Enough for thousands of men on foot to pass without them noticing.

There'd be hell to pay when they got back south of the Wall. His commander did not take kindly to failures, didn't take kindly to Victorinus on the best of days.

'And where are they going? And why?' Drost added, eyebrows furrowed together in a frown.

Victorinus looked at the young man from the corner of his eye, mounted as he was, just to his right. Drost was a recent addition to their little band, the only one of them with ties to the tribes north of the Wall. 'Was about to ask you the same thing.'

Drost looked at his commander, his young face a picture of innocence. 'How would I know? I've been with you for the last year.'

'Must have friends though, right? Family?' Cassius asked, dismounting and walking towards Halfhand, who was once more on his feet.

'You miserable old bastards are all the friends I've got,' Drost said with a scoff. 'As for family, can't say I've got any of them either.' His frown returned as he spoke. 'And anyway, it was you, Cassius, who led us on that winding route through the hills. We might have caught a sniff of the bastards if we'd just stuck to the tracks we know.'

Victorinus knew the young Caledonian was hiding something. He'd turned up at Fanum Cocidi the summer before, speaking perfect Latin, practically begging to be enlisted into the miles areani. There had been something off with that. Couple of things, if Victorinus was being honest.

Firstly, no one begged to be let into the areani. Plenty of good men have begged to be let out, but none let in. The pay was less than even that of a border legionary, the length of service the same. The survival rate was also a good deal lower, since instead of spending your twenty-five years' service tucked up in some cushty fortress surrounded by your comrades and high stone walls, you operated in small groups, out beyond the frontier, hunting enemy soldiers.

Lastly, it was the job of the miles areani to keep tabs of the tribes north of the Wall, the very people Drost had come from. They were the ones sent into tribal territory to negotiate with the chiefs; they were the ones who risked being invited into a round house with a smile and the promise of wine and food, only to never leave again. It was the way a lot of Victorinus's old comrades had met their end. Had nearly happened to him a few times, and he had the scars to prove it, didn't he? Luckily for him, he was pretty good with the sword he wore strapped to his waist; not bad with a spear either.

But Victorinus had been desperate for men. He was always desperate for men. So he had taken Drost, and so far, the lad had given him no bother. The suspicion, though, never went away. He was, however, right about one thing: it had been Cassius who'd suggested they take the longer route through the hills. He had no time to wonder why, just now.

'How long back to the Wall?' Victorinus called to Halfhand.

Halfhand was a natural scout, had been a natural soldier until he'd lost half his left hand fighting in the last civil war some thirty years ago. He'd been in the Sixth Victrix, fighting his way south through Gaul and into Italy, waging war for the usurper Constantine as he fought his brother for the throne. Both men had been sons of Constantine, the man whose rise to power had begun right here, on Britannia's northern soil. Halfhand had got his shield arm caught in the crush outside Aquileia, the fingers cleaved off by a probing sword. The army's loss had been Victorinus's gain. Nearly in his sixtieth year now, Halfhand was still the best man in the unit.

'Half a day's ride, we won't make it before sundown.'

'To Vindobala?'

'Aye.'

Victorinus nodded, tipping back his hat to view the foreboding cloud. 'We keep going, no stopping until we're back amongst friends. Won't let a bit of rain dampen our shine, will we, lads?' he said, smiling at the mutters his men returned.

There were six of them in total. Victorinus was their leader. Men often joked that in the history of the empire there had never been a tribune who commanded a unit so small. Victorinus didn't mind. He'd had grand plans once, a burning ambition to rise through the ranks, to lead men in war and earn himself fame and fortune. Life, though, had chipped away at those dreams, dug at the foundations and watched as they crumbled to dust.

He was not old, not by any standard. In his middle thirties, he should have been at the height of his strength and power. Though already he was beginning to run to fat, a once toned body now sitting too snug under his mail. Mirrors were his biggest foe these days. Trouble with mirrors is they show you the truth, not what you want to see. Victorinus much rather preferred the company of whores to mirrors. Whores at least will tell you anything you pay them to.

He knew his once gleaming eyes were now a dull,

lifeless brown. His chin sunken, nestled in a beard that melted into a fattening neck. His nose and cheeks had a red sheen from the copious amounts of wine he poisoned his body with daily. He had collapsed in a barn once, lost in a drunken slumber. His men had been so worried for him they had called a local doctor, who told Victorinus in no uncertain terms when he eventually rose to consciousness that if he did not change his ways, he would be dead by forty. Part of Victorinus had been disappointed the quack had thought he'd live that long.

'Shall I scout ahead, sir?' Pastor asked, reining in his mount alongside Victorinus.

The tribune smiled at the boy, amused by his endless enthusiasm. 'Sure. Though what is the golden rule?'

'Always stay in sight of the column.'

'Always,' Victorinus agreed with a nod. 'Especially today.'

With a salute, Pastor was off, kicking his mount into action. Pastor Benedictus had been with them a matter of weeks. He was an orphan from Eboracum, and Victorinus had found him cleaning the floors in a local whorehouse. After a flagon or two of wine he had asked him if he was up for a bit of adventure. He was a bright kid, pale skinned and wide eyed, a short body still coated in the puppy fat youth should have melted away. He was keen and intelligent, eager to learn the ways of the areani and desperate for a chance to use the sword Victorinus had gifted him for real.

The fool of youth, Victorinus thought. The young dream of battle, of the glory and fame. They see it as a ticket up the ladder, a way to propel themselves to stations their parents could only dream of. Only a man who has actually fought knows war's hidden truths. The stink of blood and shit, the terror of the clash of shields, the screams of agony, the squawk of the crows as they feast on the dead as the sun sets in the west. There is no glory in war. Just those who survive and those who don't.

The rain came. A soft chink on their armour and helms at first, then a torrent so vicious even the fish must have swum a little deeper. 'Can't see the lad.' Halfhand raised his voice to be heard over the rain.

Victorinus cursed, squinting into the distance. How long had he been gone? A matter of minutes, surely? 'He'll be okay,' he said, though he lacked conviction.

Cassius was riding ahead of the column, reaching up from his mount, his eyes fixed on the distance. Victorinus afforded himself a wry smile; things must be bad if that lazy youth was suddenly on the alert. With a start he reared his horse and rode back, hoofbeats dull on the squelching mud. 'That smoke on the horizon?' Cassius pointed south. Through the murk a column of smoke could be seen, a dark spiral in an already dark landscape.

'Halt,' Victorinus called, tipping back his sopping hat to see better. The smoke was pitch black, no hazard of nature. It was made by men. A warning. 'Good spot,' he said to Cassius. 'How far away is that?' This was to Halfhand.

'A mile? Bit more? North of the Wall.'

The tribune nodded in agreement. The hairs on the back of his neck prickled as a cold rush of fear swept through him. It was a warning, a warning for them. 'Can anyone see Pastor?'

Silence greeted his question, just the hammering of the rain and crush of the easterly wind. 'Skirmish line, move forwards at a walk.'

They spread out. Five men, fastening helmets and baring swords. Victorinus had the centre, Halfhand to his left, Cassius to his right. Drost had the far right and Severus the left. They moved forwards, dull yellow cloaks billowing around them. Victorinus had swapped his hat for a helm, his lank dark hair a tight fit under his drenched leather head protector, though it stopped the helm rubbing against his scalp.

The smoke got closer, and Victorinus felt the unease in his stomach like a sinking stone, weighing him down. He had grown accustomed to strange goings on north of the Wall. The Caledonians were a barbarian people, capable of unspeakable horrors, but not usually a people to do the unexpected. Thousands of footprints imbedded in the wet grass pointing south was not what Victorinus had expected to find when he had roused from his slumber that morning. Something was afoot in the wildlands, something strange and unnatural.

And now a vast column of smoke had appeared on the horizon. What would his commander say?

Come on, Pastor, where are you? He liked the youngster, liked all his men, truth be told, even Drost. He would not forgive himself if he lost one of them on his watch. Victorinus was many things – unreliable, hard to like, an outcast in every sense. But his men all knew he would not see them come to harm. He was respected, even if he would never be loved.

They climbed a steep ridge, the column of smoke growing closer. Victorinus held his breath, the stench of pitch and smoke attacking his throat and nostrils, and he felt the first hint of water in the corner of his eyes. It would become unbearable the closer they got. The wind seemed to whisper to him, a calling or warning Victorinus could not decipher. He felt as if he was riding towards something unnatural, something gods made. He wondered if he should turn his men around. Cassius was once more ahead of the line on the right, urging his horse up the hill, an urgent look on his soft-skinned face.

They were just about to crest the top of the rise when a figure on horseback appeared, flying at full gallop towards them. Victorinus just had time to make out the white of the beast's eyes, the rider a black silhouette, a sword held high over his head.

'Break!' Victorinus called, and at once his men obeyed, splitting left and right. Victorinus, though, stopped his mount and stayed rooted to the spot. He wanted to move, to turn and flee from this cursed hilltop, but something held him in place.

The rider drew nearer, and over the howling of the wind he heard a manic scream, saw spots of blood fly from the raised blade. And then he sagged in relief as he recognised the wide-eyed boy who rode past him, screaming incoherently as he did. 'Pastor!' he called as the boy rode down the hill, no sign of having heard. 'Pastor!'

The others had heard though, and they raced off

down the slope after the youth. Halfhand reached him first, grabbing the reins of Pastor's horse and bringing them both to a stop. Victorinus hadn't moved, still rooted to the spot, unwilling to crest the ridge and see what Pastor had been fleeing from. Once more, the wind seemed to whisper in his ear; again, he felt the presence of the gods in the wilderness around him. What trick was this? What heathen lord had penetrated his mind?

Pastor was being led back up the hill, flanked by the four men of the areani. 'You're going to want to hear this, boss,' Cassius said as they approached. The rain pounded them, the clang of it striking six helmets almost deafening. Victorinus thought he caught a smirk twitching the corners of Cassius's mouth, and he was about to curse the foolish youth, then stopped himself and sighed instead. 'Am I, though?' he muttered under his breath, reluctantly turning to face Pastor.

The boy's face had a blue tinge, the sickly edge a man has after a night spent drinking too much wine. His wide eyes quivered in fear; jagged red lines ran along the edges; tears cut rivets in the black pitch marks that lined his face. There were the same black marks over his cloak and mail, fresh mud on his boots. His horse, though, a grey gelding, seemed to have no such marks, as if the beast had been kept well clear of the smoke.

'What happened, Pastor?'

'F-fire,' Pastor stuttered out.

'No shit,' Severus scoffed, earning a cuff round the head from Halfhand and a burning glare from Victorinus.

'Pastor?' Victorinus said in a soft voice, moving his mount so he was side by side with the boy. The wind swept through them once more, breathing wordless whispers into Victorinus's ear. 'Pastor?' Victorinus said again, brushing the rain from his eyes.

'Men. Fire. I... I killed them,' Pastor said in a distant voice, his eyes lost in the horror he had just witnessed.

'Severus, stay with Pastor and give him some wine, try and rouse him from this. The rest of you, with me.'

They rode at the trot now, cresting the ridge and seeing the landscape open up before them. A wide flat plain, void of trees or bushes or streams. Unremarkable in every sense of the word. Except for the huge fire that roared in its centre.

Approaching, scarfs or scraps of cloth hastily wrapped over noses and mouths, they began to appreciate the sheer scale of the fire, in height and width.

'Seems to be in some sort of shape,' Halfhand

called over the wind and rain, his voice muffled by the cloth over his face.

He was right, Victorinus realised as he stopped his mount fifty feet from the flames. A straight run of flames stretched from east to west before them, and what appeared another straight line ran from the east towards the south.

'Looks like a V?' Victorinus moved. Was this some message to him? A warning from one of the tribes? How did they get it lit in this rain?

He looked down at the ground, made out the footprints imbedded in the grass. They were going south.

'They passed this way,' Halfhand said, as if reading the tribune's mind. 'Yesterday, morning I'd say, though the rain makes it harder to tell.' He had dismounted and was once again on all fours. 'No wagons though, no wheel marks that I can make out. That fire was made with pitch, and you'd have needed wagons to drag enough fuel up here to get it going like that, especially in this weather.' He squinted as he looked up into the dark clouds.

'Wasn't lit yesterday though, was it,' Drost added, dismounting himself. 'Wasn't a column of smoke in the sky this morning, and we haven't travelled that far today.'

Victorinus said nothing, but he agreed. The fire

was fresh, still growing, the flames still roaring, defying the rain. This had been lit today. He looked up at the rain-sodden sky, seeing the lighter patch of cloud to the west, revealing where the sun hid. It would be dark soon.

'Bodies!' Cassius called, some way ahead of them, still mounted. Victorinus followed him, drawing up his mount before two lifeless bodies, heaped one atop the other. 'Halfhand,' he called. 'See what you can tell me about these two.'

Halfhand duly obliged, rolling the first over to get a better look. The first thing that struck Victorinus was that the men were not from amongst the tribes. The Caledonians painted their faces, tattooed their bodies and dressed a certain way. This man had no tattoos, and he was dressed in Roman cloth and boots to match. His hair was a dusty brown, his eyes wide with terror, and there was a gaping hole in his chest.

The second was still face down in the dirt. Everyone jumped when Halfhand rolled him over and he coughed and spluttered.

Victorinus was off his horse in a heartbeat, kneeling down in the rain as the wounded man gasped for breath. He had an almighty gash through his stomach. He hadn't been stabbed, but swiped at with a longsword, his guts half poking out through his tunic. Victorinus studied the wound with a veteran's eye. He saw the entry point, on the man's right hip, the exit on the left hip where the wound grew shallower. He was wounded before the other man was killed; must have been, as the dead man had been almost on top of him.

'What happened here?' he said, leaning in close, smelling the blood and rot on the dying man's breath.

'He... killed... us,' the man whispered through heaving breaths.

'Why?'

'We... weren't... supposed... to die,' he said again in a whisper.

'Who are you?' Victorinus asked, urgent now, seeing the life slip from the man's eyes.

'Valentia,' he whispered with his dying breath, the word dragging out until at last his lungs emptied. His head flopped back to the mud, mouth still open, eyes fixed on the sky.

'What's Valentia?' Drost asked. Victorinus hadn't realised he had been standing at his shoulder.

'I've no idea,' he said, rising to his feet. 'But I've a horrible feeling this isn't the last we'll be hearing of it.'

'Three hours to the Wall,' Halfhand said, looking at the sky.

'And an army of Caledonians ahead of us. Something is afoot. Come, let us be away.'

Victorinus cast one last look at the bodies, and then the raging fire. The two dead men were covered in soot and their hands were black. He was in no doubt that they had lit the fire. But why? What, or who, was Valentia? And how had young Pastor managed to kill them both on his own?

They waited for Severus and Pastor to catch them. The youngster was still in a state of shock, unable to explain what had happened. Cassius had his arm around his friend and whispered urgently into his ear. *Let him recover at his own pace*, Victorinus thought. *Let his friend comfort him. After all, he's just a kid.*

Severus was of an age to Victorinus. He had served as a marine on the Rhine flotilla for ten years, fighting the Alamanni on a fair few occasions. Victorinus wasn't exactly sure what had made him swap the bows of a ship for the nomadic life on horseback they led, but as usual, he hadn't asked too many questions.

Always grateful for men.

They carried on south in the pouring rain. Each man lost in his own private thoughts.

2

A weak sun broke across the eastern horizon. The rain had stopped sometime in the night, though the strong winds continued to bluster their way in from the North Sea, rolling off the steep hilltop to the east.

Gaius Felicius, prefect of the Fourth Cohort of Gauls, stood on the northern wall of Vindolanda, his mouth hanging open in shock. He wore just his night-shirt and sandals and would have felt the cold from the biting wind if he had not been numbed by the sight that lay before him.

'And you heard nothing in the night? Saw nothing? No flames or shadows? No screams or shouts?'

The optio, in charge of the last watch of the night, shifted uncomfortably under his commander's gaze, wishing he were anywhere but there. 'Nothing, sir. None of the lads did.'

'And you patrolled on the hour every hour, as you are supposed to?'

'Aye, sir. None o' the lads were sleeping at their posts, none complained of hearing or seeing a thing. Though the wind and rain would have provided perfect cover for them,' the optio said, jerking a nervous thumb to the north.

Felicius puffed out his cheeks in shock. It was not unheard of for a small group of tribesmen to sneak over the Wall under the cover of darkness. Maybe they'd steal a few sheep, maybe they'd force themselves on a woman or two. But they were always caught, always punished; the areani saw to that. But this, this was something entirely different.

Looking out, over the wall, the fields to the north were a sea of painted tribesmen. Spears reflected the pale sun's light, swords shone in the dawn. Felicius had never seen anything like it.

'What do we do?' Vitulus said in a low murmur. He was Felicius's senior centurion and commanded the first century of the Fourth Cohort. Battle hardened, with the scars to show it, he had become invaluable to Felicius. But Felicius could see the fear in his eyes. That same fear, he knew, reflected in his own.

'Have the men form up ready to march in an hour. Every man ready for battle, and we take only the provisions we can carry.'

With his orders given, Felicius walked towards the steps, leading down off the battlement, to get himself ready to depart. He cast one last look around the fortress before he did, as if saying goodbye. Vindolanda had been the home of the cohort for longer than he had been alive, and not once had it fallen into enemy hands. He wondered how this could have happened in his time.

Felicius was an experienced commander, in his late thirties. He had fought in both the east and the west, placing himself in high regard with every general he had fought under. He had been wounded on the Danube frontier, fighting the Alamanni under the magister militum Valerius Jovinus. A spear had struck under his shield, piercing the calf muscle on his left leg. His appointment to the command of the Fourth Cohort of Gauls had meant to be a sort of early retirement for Felicius, who even now still walked with a limp.

Though Felicius had never seen it that way. His cohort was the best fighting unit left on this windswept isle, even finer than the Sixth Victrix and the Second Augusta, whose names were famous across the breadth of the empire. Those legions though, like most of the famous names of old, were nothing more than border forces now. Commanded by tired old men, filled with cutthroats and duty shirkers, they were a shadow of their former selves. They may still carry honours on their standards, but the men who had fought to earn them had long since joined their gods.

The Fourth Cohort of Gauls were going to earn their own honours, and Felicius himself would have the privilege of attaching them to their standard. That was what he had promised his men when he had been appointed their commander, five years previous.

And now, at the first hint of action, he was ordering them to run away.

'What in God's name is happening?' a woman's voice said. A shock of dark hair appeared in the stairwell, followed by a pale face and a bright red dress.

'Lucia, my love, you should not be up here,' Felicius said, approaching his wife and embracing her. 'Go back to our rooms, make sure Marcelina is okay.'

'She is with the nursemaid, she is fine,' Lucia said in that fiery tone of hers.

Lucia was highborn, cream, as Felicius's friend Victorinus would have said. The cream were the elite, the cream of society. Senators, governors, high-ranking generals; they were the men from the old families, the men who really ran things in this empire. Sure, there were emperors, and they held their courts in the east and west, gave orders and painted their faces and pretended to be gods. But it was the cream who carried out those orders, the cream who whispered in the emperor's ear, planted the seeds and watched them blossom.

Lucia was the eldest daughter of Julius Narcissus, governor of Britannia's most northern province, Flavia Caesariensis. Her father was in the fortress, though Felicius had not yet mustered the courage to go and rouse him from his slumber. His guard were here; surely one of them had been on the walls this morning? They would let him know.

Felicius had not been an obvious suitor for the governor's daughter. He was not highborn. His father had done his twenty-five years in the army, serving the great Constantine. He had saved his money well throughout his service, bought himself some land in northern Gaul on his retirement. There he had met Felicius' mother, and, well, the rest was history.

Lucia, though, was a woman driven by passion. She had first laid eyes on Felicius when he had arrived at Vindolanda to take up his new command. He was dust covered from the road, limped as he dismounted his horse, and Lucia had thought there had never been a finer man. They had been married within the month.

'She won't be for long, you need to make ready to leave,' Felicius said, already wincing as he anticipated the backlash from her tongue.

'Leave? Retreat from that rabble? Are those my father's orders?'

'No, my love. They are mine.'

'Well, I never thought I'd see the day,' she said, sticking out her chin and casting her eyes to the clouds.

'We cannot hope to fight so many,' Felicius said in a pleading tone, chiding himself as he did. What did a woman know of warfare, after all?

'And do that rabble have ladders? Siege engines? Are they going to batter down our gates and climb our stone walls?'

'Lucia, there are over two thousand men there, by my reckoning. They are thirty miles south of the Wall, and I have no idea how they got there. This isn't normal; this is no mere raid. Something is happening here, and I don't know what. Until I know more, my orders are to retreat to the south. We gather more men as we go and then we can coordinate our attack plan.'

'And the people in the vicus?' she asked, gesturing

to the settlement to the west of the fortress. It was common for the locals to build a small town on the outskirts of a military base. There was custom for whorehouses, smithy's, taverns and barbers, plus they had the added advantage of being near high stone walls should the worst happen.

Well, today the worst had happened. 'They are already overrun, there is nothing we can do for them,' Felicius said, full of regret. He, like most within the fortress's walls, had friends out there in the honeycomb alleys.

'Have they tried to attack?' she asked, her eyes roaming the buildings to the west, seeing for the first time the bodies of the dead on the flagstones.

'Not yet. They seem to be building something, can't make out what.'

And then it happened. With a roar and a blaze, a fire erupted on the northern plains. The tribesmen cheered and hollered, whooping for joy as they danced around the flames. The fire grew in strength, thick black smoke wafting towards an already dark sky. 'Is that a V?' Felicius asked, his face pursed in puzzlement. 'Have they meant to do that?'

He looked to his wife. He saw it, the briefest look of fear, before her face set in a heavy frown. 'My father needs to see this immediately. And you are right, my love, we should leave.'

'Lucia, what is it?' But she was already gone. Clattering down the steps, she raced into the fortress.

Felicius paused for a moment. Why had the fire scared her so much? In fact, that had seemed to be the only thing that had scared her this morning. And why was it suddenly important her father come and see it? Surely the two thousand warriors who had built it were more of a concern. He wasn't sure what concerned him more, the two thousand warriors at his door, or his wife suddenly agreeing with him.

He walked down the stairs, shouted orders at his centurions as he made his way through to the praetorium, the beating heartbeat of the fortress. It was there the clerks and the slaves kept the clogs of the cohort moving forwards. There where the men were paid, where rations were issued, new armour bought and records kept. There it was decided when a soldier would be discharged, when they would have their annual leave, when they would be free of their monotonous routine to see their families.

Felicius had, of course, given up his quarters for the governor upon his arrival, and it was to there he rushed, following the echo of his wife's footfall. He was fifty paces from the door when he heard her scream. He was in there with her before she could utter another sound.

'Lucia, what is it—'

He barged his way into the chamber, pushing past the two guards who stood either side of the door, their spear tips glistening in the glow of a nearby brazier. They hesitated to get out of his way, then hesitated again, unsure whether to follow him in. For surely nothing could have happened to the governor inside? They were guarding the only door in and out.

Lucia was on her knees, quivering hands covering an ashen face. She whimpered and sobbed, rocking back and forth, shaking her head. He was struck by a wall of stench all too familiar to a man of war: the iron tang of blood, rotten bowels leaking from a dead man's corpse.

'You should leave, my love,' Felicius said gently, trying to raise her to her feet, his eyes all the while fixed on the sight before him.

The governor was dead. Throat cut, a bloodied knife resting in his right hand. That, though, wasn't what held his attention, and he'd wager it wasn't what had set the governor's daughter into a frenzied state, for they had never been close.

It was the V on the governor's chest, burned through hair and skin, smoke still drifting from the brand. The brand itself lay on the floor by the bed, the scorched metal still sizzling.

'What in the gods names is happening?' Felicius muttered, still trying to drag Lucia to her feet.

There was a gust of wind, strong, unnatural, and its force slammed the door to the chamber shut, leaving the mortified-looking guards alone outside. The brazier, roaring just moments before, blew out, and white smoke filled the room.

Coughing, Felicius moved over to the window and forced open the shutters, the smoke clearing in moments. When he could see again, his eyes were drawn away from the mutilated corpse to the wall behind the bed. 'Valentia' was written on the plaster in blood. Still wet, slithers of it ran down the wall.

Felicius felt panic grip him like winter. The fear had hold of him, rooting him to the spot. His mind froze, heart thumping like he was riding into battle. And still he stood there, his grieving wife all but forgotten next to him.

3

'How many do you think there are?' Halfhand asked. He bit into an onion, its sharp scent carrying on the breeze, causing Victorinus to wince. He never could understand how his friend ate them raw. Put them in a stew, sure, but to just bite into one like that? Not for him.

'Two thousand?' Victorinus mused, rubbing his mare's flank as she shied away from the noise and smoke.

They had ridden through the night, entering Vindobala under the cover of darkness. The fort had been deserted; the gates left open. There was no sign of a battle; in fact, Halfhand had guessed the legionaries manning the fort had left before the Caledonians had arrived, their hobnailed footprints being shallower in the grass. On every door and wall a V had been painted in red, a couple of them still wet, the paint running down the walls like blood. The store rooms were empty, so too the armoury, and judging by the smashed locks and broken doors, they hadn't been emptied by the legionaries.

Riding on as a weak sun broke through the heavy cloud in the east, their progress had been hampered by refugees blocking the roads. There were people from every local farm, village and town for a hundred miles, all running south down the main roads. They flocked to Victorinus and his men when they saw their yellow cloaks billowing in the wind as they rode. 'It was Saxons, Lord! Saxons, this far inland! They took my daughter, my little Amia. Please, Lord, please help me get her back!'

'Franks! It was Franks, sir, I know, I fought in the field army for ten years! Got this scar, look, right here, was a Frankish axe that did that! Must have been a hundred of them. They burned my barn, killed all my slaves and filled their packs from my granary before they burned that too! Where is the army, sir? When are we going to get help?'

'Northmen loose on the roads! Everywhere! They came in the night, burnt everything. We managed to get out, thank the gods, but our neighbour Cato was caught. They forced him to watch whilst his wife was raped, and then they started on his children...'

'Valentia! That was their war cry! Just kept screaming it over and over. What is it, sir? What is happening? You're an officer, aren't you? Can't you tell us anything?'

'The fires, sir! They are setting fires everywhere! Great big things, burning brighter than the sun. Look! Look! In every direction! What do they mean, sir? What's happening?'

And sure enough, everywhere they looked, stretched beyond every horizon, were thick, black columns of smoke.

Victorinus cast an uneasy look to the west, where yet another column of smoke had appeared. He rubbed his tired face, fat fingers rubbing through a lank beard, and sent up a quick prayer to the gods, the true gods, not the Christ god, for he had never succumbed to Christianity, no matter how many thousands of other people in Britannia had. Not that he'd ever speak to anyone about his own religious beliefs. Way he saw it, religion had done more bad than good in its time. Wasn't that long ago Christians had been persecuted right across the empire. He had no interest in getting into some argument or another about which god he should be praying to. Wincing as his knuckles dug too far into weary eyes, he looked once more to the west and felt the familiar pang of guilt as he did. As much as his heart pulled him that way, over those rolling hills, towards that column of smoke, his head was telling him to keep going south.

'Go, if you need to,' Halfhand said, seeing Victorinus's gaze.

'No.' The tribune shook his head. 'I won't leave you, not now.'

'What's in the west?' Pastor asked. He had recovered on their night ride, in a way only the young can. He was back to his usual self now, if still a little pale.

Victorinus still had questions to ask the boy, but he figured it could wait out the day. Just why had he dismounted his horse? He looked once more at the youth's soot-stained cloak; at the grey mare he rode that was suspiciously devoid of the same marks. The tribune tried to picture the youth riding over the same ridge he had, seeing the fire. Why approach? Especially when there were two armed men in plain sight. Pastor was no warrior, had never used his sword in anger until the previous day. Didn't seem the logical thing to do.

'Nothing that concerns you,' Victorinus said, rather harshly. He chided himself; he had no reason to be so hard on the boy, just a nagging feeling in the back of his head.

'So, what's the plan, Chief?' Drost asked. He carried a single-headed war axe, a weapon he always claimed to be far superior to the sword. He hefted it now in his right hand, reins gripped in his left.

'Recognise any of them?' Victorinus asked with a nod down the slope.

The six men were atop a small cliff, unassailable from their front, which was just as well. For below them were two thousand or more tribesmen, their blue faces streaked with black smoke and soot. Another fire had been lit, once more in the shape of a V, and they seemed to dance around it as if it were some sort of god.

'Aye, I see the same colours as you.' Drost spat on the ground to show his disdain. 'Don't know what the bastards are doing here though, if that's what you mean.'

Victorinus nodded; he had expected no less. He was feeling more comfortable with the Caledonian than he was the previous afternoon when they had first seen the fire. Drost had been nothing but loyal and dependable since signing up to the areani, and whatever lay in his past, he'd proved himself when it counted in the last year. Drost had taken no leave

since joining with Victorinus and his troop, and neither sent nor received any correspondence with
anyone from the tribes. *He is loyal*, Victorinus assured
himself.

'Cassius, you have the best eyes. Can you see any
of our lads on the walls of the fortress?'

Cassius had been with Victorinus for two years.
His father was a blacksmith by trade, making swords
for the legion based at Eboracum, or so Cassius has
said. The two had gotten into a fight, the father
kicking Cassius out into the street. Cassius had never
said about what, had looked half starved when he'd
approached Victorinus on his way out of the city one
morning. Victorinus had taken the lad in, always desperate for men.

He was small, Cassius, slight of build and lacking
in height. His blond hair as bright as the sun, pale
cheeks still smooth. He looked no older than Pastor,
though Victorinus mused he must be nearly twenty by
now. He could have passed for thirteen at a push. He
was lazy by nature, though quick witted and usually
the first to jump on any opportunity to get a dig in at
his colleagues, though to Victorinus's surprise, he
seemed to have given Pastor nothing but support in
the last day. In fact, he hadn't let the lad out of his
sight.

'No, sir,' Cassius said after a moment. 'Dust column far to the south of the fortress though. Maybe they've legged it?'

'Not like the prefect to run from a fight,' Severus said, removing his helmet and scratching his bald head.

'No, it isn't,' Victorinus agreed. He stared at the walls of Vindolanda, the beating heart of the Fourth Cohort of Gauls. Prefect Gaius Felicius was a good friend of his. They had met shortly after Felicius's arrival to Vindolanda. Victorinus had been there, checking in with his commander, and the two had been introduced. By the following dawn, after a fair few jars of a good Spanish red, the two had declared themselves long-lost brothers. Despite their many differences, and Victorinus's initial jealousy of the esteemed career Felicius had enjoyed – one which a youthful Victorinus had assumed was his for the taking, many years ago – they hadn't had so much as a minor disagreement since.

'So, what's the plan, Chief?' Drost said again, as restless as the skittish horse beneath him.

'Well, we ain't getting through that lot.' Victorinus gestured to the milling tribesmen below. 'They don't look like they've made any attempt to attack the fortress, or even surround it,' he said, more to himself than anyone else. He looked to the fortress's west, to the smoking ruins of the Vicus. The people there, it seemed, had not been so lucky. 'Not exactly famed for their organisation, are they, your people.'

Drost laughed. 'We tribesmen are many things. War lords, we are not. If Felicius had got five hundred men out of there without these curs noticing, I wouldn't be surprised.'

Victorinus chewed his bottom lip. Once more, his gaze was drawn to the west. 'So, what do we know?'

'Sir?' Halfhand asked, eyebrow raised.

'I said, what do we know? We know an army of Caledonians has crossed south of the wall, possibly after assisting with the fire we saw yesterday. We know they have attacked other settlements from the refugees we met on the road. We know there are potentially Saxons and Franks to the east, presumably come over by ship, which isn't uncommon. We know the north is in chaos; there are people crammed on the roads, panicked, leaderless, with no idea why this is happening to them.'

'Caledonians south of the Wall isn't unheard of. Saxons and Franks raiding from across the sea is standard, especially considering the state of the Navy these days. For it to all happen at the same time though?' Severus let his question hang in the air.

'Yes, that is odd. And we know that for some reason everyone seems to be obsessed with this Valentia, whatever that is.'

'And we know there are Roman troops abandoning their posts and letting the whoresons through the Wall,' Drost added.

'Do we?' Cassius said. 'We know the cohort at Vindobala left; we don't know they are traitors. Maybe they just saw the numbers coming towards them and lost their courage?'

'No,' Halfhand cut in. 'I'm sure they left before the Caledonians were even in sight. In fact, the more I think on it I'm sure they did. And it ain't like we've seen any sign of them since crossing back to our side of the Wall.'

'We need information,' Victorinus said, speaking before his men's debate turned into an argument. 'Halfhand, Severus and Drost, I want you to go back to Vindobala. Go east and speak to the men at the forts, if they're even still there that is. Find out what you can. We'll ride north and meet you in one of the forts along the Wall, one week from today. We need to know if they've seen any other Northmen coming south, and what they know of the Germani landing on the eastern coast. And if they've heard of this Valentia, of course.'

Halfhand nodded. 'Where will you go?'

'I'll take Cassius and Pastor and catch up with Felicius, if that is his cohort's dust cloud on the horizon, see what he knows. Then I'll head for Eboracum and see if I can find either the Vicarius or the governor. One week,' he said, looking each man in the eye. 'Are we agreed?'

Hands were shaken, jokes made, and then the six men split into two groups, heading opposite ways. Below them on the open plains, tribesmen yelled and whooped as they finally realised they were being watched, but the men of the areani were long gone before they could get within spear range.

* * *

Victorinus rode west, Cassius and Pastor in tow. The weather turned for the better as they travelled, skirting the southern plains littered with armed tribesmen. The sun broke through the low banking cloud, though the grass and trees still glistened with the night's fallen rain.

'Maybe your father could help us?' Victorinus said to Cassius, who was chewing furiously on hard tack as they rode.

'Help with what?' Cassius managed to say around his mouthful.

'He must be a man with many contacts. He must have heard something. Doesn't he still supply swords to the Sixth Victrix? I'd wager their commander knows more of what's going on than we do.'

'We know nothing,' Cassius said, swallowing with a wince. 'And I doubt my father does, either.'

The tribune studied Cassius a moment, wondering at the sharpness of his voice. He'd never actually met Cassius's father, knew the lad had gotten himself into some sort of fight with the man. Maybe he wasn't ready to reconcile their relationship? The thought made him feel uncomfortable. Fathers and sons. He looked west, over the horizon, then pushed it from his mind. The gods knew there was enough going on in there. He looked over his other shoulder at Pastor. 'Tell me what happened.'

'Huh?' Pastor said, as if snapping out of a dream.

'Back over the Wall, the two men you killed. Tell me what happened.'

'I don't understand,' Pastor said. Victorinus saw the boy pale under his gaze.

'You rode off. When you left us there was no smoke, yet when we caught up with you there was a roaring fire in the shape of a V and you had killed two men. Tell me what happened.'

'Not much to tell.' Pastor shrugged. Victorinus felt his impatience grow.

'I want you to tell me what happened in as much detail as you can and then explain your actions.'

Pastor seemed to consider this a moment, before shrugging reluctantly and beginning to speak, slowly at first. 'I rode off, crested a ridge and rode down the other side. Realised I had broken the golden rule and had gone out of sight of the rest of you. But then I saw the smoke, just over the next ridge. Curiosity got the better of me.' Another shrug. He wouldn't raise his eyes to meet with Victorinus.

'You could have been killed,' Victorinus said through clenched teeth.

'I wasn't.'

'What happened when you crested the second ridge?'

Pastor sighed. Victorinus wondered if it was through frustration at having to relive the previous day's events or something else. He hoped it was the former.

'I saw two men lighting the fire. They had flaming torches, stunk like pitch. They saw me the same time I saw them, so I drew my sword and rode down to meet them.'

Victorinus grunted, though already deep in thought, remembering the wounds the two men had received. Neither had been killed from horseback, he didn't need Halfhand to tell him that. Both men had been killed by sword wounds by a man on foot.

'Why did you dismount?'

'What?'

'You said you rode down the hill, sword drawn. But those men were killed by a man on foot, not a man on horseback. Your cloak was covered in black grime from the fire, the skin on your arms and face too. Your boots were coated in mud, yet your grey mare had no marks on her at all. What I'm saying, Pastor, is you got closer to the fire than your mount did. So why dismount?'

'I... I don't know. I don't know why I did any of it,' Pastor said, a quiver in his voice now. 'Never killed anyone before.'

'Knew how to use that sword though, didn't you? Weren't one of my lads who showed you that, not in the short time you've been with us. Where did you learn?'

They rode on into a small crop of woodland. The track narrowed so they had to ride single file. Victorinus pulled aside and let Pastor go through first, his right hand straying from the reins to the hilt of his sword. It was quieter under the canopy of the trees, just the rustle of the wind through the branches and the birds serenading them with their songs.

'I used to watch the men who came to the whore-house,' Pastor said after a while. 'Had a friend, a kid my age called Fullo. We'd practise with wooden swords in our bedchamber, doing the moves they did.'

'Different doing it for real than it is with practice swords, though.'

'Yes. It certainly is.'

They left the woodland and rode into bright sun-light, riding in stoic silence. The wind had blown most of the clouds away, the sky above a pastel blue. Ahead of them a track ran through a valley, and at the end they could see the main road south. Victorinus looked to the west once more, at the foreboding column of smoke. Seemed more menacing in the sunlight, the whirling black somehow darker against the lighter sky.

Halfway down the track they came upon a small farmstead, a lone man on the roof of a rickety old barn, checking the damage the rain had wrought.

'Salve, brother,' Victorinus called. The farmer looked up from his work, seeing the faded yellow cloaks and the mail beneath. Reluctantly, he descended a bowed wooden ladder and approached.

'Salve,' the man said, removing a cap from his head and using it to wipe the sweat from his forehead. 'Can I help you, sirs?'

'Never been called sir before!' Cassius said with a snort. Victorinus silenced his man with a hand, before turning back to the farmer.

'Have you seen the Fourth Cohort of Gauls come past this way? They're the cohort based at Vindolanda.'

'Aye, came by not two hours ago.'

'Going south? Did any of them speak to you?'

'Aye, they took the road south. One of 'em came over and knocked on the door, said I should get my family out of here and join them on the road. Said there was something coming, something we couldn't survive if we stayed. He was an officer of some sort, long blond hair.'

'Felicius! Good, that's good. Two hours ago, you say?' Victorinus was relieved to hear news of his friend. His death would have been unthinkable.

'Yes, sir, give or take.' The farmer looked up at the sun and gave a shrug. 'Should I be worried?'

'You have a family?'

'Wife and daughter in the house. The girl's only a

babe, not sure how long she would survive out on the road.'

'She has more chance than if you stay here. A storm is coming, brother, best get yourself out of its path.'

* * *

They reached Felicius and his cohort at high noon. The rain clouds were a distant memory, the sun scorching, the wind non-existent.

Victorinus sweated in his mail, and his wide brimmed hat rubbed at his scalp as he removed it, lank hair immediately sticking to his face. The prefect and the tribune clasped arms in the warrior's embrace, each man giving the other a warm smile, despite the desperate circumstances.

All around them was the clamour of armoured men on the march. The smell was of leather and horse dung, the dust cloud around them a whirling mass. Men shouted and sung, insults were traded along the column, the air full of the usual banter between the horsemen and infantry.

'Do you have any idea what's happening?' Victorinus asked Felicius in a low tone, not wanting to be overheard by the marching men.

'I was hoping you would, brother.' Felicius grimaced, blue eyes downcast. Victorinus saw fear there, in those crystal blue eyes that normally held so much life. He did not think he had seen that in his friend before.

'We should talk. Shall we go for a ride?'

Felicius looked up and around, blinked, as if seeing his men for the first time. 'Yes. Yes, I think we should.'

They gave their orders then took their leave, riding south for two miles before stopping their horses under the shade of a small crop of trees at a junction on the southern road. Dismounting, they shared a small lunch of fresh bread, ham and cheese, washed down with a small amphora of red wine. It was strong, un-watered, and just what they both needed to take the edge off.

'You want to go first,' Felicius said after a while. Victorinus had been enjoying the peace. There were no refugees crammed on the road this far south, no people in widespread panic. For a moment, it just felt like a normal summer's day, out for a ride with an old friend. He sighed, sitting up from where he had been lounging, knowing the moment could not last.

'Was just a normal summer. We'd been out over the Wall for a couple of weeks. There had been some unrest in the west and we had been staying at the fort at Fanum Cocidi for a few days, riding out with the dawn and coming back in the evening. Seemed one tribe had taken offence to another tribe's leader turning down a daughter's hand in marriage. Nothing major.' Victorinus stopped, swirling the last of the wine around in his wooden cup.

'Then one day I sent Halfhand out east with one of the lads, the new one, Pastor, just to check in on some of the other tribes, make sure all was in order. And they weren't there.'

'Weren't there?' Felicius scowled. 'People don't just vanish.'

'You've not spent much time in the north, have you? People do just vanish, all the time as it happens. But normally it's one man, or two, maybe a small group. I'm talking about thousands of the bastards, whole tribes gone from their settlements.'

'You had no idea about any of this? No clue where they were going?'

Victorinus shook his head. 'None. We rode east once I'd heard, entered every settlement we came across, saw no one. All the huts were empty, fires cold. No livestock, no grain.'

'So what did you do?'

'Halfhand tracked them. Got easier when the rain

came; there being no roads up there, we just followed the flattened grass. And that's when we found it.'

'Was it a giant fire in the shape of a V?'

Victorinus nodded. 'Same as the one outside of Vindolanda.'

'Ah, you saw that then?' There was shame written all over Felicius's face. Victorinus knew too well it would have hurt the prefect to abandon the stone walls his cohort had called home for a generation or more. More than he would ever admit.

'You did the right thing, leaving.'

'Did I? We don't even know what we're running from. We're just running.'

'Where are you headed? To meet with the governor?'

'He's dead, Sixtus.' Weren't many men who used Victorinus's given name, was normally reserved for family. Not that he had one any more.

'Dead? How?'

Felicius spoke of finding the body in his quarters at Vindolanda. He told of the branding on his chest, of the smell of rotting flesh, the iron tang of spilled blood. He spoke of a gushing wind that tore the shutters off the windows, the writing in blood on the wall.

'Valentia.' Victorinus said the word before Felicius did.

'How did you know?' Felicius said in a small voice. He had grown pale, and looking at him, Victorinus could see his usually well-groomed blond hair and beard were ragged, standing on end. The tribune wasn't sure what to make of his friend's story, wasn't sure what to make of anything that had happened in the last couple of days. But he could see his friend was well and truly scared, and that was enough to scare him.

'The fire we found in the north. Pastor had gone ahead to scout; he came across the fire before we did. There were two men, I guess the two who had lit it, and Pastor fought them. He killed the first, but the second was still alive when I got there. I tried to get him to talk before he died, but he only said one word.'

'Valentia,' Felicius said, rubbing his face aggressively, as if he could rub this all away.

'Don't suppose you have any idea what, or who, Valentia is?'

'Nope.' They sat in silence a short while. Victorinus looked across the junction to the west, the black column of smoke still visible beyond the horizon.

'You should go to them.'

'It was made clear to me that my presence there was no longer welcome.'

'Sixtus, this is different. They could be in danger.

Also...' Felicius trailed off, as if he was unable to find the words.

'What is it? Has something happened to them? If you know something, brother, then you'd better tell me!'

'No, no, nothing has happened that I know of.' The prefect raised his hands in defence. 'It's Lucia.'

'What about her?' Victorinus scrunched his face in confusion.

'When we found her father's body, I saw something in her face I had never seen before. It was more than just a daughter's shock at seeing her father's corpse. She was terrified. It has something to do with this Valentia, but she won't tell me what it is.'

'She'll speak when she's ready, I'm sure. You two have always been rock solid.'

'She won't come south with me. She insists on going west, to the farm.'

'And you want me to take her?'

Felicius shifted uncomfortably. 'You need to go, Sixtus. You need to make it right.'

The tribune sighed, rubbing his weather-beaten face with one of his paw-like hands. 'I know I do; I just don't know how.'

'You always were shit with women. Shit with people in general, actually.'

They both laughed. 'Why do you think I took this job? I can go weeks without speaking to anyone apart from one of my lads over the Wall. It's bliss.'

Felicius shifted uncomfortably, rubbing his back on the tree trunk he was perched against. 'You got something to say, just say it,' Victorinus said, knowing too well when his friend was about to say something he didn't want to.

'It's just...'

'I could do more! I could stop drinking! I could still be the soldier I always thought I wanted to be!' Victorinus finished with a flourish, wine slurping from his cup as he waved his hands extravagantly through the air. 'I could put up with it, coming from her. Still seems to hurt more coming from you.'

Felicius winced. 'It's not a lecture, I promise you I'm done with those. But this job you have, the time you spend away over the Wall, it isn't healthy. Think of all the time you have missed out on with—'

'Don't mention them, brother.' Victorinus spoke in a low murmur, his tone laced with venom. 'Please, don't.' He didn't know what hurt him more – Felicius having the gall to say those words to his face, or Victorinus knowing his friend spoke true. Trouble with the truth is it ain't always what you want to hear. Easy to lie to yourself, tell yourself you're doing the right thing, even when you know you're not. Victorinus had mastered it over the years, falling down the same rabbit holes, pulling out the same self-destructive tricks. He knew what he had become, what he had let himself fall to. He snorted to himself. What was he doing here, anyway? What business did he have involving himself in some disaster or other? Rome would come, Rome would put things right, just like she always did. Would be men like Felicius who saw to that. The straight-backed officers of the army, shepherding their men into line, putting steel in their men's veins. What good could Victorinus add? He was just an outcast, a scout. Good for nothing, best kept out the way. That's what she had said to him, last time he'd come knocking.

From the north they heard the distant rumble of men on the march, some background noise to drown out their awkward silence. The dust column from the Fourth Cohort of Gauls appeared a moment later. It seemed their time alone had come to an end. 'Will you go?'

Victorinus stood, wiping the dirt from his tunic. He pondered a moment, waiting for his courage to fail. But it seemed it held on yet. Draining his wine cup helped. 'Aye, I'll go. Seems like we might all be dead soon anyway, might as well try and make things right whilst I can. What will you do?'

'Head south, find the Dux. Fullofaudes is not perfect, but he's an experienced military commander. He'll know what to do.'

'Keep in touch, brother. We're going to need to stay close if we are to survive this thing. I'll try and make contact with some of the commanders of the northern units. There must be some who haven't deserted.'

Felicius stood with a wince. 'Damn leg,' he muttered, rubbing at his left calf. 'We've barely covered any ground, not sure how it's going to hold up if we end up marching the length of the country.'

'You want me to find you a cart to ride in?'

They embraced, sharing a laugh at the cheap joke, the tension between them easing. Victorinus could not shake a sense of looming foreboding though; even the wine hadn't helped shift that. He felt a stranger in a country that should have been home. He scanned the horizon in every direction, dreading the sight of more black smoke pluming to the sky. 'I'm going to stay off the roads as much as I can. I'd suggest you and your men do the same, though it will hardly improve your progress.'

Felicius offered a shrug before speaking. 'I have five hundred battle-hardened men at my back. Reckon

I've a better chance on the roads than I do cross-country. Lot of space up here, lot of miles to cover. I think we'll be safe enough.'

'You sure your girls aren't better off with you? I'm lacking in manpower if it comes to a fight, can't see how I'm going to keep Lucia safe if we meet a band of raiders.'

'Tell me something I don't know. But you know what she's like, stubborn as an ox. If she wants to go west, then she's going west. And something tells me she doesn't want to be too far from the north. As I said, there was something, some flicker of recognition, fear, I don't know, when she found her father. Whatever this is, it feels like no mere summer raiding season. Look after her, best you can. Please.'

4

The easterly wind returned as they rode west, harrying their backs along the dusty track. They were five men, two women and a girl, all on horseback. They had ridden for two hours, mostly in silence, each person seemingly lost in their own thoughts.

Victorinus rode with a knot in his stomach. An anchor fit to halt a ship, though he rode on without complaint. Had been a long time since he had ridden this track, a long time since he'd wanted to.

'It will be easier than you think,' a female voice said from behind him. 'Time is a great healer.'

Craning his neck, he looked Lucia in the eye. She was a handsome woman, if not overly pretty. All cheekbones and chin atop a long, slender neck. Felicius was besotted with her, though Victorinus had never quite gathered why. She was amiable enough company, if a little snooty in the way all people born to high society are. Lucia was a force of nature, a woman of such single-mindedness that the mere thought of her not getting her own way was so unimaginable he doubted it had ever crossed her mind. She did what she wanted, when she wanted. Hence why she was riding this road, Victorinus supposed.

Being in the company of a woman with such a strong character was not, however, a new experience for Victorinus. 'Not sure enough time has passed for me to be forgiven.'

'It's been months, hasn't it? How much more time could she want?'

'Another fifty years or so I'd imagine,' Victorinus said under his breath. Pastor frowned at his tribune. The lad didn't know where they were going, and Victorinus hadn't yet mustered the courage to tell him. Cassius grinned. He had ridden this road with Victorinus before. The tribune was sure his men still whispered about their last visit when he was out of earshot.

'Felicius told me of what happened in Vindolanda. I'm sorry about your father.' Victorinus had never spent any time with the governor. He had attended a couple of dinner parties at the behest of Felicius, but had always been seated well away from the more important men in the room. He thought Lucia had probably had something to do with that.

'A horrible business,' she said, her masked expression not changing. She was every inch the patrician, Victorinus thought; 'cream' to her core. He turned back and faced the front, a half-smile on his face. Was it that haughtiness that had attracted Felicius to her? Was it the same feature that had bewitched Victorinus all those years ago? If it had been, he guessed it was just more evidence to the saying that age changed a man. Or a woman.

'Do you know why it happened?'

'Excuse me?'

'Do you know why your father was branded like that?'

Lucia pouted into the silence, lips working like a fish out of water. 'How in God's name would I know?'

Victorinus shifted in his saddle. His grey mare was tiring underneath him. He patted her neck, aware of the strain the miles they had covered in the last three days must be taking on her, especially carrying his considerable weight around. He lowered the brim of his hat. The sun was coming round to the west; he judged it would be setting in the next two hours. 'Something Felicius said to me.'

'And what exactly did my husband see fit to say to you that he did not say to me?'

Victorinus took a deep breath. When you start off down a path, you have to see the journey through. His father had told him that once. 'Just that there was a look in your eyes. As if you had just seen all your worst fears come to fruition.'

Lucia looked to her daughter. Marcelina rode with her nursemaid, the elder woman's hands gripping both the girl's waist and the reins. She had a shock of dark hair like her mother, pale skin like her father. She was looking from Lucia to Victorinus, following their conversation. Two men from the Fourth Cohort of Gauls rode at the rear, sent as an escort for the governor's daughter. Each man was looking over the countryside, studying the rolling hills and columns of smoke that swirled to the sky over every horizon. They appeared to be paying no attention, though both Victorinus and Lucia knew they would be.

Lucia was about to respond when Pastor shouted from the front, 'Riders! Coming towards us.'

Victorinus snapped his head around, alert at once. There was only one place this road led to, and armed men had no business travelling it.

There were three of them, red cloaks billowing as they rode at the gallop. They slowed as they saw the approaching party, the lead man turning and gesturing to the other two. Each man wore mail and a helmet. Victorinus could see their spear tips glisten in the sunlight, the swords strapped to their waists.

The two groups grew closer. The lead rider from the three approaching men wore a cavalry helmet. He lowered the face guard as he approached, showing Victorinus nothing but a face of polished steel.

'Salve,' he called, his voice muffled through the steel.

'Salve. Who are you? What is your business here?' His hand already gripping his sword hilt, Victorinus walked his mount forwards so he was at the front of the column. He felt Cassius and Pastor converge on either side, heard the two men from the Fourth Cohort move up behind them. Safety in numbers.

'That is of no consequence to you, Tribune Victorinus.' The man spoke in a deep, toneless voice. He was out of breath from the hard riding, his deep breaths audible through the helmet.

'You know who I am? Then I'm afraid you have me at a disadvantage,' Victorinus said, trying to keep his own tone light. 'You are travelling on a road from a private settlement. Men armed such as yourselves have no business there, unless they are looking for me.'

'Why would I be looking for you, Tribune? It has been a long time since you lived here.'

Cassius half withdrew his sword from the scabbard, the steel scraping as the blade was freed. Victorinus held out a calming hand. Cassius returned the blade.

'What do you want?' Victorinus felt his skin prickle, and his heart rocked in his chest. Something was very wrong here. He looked past the steel helmet of the lead rider. The two men behind him were greying under their helmets. Both of them had black marks on their red cloaks. The same marks Pastor had borne when he got too close to the fire north of the Wall.

'I want you to give me the road, Tribune. I have the right of passage.'

'I am a tribune of Rome, escorting the daughter of the governor of Flavia Caesariensis. The rite of passage is mine. Now, I shall ask once more. State your name and business.'

His breath was shallow now, growing more urgent with his desperation. It showed in his voice and he knew it.

'My name is none of your concern, as irrelevant as

your rank. As to the governor, we both know that he is now with his maker.' Lucia pushed her horse forwards, iron in her eyes. She withdrew a dagger from beneath the folds of her dress and looked as though she would have charged the man on the spot were it not for the two auxiliaries behind her, who grabbed hold of her reins and pulled her back. She screamed in protest, to no avail.

'And as for Flavia Caesariensis, it no longer exists. You are in Valentia, Tribune, a realm outside the control of your emperor. I suggest you go south with your good friend prefect Felicius. If you value your life, that is.'

'And if I don't?'

The masked man sat straighter in his saddle. He raised his hands to the blue sky and inhaled loudly. Victorinus thought he could make out the whites of his eyes through the slits in the helmet before the helmet was lowered and once more, he could see nothing but iron and bronze.

The horses, though, must have smelt something to fear in the masked man and his companions, as suddenly they began to neigh in terror. Victorinus fought for control of his own mount, and once the beast had settled, he turned to look at his people behind him. One of the auxiliaries from the Fourth was struggling to hold on to his mount. Cassius peeled off from Victorinus's shoulder and rode to the struggling soldier. He reached out an arm to grasp the reeling beast by its saddle, but the saddle snapped and the rider was tossed to the ground with a thump.

'You asked who I am, Tribune. I am a messenger. Cocidius speaks to me. Through his guidance we shall take back this island one province at a time, forge ourselves a new path, a new destiny! You Romans shall fade away across the Narrow Sea, taking your Christ god with you. And when you do, we, the loyal citizens of Britannia, shall be free.'

'You and what army?' Victorinus said through a half laugh, sounding more relaxed than he was. His eyes darted from the masked man to the horsemen behind him. 'No one stands up to Rome and wins. Rome is inevitable, undefeatable. You cannot win.'

'Rome has been defeated before, and she will be again. Nothing is eternal, Tribune. Nothing lasts forever.'

The auxiliary that had been thrown to the floor slowly rose to his feet. His companion had hold of his mount, which was still skittish. Victorinus risked another glance behind him and saw Cassius sheathing a knife, but had not time to ponder why he would have drawn it in the first place.

When Victorinus turned back to his front, the masked man had freed his sword from his scabbard with a screech and kicked his mount forwards. Fifteen paces separated the two and Victorinus was half stunned by the sudden movement. By the time the man was on him, Victorinus just had time to duck a savage blow that would have severed his head before pulling free his own blade and charging at the other two men.

'Roma!' he bellowed as his mount lurched into action. He snarled and aimed himself for the left-hand man, who looked as shocked as Victorinus had moments before. Victorinus pulled back his right arm and slashed down with his blade. The sword struck the man on the shoulder, shattering the links of his mail and biting down through flesh into bone. Blood erupted from the wound, and the man screamed and slumped from his horse.

Victorinus slowed his mount. Turning, he saw Cassius charge the other of the two. Cassius swiped with his sword but missed. His opponent raised his spear and jabbed forwards, aiming for the neck. Cassius jerked to the right to miss the blow before bringing his sword up to knock away the spear. Unbalanced and overstretched now, the man could do nothing as Pastor charged in and buried his sword in his guts. He slumped from the saddle without a sound.

Looking back along the column, Victorinus saw with dismay the masked man had ridden clean through. The two auxiliaries were caught by surprise, one still helping the other after his fall.

The masked man rode off at the gallop, without a second glance back at his two fallen comrades.

* * *

Victorinus sat under an awning, watching the sun set in the west. He felt such a tiredness sweep over him that he had not felt in all his days. His thighs were sore from the constant riding and his right shoulder ached from striking the killing blow on the man on the road that afternoon. Getting old, he thought with a sad smile.

He turned the events of the last days over in his mind, trying to make sense of them, and couldn't. What was Valentia? A person, a place? What was it the masked man had said on the road? 'You are in Valentia, Tribune, a realm outside the control of your emperor.'

A place then. He closed his eyes and tried to empty his mind of the torrent of dark thoughts. This was a plot. A plot against Rome and her emperor. A plot to overthrow Rome's control of first this province and then the island. The thought only darkened his mind further. Who had the power to arrange this kind of thing? Had the Caledonians been paid to attack? But they cared nothing for money; cattle was their coin, pelts their wealth. The soldiers on the Wall, had they been paid to leave their barracks? Gods only knew where they were. Pawing at his face, he wondered what he should do. Had splitting his small force been a mistake? He'd no way of contacting Halfhand, no way of knowing where his friend was.

And to make it worse, the panicked people cramming the roads spoke of Saxons and Franks raiding in the east. Even to his wine-soaked mind, it didn't seem like a coincidence. Who could unite these peoples? Who had the power and the strength of will to bind them to the same cause? Whoever it was, they seemed to have the gods on their side too.

He rose to his feet, wincing at the dull pain in the bottom of his back. He was about to move off when he remembered something else. Cocidius. The god of war and the hunt. The Romans had adopted him; well, the ones in the northern provinces of this island anyway. He was Mars and Mithras reborn, a soldier's god. The masked man had said he was a messenger, that Cocidius spoke through him. But what business did a Roman god have slaughtering his own people?

He walked a few paces, out from under the awning just as the last rays of the sun's red glow sunk below the western horizon. The land was plunged into darkness, the star-filled sky above a haze of purple. Turning a corner, he came to a small farmhouse with an old, dilapidated barn to its right. He had meant to repair the barn. Tear it down and build a new one if necessary. He'd never got around to it, just as he'd never got around to a hundred other important things he should have been focusing his energy on.

Hindsight always gave a man a different perspective. It was easy to evaluate your mistakes once you'd made them. The little decisions you made on the road of your life, the ones you thought had no consequence or little meaning. But just because they had little meaning to you, didn't mean they did not mean the world to someone else.

He breathed in through his mouth and exhaled heavily. He had put it off long enough.

Walking down the road towards the house, he nodded to Pastor and Cassius, who were rubbing down the horses and settling them into the barn for the night. They were talking in hushed tones and grew silent as their tribune approached, each man nodding to him.

Victorinus walked past his two men and approached the door to the house, stopping at the threshold. He heard the voices within and was about to knock when his courage failed him. Turning away, already ashamed of himself, he was about to walk away when the door opened behind him.

'Father!' a boy shouted excitedly and ran out, gripping Victorinus tight around the waist.

Victorinus smiled and, kneeling down, he pulled the boy tight, breathing in the scent of his hair. 'My boy,' he said quietly, a single tear forming in his right eye.

'Where have you been, Father?' the boy asked. 'We had men with swords come to the house. They asked for you but Mother said you weren't here. Then they said they were going to take us and Mother chased them away with a pitchfork! It was really exciting!'

Victorinus could not stop himself chuckling, despite the eerie feeling that crept over him. 'You were not harmed?'

'No, Father,' the boy said, shaking his head.

'Where is your mother?'

'I'm here,' a sharp voice said from the doorway. 'Been a long time since you bothered to come home.'

'Well, you did tell me never to come back,' Victorinus said, and regretted it immediately. Sarai shot him
daggers, and a small part of him died inside.

They had been married for eighteen years. Victorinus was sixteen, she fifteen, when their parents had
escorted them to Eboracum and paid for them to be
wed. They had been so happy. Sarai had been his
childhood crush; Victorinus could not recall how
many days he had spent following her around like a
lost puppy.

In the years since she had proven to him every day
why she was the perfect woman. She stood a head
shorter than him, dark blonde hair cut short so it
didn't reach her shoulders. Her eyes were blue-green,
her cheekbones well defined, and despite birthing
three children, her figure was still slight and firm.

'So why have you?' she said, turning away and
walking inside. Victorinus followed her into a small
kitchen, one of the two downstairs rooms in their
small farmhouse. She reached into a wooden crib in
the corner of the chamber and picked up their
youngest son.

'There's a conspiracy afoot,' Victorinus said absently. He could not take his eyes from her. Truly there
is nothing worse in this world than loving someone

and not having that love returned. Victorinus thought he would rather face a shield wall on his own than Sarai. Though he also knew he could not be without her.

Love. Nothing good ever comes of it.

'Oh, is there really? I hadn't noticed. Oh, no, wait, we did have three men with spears come by here earlier today. They threatened me, saying they would kill our children if I did not tell them where you were. They even threatened poor Publius and Amata, said they would take their daughter.'

Publius and Amata were their neighbours. A lovely old couple, who always thought the gods had cursed them as, try as they might, Amata never could fall pregnant. But not long after her fortieth birthday, when they both assumed all hope was lost, a miracle happened. That miracle was Delphina, their daughter.

'Gods,' Victorinus muttered, 'were any of you hurt?'

'You mean did they defile me? No, they didn't, thank you. Though for once I wished you were here. You could have come in handy with your armour and that ridiculous sword you carry. Not that you would have known which end to point at them!'

'I killed one of them!' he blurted out. He didn't know why really; thought he was just sick of her thinking him so worthless. Without thinking of what he was doing, he told the story of all that had happened to him and his men in the last few days. He spoke of the fires that lit up the night sky, the marauding Caledonians and their siege of Vindolanda. 'This is a conspiracy against Rome, and I am going to stop it.' Even surprised himself saying that.

'You? What have you ever done? How are you going to stop the tribes from retaking lands they think are theirs by rights? You're a drunk, Sixtus. Know your place in this world.'

Victorinus felt his cheeks burn with shame. Here was the root of their problems. The wine. Too many years he had spent finding solace in the bottom of a jug, spent too much of his leave from the areani in Eboracum with his friends, drinking and revelling, when he should have been at home with his family. He had turned a corner in the last months, kept himself out of the taverns and the brothels. It had not been easy, and his men had noticed his struggle, he was sure. But he had told himself it would be worth it in the end, when Sarai saw the change in him, when she would finally let him return home once more.

'I... I...' he stuttered, unable to find the words. 'I know, but—'

'But this time you're going to make it right? Heard it all before, Sixtus, don't make promises we both know you won't keep.'

'But this time I will! I swear it. I'm going to get to the bottom of this uprising, kill those responsible and come back to you, and the boys.'

'We don't need you any more, Sixtus!' she screamed, waking the baby in her arms. 'I haven't needed you for years now. Where were you on the long winter nights, with me left alone to entertain the children, making sure the livestock was fed, the grain wasn't going mouldy in the store house? Drinking and whoring north of the Wall, with all your sad little friends, that's where you were.'

'Sarai, please—'

'And even when you were here, getting two words out of you was like pulling teeth! I tried, Sixtus, for years I tried to connect with you, but you weren't interested. All you did was take me for granted. You neglected me, neglected your children!'

'I know,' he said. Tears of shame fought to be free from the ducts in his eyes, and he tried desperately to hold them back.

'Where were you when our child died?'

It was too much. He slumped to his knees. Beaten.

'I had to bury our little boy alone. Publius helped, even said some lovely words once the deed was done. You should have been here, Sixtus! You weren't.'

He lost the battle with his tears. They fell from his eyes, staining his face. He wiped them away, tasting their saltiness on his tongue. Her words had left him as nothing but a shivering puddle of raw emotion, and he felt his anger rise to force away the sorrow that had been crushing him. 'What neglect do you speak of?' he said, rising back to his feet. 'Have I not provided for you, given you and our children everything you have ever needed? I didn't neglect you, Sarai, I went to fucking work!'

Spittle flew from his mouth as he vented, hands clenched in tight balls, knuckles white, shoulders tense. He wouldn't strike her; would not be able to live with himself if he did. Victorinus had many vices; a woman beater, though, would never be one of them.

'Watch your language in front of your children! And don't preach to me about going to work, you've never done a hard day's work in your life and you know it! Even your father had to pay for you to get that job you love so much.'

The baby wailed, a high-pitched screeching cry that would on a normal day have had Victorinus grinding his teeth in frustration. Today he just wanted to hold him, to tell him he was loved. He heard it said once that a man must lose everything he possessed to appreciate its true value. No man had ever spoken truer.

'I messed up!' he said, holding up his hands in admission. 'I see now how wrong I was, how badly I treated you.'

'We've been through this, Sixtus. I do not wish to tread over old ground.'

'Just give me another chance, Sarai, I beg you. You are my queen, let me treat you as such.'

She moved away. They were still in the kitchen. It was a small chamber, the walls a bare white. He had promised her he would have them painted, bright colours, epic landscapes, vivid in detail. Alas, he had promised her many things.

In truth, he had known the marriage to be over for some time. Since little Leonius had passed from the world, two winters past. He had been north of the Wall, scouting – or drinking and whoring, as Sarai would say – and did not return until early spring.

Sarai had been standing in the doorway to their

home. Their eldest child, Maurus, clutched in her arms. He had known something was wrong when Maurus did not immediately run to him, as he always had when he came home. That time he just stayed in Sarai's arms, his little hands wrapped tight around her neck. 'Where's Leo?' Victorinus had said, not even saying hello to his own wife. Gods, what an ignorant prick of a man he was.

She had said nothing, Sarai, just walked from the front door, past the old barn, to a small patch of grassland, fenced off, sheltered from the sun by an old beech tree. 'He's there,' was all she said, before turning and leaving him alone.

Victorinus had blamed Sarai for his death. Cursed her for not taking better care of his son. He had been just two years old, every bit his mother's son, in looks and spirit. He often wondered if that was why he had loved him so fiercely. Sarai said he had woken one morning with a fever and a rattling cough. The next morning, he had not woken at all.

'I'll not have this conversation again, Sixtus. It is over. I do not love you nor need you. Here,' she said, handing him the baby. 'Say goodbye to your children and run off and save Britannia if you must. Just promise me one thing.'

'Anything,' he said, cradling the babe in his arms,

who had quietened now and looked up at him with giant, dark eyes he knew resembled his own.

'Come back when it is over. Not to me, but to them. I may have no further need for you, but you are still their father, and they need their father in their lives.'

'I promise,' he said. He reached out a finger and stroked Silvius's hair. He was eight months old, conceived, Victorinus thought, out of last gasp desperation on Sarai's behalf, as she sought to bring her pig of a husband back to his senses. He dearly wished she had succeeded.

Sarai left, out through the front door, her scent lingering on the air. He savoured it.

'Why don't you and Mother love each other any more?' Maurus asked, a slight quiver in his voice.

'Oh, my boy,' Victorinus said, once more lowering himself to his knees. 'The thing is...' He tried to find the words and failed. He was a liar and a drunk, lazy and rude. He did not deserve something as pure as a child's love. *Be honest*, a voice said in his head.

'The thing is, your father has not been very kind to your mother, and now your mother is cross with me, as she should be.'

Maurus moved towards him, buried his head in his father's chest. 'It's okay, Father,' he said in a small voice. 'Sometimes Mother gets angry with me too, normally when I don't eat all my dinner.'

Victorinus smiled, a single tear running down his cheek. 'Yes, well, I've been a bit naughtier than that. Listen, Maurus, I have to go away for a little while.'

'You going back to work already?' he asked. His little arms reached around Victorinus's body and hugged him tight. Victorinus lowered his head, breathing in his son's scent once more.

'I know. But when I come back, things will be different. I promise, I'll find a way so we can spend more time together.' Again, he thought back to all the leave he'd taken from the areani, the time he had spent in Eboracum, drinking and catching up with old friends. He should have been here, should have been with them. Maybe if he had been here that winter two years ago, he could have ridden off with the dawn and found a doctor, rushed him back, and little Leonius need not have died.

He should have done a lot of things.

Tears ran in rivulets, splashing on Maurus, who winced as one hit just above his eye. 'It's okay to cry, Father,' Maurus said, giving Victorinus another squeeze. 'Mother says even the clouds rain too when they get heavy.'

Should have been the father doing the comforting,

telling his son it was going to be okay when life got him down. If that wasn't a father's job then what was? Instead, it was the other way around. Maurus was only seven.

'There are some bad people, Maurus, and they are going to do a lot of bad things if I don't stop them. Do you understand?'

The boy nodded. 'Are you going to kill them?'

'Yes,' Victorinus said. 'Yes, I am.'

He paused at this. 'Good,' he said after a while. 'Bad men should be punished.'

'Yes, they should,' Victorinus said. Though he did not think of Valentia and the mysterious rebellion. He thought of himself.

Maurus moved away, and Victorinus rose slowly to his feet. The baby, Silvius, had nodded back off in his arms. Maurus ran to his toys. They were wooden fig-ures, carved by their neighbour Publius as a gift not long after they had moved here and Maurus had been born. He picked up a horse and brought it back. 'Here, Father, take this with you.'

Victorinus walked over to the far side of the kitchen, kissed Silvius gently on the head and lowered him back into his cot. Turning, he took the horse. 'Thank you, but won't you miss it?'

Maurus nodded. 'I will, that horse is my favourite, but I want you to have it.'

Victorinus reached out and grabbed his son, squeezing him tight and kissing him on both cheeks. Maurus squirmed and laughed. 'I'll bring him back to you, once I have beaten the bad men.'

'It's not a him, silly! She's a girl. Mother and I named her Amor.'

'Amor,' Victorinus said with a smile, tears once more pricking at his eyes.

'Mother says it means love.'

'It does indeed.' Victorinus pulled him close once more. His hair was sand coloured, his eyes pale blue. His nose was small and round, and his cheeks dimpled when he smiled. Victorinus savoured each of his son's features, imprinting them on his mind. When he was drunk and feeling low, he chided himself that he had done nothing good in his life, that he had nothing to strive for, no reason for being. He realised now that he was wrong. He had done something right; he'd made these beautiful children.

'I shall cherish her,' Victorinus whispered, and kissed his son once more. He heard a noise upstairs, and realised Lucia must be up there with the maid, putting Marcelina to bed. He wondered briefly if they would have heard the argument between Sarai and him, then reddened as he realised Cassius and Pastor must have heard outside. 'Why don't you go up to bed. I'll come and give you a kiss goodnight in a minute.'

Maurus ran upstairs and Victorinus walked slowly outside, stroking the wooden horse in his hand. He passed the barn. Cassius and Pastor were still there. Neither man spoke as their tribune walked by; they couldn't even bring themselves to look at him. Shame burned in Victorinus once more.

He reached the small patch of grassland under the beech tree. It was fenced off with a small wooden barricade, and Victorinus stepped over easily to stand at the foot of a small, unmarked grave.

He had not been able to summon the courage to come here since that day he had returned home two years before. His son, his beautiful little boy, who died without really knowing his father at all. He stared at the grave, the blank, decaying, wooden headstone, and promised his son he would have one cast from stone or even marble, a fitting tribute to a perfect little boy.

'Tribune?' a voice said to his rear.

Victorinus turned to meet the face of Publius. His elderly neighbour was well past his sixtieth year now, and his thin hair sat as white as snow atop his pale face. His pale eyes quivered and Victorinus saw the tremor of fear in his lips as he spoke. 'I am glad you came,' Publius said in a small voice.

'I'm glad someone is, at least. How are you, old friend? How are Amata and Delphina?' Delphina, their daughter, was approaching her fourteenth birthday, if Victorinus remembered correctly.

'Amata is fine, she's tough as old leather, always has been. Delphina is scared though. Those men, they said they would take her from us if we didn't say where you were.'

Victorinus did not know what to say. He wondered briefly why these men had been so desperate to find him. He was no stand-out officer; he commanded a small party of scouts and their job was north of the Wall. All the Caledonians, it seemed, were currently south of the Wall, so what did it matter where he was? Once more he thought of the man who could be behind this coup. Who had the power to finance it? The ambition to drive it? And did that person have some connection with Victorinus? If there was even a man at all. So many questions, no notion of how to find the answers.

'I am sorry, Publius,' he said eventually. A pointless gesture, he knew. 'You should go south, spend a few months at the coast, wait for this to blow over.'

'Will it? Blow over?'

'I don't know. I wish I could tell you more.' He wished a lot of things. His eyes looked past Publius to the house. Sarai was walking back inside. She turned at the threshold and looked at the two men, talking under the beech tree. Victorinus shivered, told himself it was the night breeze and not his wife's icy glare.

'She loves you, you know.'

Victorinus laughed. 'If only that were true.'

'She does, Tribune, I can tell. She will come back to you, when she is ready. You are a good man, Sixtus.'

Once more Victorinus felt tears well in his eyes. He turned back to his son's grave, to all that was left to remind people that little Leo had once been in this world, and he had been as bright and perfect as any little boy could be. 'No, Publius, I am not.'

He had pushed his wife away, neglected his children. His son had died whilst he was out drinking with his friends, and for that he had blamed his wife. He had nothing left of value, nothing to live for, nothing to strive for.

'You are a better man than you give yourself credit for. Those boys in the barn think you're a hero. Perhaps it's time to become one.'

'I'm no hero,' Victorinus said in a small voice.

'You are. And we need a hero now, Sixtus. Rome

needs a hero, and she probably still has no idea how badly.'

* * *

Dawn broke across the small settlement. The first red rays of the sun brought colour to the clutch of small farmhouses; birdsong filled the air.

Victorinus sat under the beech tree, unable to sleep, but not really awake. He had spent the night thinking of his children, the two still with him and the one who had passed on. He had never felt the need to do something as strongly as he did then. The need for action, for violence and revenge. Problem was, he still had no idea who he owed his vengeance to. He'd spent his youth dreaming of growing up and becoming a famous general. His father would regale him with tales of days gone by, of the glory of Rome's mighty legions, and the heroes who commanded them. How had it come to this? Sad thing was, he could have been talking about himself or the empire; both were in such a state of decay.

Around him the world began to come to life. A dog barked, cattle awoke and complained as they did. He smiled. It wouldn't have been a bad life, living here with his perfect wife and children. Raising cattle, growing crops, picking fruit from the trees as it ripened.

Once again, he turned over the decisions he had made in the past. He remembered him and his friends playing soldiers whenever they got the chance, each boy wanting to be Caesar or even Hadrian, the soldier emperor who had built the great Wall.

Maybe that was why he had been so determined to join the areani when he came of age. It was right, what Sarai had said to him the night before. His father had bought him his commission as a tribune, and ten years later he had still risen no further. It was supposed to be a starting point, a foot in the door. Ten years. He still hadn't managed to squeeze his sagging torso over the threshold.

But what else was there to rise to? The only person above him was his commander, the vicarius, which was a civilian position. With a sigh, Victorinus surmised that it was to him he must make his next stop. Surely Secundus would know what to do, could guide him. There must be other units of the areani around somewhere, running south from beyond the Wall, tails between their legs, much as Victorinus and his men had done.

Reluctantly he rose to his feet, yawning, rubbing the sleep from his eyes. He made his way over to the barn where Cassius and Pastor were already up, saddling the horses.

'Are we ready?' he asked the two youths.

'Ready when you are, Chief. Will take us a while to load the supplies if you want to go and say goodbye,' Cassius said, motioning to the house.

Victorinus shook his head. 'I've said my goodbyes, for now at least. Let's go north this morning, catch up with Halfhand and the others, see what they've learnt. Then we go to the vicarius.' He wondered briefly how Felicius was faring in his march south. He knew his friend would have driven his men on through the night, desperate to reach Eboracum, hungry for news.

He walked over to his horse. The grey mare seemed in a sullen mood, matching his own. He rubbed her flank, a small smile playing over his mouth as he whispered to her, watching her ears prick as she listened. He had never bothered to name his mounts before. Too often they would go lame in the rough terrain of the north, and he would either have to sell them at the nearest village or butcher them for the meat.

'Amor,' he said softly, reaching into the leather pouch he wore strapped to his waist, pulling out the wooden horse Maurus had given him. It was a fitting name, for both the toy and his mount. He breathed deep, relishing the warmth of the early sun. Today was his first day on the road to redemption. Today was the day he would finally put his past behind him, become the man his childhood self had dreamed of being. But how many times had he said that to himself? Even right here, in this very stable. His body trembled with the first cravings for wine. He knew it wouldn't be the last, but he forced himself to quash them down. 'Come, Amor. Let us ride to war together, and victory.'

5

JULY, AD 367

'Dress the line! Dress the line! Re-form, you bastards!'
Felicius screamed over the cacophony of battle.

They had marched solidly for two weeks, their
journey taking them through the heartland of Britannia. Every day they were delayed by the mass of the
civilian population, running north or south, blocking
the military roads and clinging to the soldiers, tears in
their eyes, as Felicius ignored their pleas and ordered
his men on. Desolate mothers begged the soldiers to
take their children, to keep them safe, but the prefect
hardened his heart. He had just five hundred men; he
needed to link up with the Dux.

The panicked population spoke of raiders in the
east, Saxons and Franks beaching their ships and

plundering all they could carry back. Felicius thought that worrying enough, but when people fleeing from the west told tales of the Scotti raiding the west coast, he marvelled at the extent of their doom.

This was bigger than even their worst fears. Every fortress they had passed had been empty or full of soldiers too cowardly to open their gates to a friend. No one had seen or heard from the Dux Fullofaudes, who was supposed to be the supreme military commander on the island. Where was he? What was he doing? Surely Rome was fighting back somehow, somewhere? Felicius was starved of news and friends, and running low on supplies.

He thought of the icy wind that had shocked him as he stood over the governor's body. The blood on the wall haunted his dreams; the branding on the chest soured his every meal. Seemed a lifetime ago now, since he had said goodbye to his wife and daughter on the road south.

They had been unable to stop at Eboracum, so overrun it was with Franks and Saxons. They were growing bolder, it seemed. He had heard already from the refugees on the road that they were raiding the coast; now it seemed they had left their ships altogether. What gave them such confidence?

On his men ploughed. Their direction a stoic

south, bypassing every town and settlement on the way. Now they were in the south, a stone's throw from Rutupiae, from high stone walls and friendly forces. They may as well have still been in Vindolanda.

The Saxon force had attacked from the forest to the east. Broke their cover with the dawn and charged as the Fourth Cohort of Gauls were still rubbing the grit from the corners of their eyes. There were hundreds of the bastards, clad in mail and armed with sword and spear. Felicius knew this was no mere raiding party.

The Germans were a poor people, the prefect knew that from the time he had spent fighting the Alamanni on the Rhine. Only the household warriors, the protectors of the tribal chiefs, had mail and swords. They were expensive to make or buy, required craftsmanship of the highest calibre, a rare quality in the wildlands of Germania. Even a chief of one of the bigger tribes would not be able to afford to armour and arm this many warriors.

And this was just one of the many bands of Germans stalking Britannia.

The Fourth Cohort were maintaining the square formation Felicius had ordered them into after the first clash of iron. He stood in the centre, flanked by a horn blower and Vitulus, his senior centurion. Between them and the fighting, the ground was littered with the wounded, some fairly minor, others mortal. Felicius knew he was going to have to order the square to move soon, to keep moving south and reach the walls of Rutupiae. But he could not bear to leave his wounded for the wolves.

And the wolves were ravenous. They snarled and spat and charged the Roman square again and again. Each time the side of the square under attack would cave in, the line almost buckling, and Felicius would extract half a century from another side not under immediate threat to bolster the line. But he was running out of men and he knew it.

'We need to do something, Centurion,' he said quietly to Vitulus. 'We can't just stand here and be butchered.' He was limping badly now. The old wound in his thigh burned with every step. He wasn't sure he would be able to hold the weight of his shield when he took his place in the line, and that time was coming fast.

Vitulus looked south, over the top of his men, seeing what Felicius saw – the top of a stone wall. 'An hour away?' he guessed, gesturing to the wall with a flung hand.

'Three, if we have to move in this formation.'

'A rider could make it in less than an hour.'

Felicius glanced behind him, to where the few remaining packhorses fought to be free of the ropes that bound them. Around them, a handful of panicked slaves fought to keep them calm. 'Who is our best rider?' Felicius asked.

The cohort did not have a cavalry detachment. There was a detachment of Tungrians based close to the Wall in the west, at Maglona. Felicius wished he'd had the foresight to get a message to their commander. The men were battle ready, well drilled and would have been a most welcome addition to his forces on their journey south.

'I know the man, sir,' Vitulus said, bringing Felicius from his thoughts.

'Get him mounted, quickly.'

Felicius moved forwards. The battle seemed to have ebbed, the Germans licking their wounds, readying themselves for another assault on the cohort's shields. His men crouched on their shields, the line around the square just three deep in places. The wounded murmured in pain, some of them prayed, others sobbed quietly for their mothers. Men sought to measure themselves in war, to prove their courage and masculinity to the world. In Felicius's experience, war made boys of all men in the end. He had seen many a heroic soldier go to his god crying for his mother. He liked to think he would be different if it happened to him, though he was in no rush to find out.

'Centurion, over here, man,' he said to the centurion of his third century, who currently held the centre of the southern line of the square.

'Sir.' The officer snapped a smart salute. He was a career soldier somewhere in his middle thirties, his heavy black beard beginning to streak with grey.

'Have your men ready to push out to the front and then left and right. We need to make room for a rider to pass through those damn Germans and reach Rutupiae.'

The centurion looked past Felicius to the rider who was already mounted on one of the packhorses, then turned his head to look at the distant walls of Rutupiae. 'I understand, sir,' he said with a salute, moving off to bark orders at his men.

'Get me a shield,' Felicius snapped to a passing slave, who had armfuls of bandages.

'You plan to fight, sir?' Vitulus asked, apprehension in his voice. Felicius could not help but notice his centurion's gaze flicker to his wounded leg. It had been the same since his arrival in Britannia, when he had first taken his new command out for a winter march through the hills. Three hours they had been marching before Felicius crumbled, leg spasming with cramp as he fought to get back to his feet.

He felt the burn of shame on his cheeks as the memory flooded back to him. Then he was back on the Danube frontier, in his commander's tent, fighting back tears of rage and shame as his transfer papers were handed to him. 'It is for the best,' he had been told. 'No shame in it, you have served us valiantly, and will continue to do so in Britannia.' He'd known what it meant, though. It had meant that his superiors thought him no longer worthy of a place in the field army, that his usefulness had run its course. Soldiers were nothing more than payroll numbers on a piece of parchment, after all. Expendable, easily replaced. He felt his resolve double, forced himself to stand a little straighter.

'Damn right I do. All morning I've stood here and watched my men be cut apart. It's about time I showed them some leadership. Don't look at me like that, I'll be fine. You hold the centre, Vitulus. The square is to stand to, apart from the southern edge. I will not abandon our wounded to those savages.'

Felicius waited for his senior centurion to nod in agreement. Both men knew the sensible thing to do would be to keep the square moving south, edging ever closer to Rutupiae and safety. But to do that would be a death sentence for the men who had fought and been wounded fighting for the cohort's standards. Felicius would never abandon his men, and they knew it too; it was part of what endeared him to them so much.

The slave returned with a shield, oval in shape, leather bound over a linden board, the cohort's standard painted on the front. He gripped it firmly in his left hand, drawing his sword with his right. 'Right then,' he muttered to himself, quashing down any self-doubt that lurked deep in his bowels.

'I don't know about you, lads,' he called as he pushed himself into the southern edge's front rank, 'but I've had enough of standing here waiting to die. When those whoresons come back for us, we meet them with a charge of our own, push out to the flanks from the centre and give our rider back there a chance to break through to Rutupiae. The Second Legion are behind those walls, one of the proudest units in the history of Rome! Soon their shields will join with ours, their javelins will darken the sky above the Saxons' heads! And we will be free to enter Rutupiae at our leisure!'

The men cheered, a hearty sound that gave Felicius courage. His men were still with him, ready to fight at his side. 'Franks, sir,' an officer said beside him.

Felicius said nothing, but gave the man a questioning look.

'You said Saxons, sir. I think these bastards are Franks.'

'Tell me, Centurion,' Felicius said in a loud voice. 'Do Franks die the same way Saxons do?'

The man laughed. 'I do believe so, sir, though I'm not certain. Shall we go and find out?'

Once more, men cheered and a ripple of laughter emerged from the ranks around the two officers. Felicius winked at the centurion, and then there was time for no more words as the German warriors charged once more.

* * *

'Push!' Felicius yelled, pressing himself against the back of his shield and leaning into it. Step by bloody step the prefect moved forwards, left leg burning, the men around him spitting and cursing, jabbing their blades through any gap in the wall of shields.

He risked a glance over the top of his shield, saw above the heads of the snarling German warriors the top of the walls of Rutupiae once more. He wondered briefly why the commander of the Second Legion had not already sent out men in their support, and prayed to any god that would listen that the legion was still there, that it was still loyal.

'Now!' the prefect screamed, more to wash away his nerves than anything else, and to each side of him men pressed harder on their shields, the soldiers in the second rank pushing into their backs, and they forced the Germans back.

Gritting his teeth, groaning at the effort, Felicius heaved once more. A burst of light appeared between his shield and the one to his right. Without thinking, he thrust his sword through the gap, feeling it connect with mail. He pushed harder, grunting as he strained, and was rewarded when the mail against his blade's tip burst and the sword slid into flesh, collided with bone.

He pulled the sword free, blood splashing his face as he brought it back behind his shield. His assailant crumpled, and Felicius was dimly aware of the soldier behind him stabbing down with a blade after the prefect had stepped over the injured man. But there was no time to think, to ponder, for the next man was on him.

An axe hooked over the rim of his shield, the blade smashing into the top of his helmet. Felicius squirmed away from the blow, ears ringing, and one of his men reached across with his shield, thrusting into the axe man's face before hacking at an exposed neck with his sword.

'Sir, are you okay?' Felicius heard, though the voice was muffled, a distant echo in a land of fog. His ears rang; a lance of pain burst through his skull, and he blinked rapidly, trying to force the pain out through his eyes. The only thing his mind could focus on was the shooting pain in his left leg every time he put a wobbly foot down.

'I'm f-fine,' he stumbled out. 'Keep the men moving forwards.' He staggered back from the fray, a numb hand removing helmet from head, tingling fingers probing his skull, checking the helmet had done its job. It had.

Someone handed him a water skin and he drank greedily, the pain receding as he closed his eyes. 'We're ready when they are, sir,' Vitulus said behind him. Felicius opened his eyes to a squint, cursing at the pain as he saw the nominated messenger trotting his horse towards the square's southern edge where the battle still raged.

'Tell the men to push out to the flanks,' Felicius told Vitulus, before turning to the rider. 'Ride straight to Rutupiae. Stop for nothing. Ask the commander of the Second Legion to come to our aid with all speed. Tell him we are still loyal to the emperor and to Rome.'

'Who is the commander, sir?'

Felicius paused. There would have been a time when he'd have known the name of every significant military commander on the island, but right now he could not recall it. 'I don't know, but I'm hoping the Dux Fullofaudes will be there. He knows me. Tell him what is happening here.'

With an almighty roar, the men of the Fourth Cohort pushed out to left and right, opening a hole in the square's southern edge. 'Ride now! Ride now!' Felicius slapped the rump of the mount, and the soldier had no time for more questions as he grabbed the reins with white knuckles and bent low in the saddle.

Felicius, hands still shaking, gingerly tied his helmet back in place and walked back to the middle of the square. Along the other three edges it was quiet; the Saxons – or Franks, or whoever the bastards were – were concentrating on the south. He gave two quick orders. Moving a half century of men from the northern and eastern edges and leaving one of his centurions in charge, he staggered back to the battle.

His men were doing well. The Germans had been forced back as the men of the Fourth had been pushed out, and now two separate battles raged to each side as his men still held the gap the messenger had ridden out of. 'We need to bring them back,' he called to Vitulus. The senior centurion nodded, and almost at once a horn blower sounded the withdraw, two sharp blasts on the horn.

Felicius moved forwards, positioning himself so he would be in the front rank when his men retreated enough to complete the line along the southern tip of the square. He saw one of his centurions fighting as he stepped back, his sword snaking out and stealing a life. He was grinning, a savage snarl that was all teeth between his blood-drenched beard. When he reached his commander, he roared in delight. Felicius didn't know whether to laugh or recoil. The man was so lost in the joy of battle he was half worried the man would take a swing at him.

The Germans, though, were far from beaten. Over the top of his shield, Felicius saw what must have been their commander, a huge barrel of a man in a silver helmet, pushing his men back into line, shouting, spitting, clearly furious his men had not managed to break through the Roman shields. Felicius looked up at the sun, judging it to be two hours past dawn. It was a clear day, the sky a deep blue. The heat would have an effect soon, he knew. The Fourth were running low on water; all that was left were what the men carried in their skins. Most of that would be being used to wash the wounds of the wounded. It was no easy thing to march and fight in mail at the best of times, but in the height of summer it was almost unbearable.

'Everyone, get a quick drink,' he shouted to the men who could hear, and he heard his officers repeat the order down the line. His stomach rumbled. He wondered when he had last eaten. His men too would be hungry, thirsty, their adrenalin wearing thin.

He thought the Germans must number around four hundred. Not enough men to attack all sides of the Roman square at once – which was why he had ordered it formed – but more than enough to break through one of the sides if they concentrated all their men on one spot.

Felicius realised he was fighting with one arm tied behind his back by maintaining the square. He reckoned they had killed over a hundred of the raiders, and he had perhaps fifty wounded taking refuge in the centre of the square. But there was no immediate threat to the square's northern line, nor the western. It was time to rethink his battle plan.

'Vitulus, the northern edge of the square is to form up in our centre, here,' he said, stamping his foot down where he stood. 'We will move left and join forces with the men on the western edge. The centuries on the eastern edge are to form our right flank. We form a line here; we hold them whilst we wait for relief from the Second Legion.' *If we are to be relieved.*

Orders were given, horns blown and the crunch of hobnailed boots on the turf could be felt underfoot. Felicius swayed on the spot. A flash of white light exploded behind his eyes and he staggered, squinting to regain his sight. 'Sir?' Vitulus said in his ear. Slowly coming back to his senses, Felicius realised his centurion was the only thing holding him up. 'Sir, you took a big blow on the head. Maybe you should sit this one out.'

'Fuck off,' Felicius snapped, not wanting to show weakness in front of his men. They were in a fight for their lives; they needed their commander. 'I'm fine.'

He reached a hand up to his helmet, for the first time noticing the great dent in the metal. How hard had he been hit? Was it an hour ago? Or a few minutes? Time seemed to have no meaning.

The Germans were rallying for one more assault. Once more, Felicius saw their commander, his silver helmet glistening in the summer sun. He stood front and centre amongst his own men, clearly feeling the same as Felicius. There was a time for a leader to give orders, and there was a time to lead from the front. The Germans would be all too aware that he was a long way from his ships, that retreat in a hostile land stripped of supplies would be difficult to survive and for his men to forget. In Germania, men ruled due to their strength and prowess, their reputation as a warrior and a leader. Stripped of that reputation, their lifespan became a lot shorter.

Felicius moved down the Roman line, a wall of shields, helmet tops and sword points. His head throbbed. Touching the dent on his helmet had somehow made the pain worse, as if he did not truly appreciate how bad the blow had been before. He positioned himself in front of the enemy commander, meaning to take him on man to man. His leg was a burning halo of pain now, each step excruciating. He had not walked the miles he had in the last few weeks since taking the wound. That was the privilege of command. Sure, after a long day in the saddle the leg would ache and he'd have to stretch it out by the fire, but nothing like this. He ground his teeth and swallowed, forcing the pain from his mind. His men needed him to be sharp.

'Who has javelins left?' he called, and those with them raised them high. 'Pass them to the front, quickly now.'

The javelins were passed forwards. They were of the more modern kind, half the length they had been when Felicius first learnt how to throw one. The one he now grasped was half the length of him, with a small weight attached to the iron head at the point. He didn't think you could get as much distance on them as the older, longer ones, but at close range they were just as deadly.

'Prepare to throw!' he called, and the order was echoed down the line. His men were all in place now. A quiet descended over the ranks of the cohort as men once more prepared themselves to face down death. It was always this way, he found himself thinking. Men start a battle with a ferocious roar, their bodies and minds sharpened by the rush of adrenalin only hand-to-hand combat can bring. But after the battle has raged for an hour or more, men grow sombre, re-signed to their fate. They do not relish the fray, just seek to endure it.

The Germans were slow to advance. Felicius could see the forlorn looks on their faces. They could see the Roman line grow stronger, the javelins passed from back to front. They knew what awaited them. Men licked their lips, tasted fear, swallowed it down.

'Ready!' Felicius called as the enemy started into a run. They had their own spearmen, and these men were in their front rank. Their spears were longer than a man, the shafts carved from ash. They would seek to use these men to break the Roman shields, shatter the wall and cause havoc in the Roman line. 'Aim for their spearmen!'

Felicius felt his palm dampen around the shaft of his javelin. As always, the urgent need to empty his bladder and bowels was overpowering but he quashed it down. There would be many a man in the Roman line with piss running down his leg, many a man in the third or fourth rank squatting down and voiding their bowels.

'Loose!' he screamed as the German advance came within thirty paces, and as one the Fourth Cohort grunted as they let their javelins fly. The sky darkened. For a moment it seemed all was quiet, and then with a whistle and a crash the javelins smacked home. Blood sprayed the air, Germans screamed and men fell to the ground. The javelins buried in mail and bone, and the field before the Roman line was a forest of shafts, sticking up from the dead and dying.

It slowed the enemy advance, but only for a few heartbeats. 'Shields!' Felicius screamed, bringing his own to bear. The Roman front presented an unbroken wall of shields to the charging Germans, swords ready. They were a wall of wood and metal, an unflinching line that stood in the name of Rome's glorious past.

And then the Germans were on them. Howling and snarling, they threw themselves on the Roman shields in a savage desperation to break through. Maybe they knew time was running out. They would have seen a rider galloping south, would have guessed help was on the way.

'Hold the line!' Felicius roared, but he was talking to himself as much as his men. He had been charged by the chief of the raiders, and the man seemed to weigh twice as much as he. The prefect buckled under the weight as the pressure grew on his shield. He was forced back a step, then another, his leg weakening. A sudden panic gripped him, a vision of his leg buckling, of him falling, a sword, bright against the blue sky, arcing down to end his life. He would not die in the mud, bested by some German chief. He felt the man behind him in the line lean forwards to stop him being pushed further back and took comfort in the man's presence. His men had his back, and he had theirs.

A sword snaked between his shield and the man next to him, hitting nothing but air. Felicius watched as the blade slid in and out of the gap once more, then readied himself. When it came a third time, he changed the grip on his sword so the blade was pointing down, and he rammed it down onto his assailant's searching sword, the metal clashing with a snap. He felt the pressure on his shield change as the chief was forced forwards and down, and he heard the man grunt in pain and surprise.

'Got you, you bastard!' he yelled in triumph, pulling back his shield and stepping back so his assailant had nothing to stop him as he stumbled forwards. Felicius raised his shield, slamming the metal-rimmed edge down onto the German's head, before plunging his blade into his unarmoured neck.

The battle changed in an instant. To his left and right Felicius could see the enemy take an involuntary step back, their courage deserting them. What was the point in fighting on when their leader was dead? Who would share the plunder at day's end? Who would give out arm rings and praise them for their courage in battle?

Heads swivelling, they looked back to the forest in the east. As if coming to an unspoken agreement, they turned and fled as one.

Felicius joined in the cheering with his men. There are few greater joys in life than standing victorious on the field of battle, your enemy fleeing before you. He considered briefly whether he should order his men to pursue, but if they were as tired and hungry as he, it would be pointless, and he could lose more men in an unnecessary battle in the forest.

He was about to speak to his men, to hail them for their courage, when a horn sounded in the distance. The cheering died away. Men looked around, confusion and fear on their faces.

'Who's that then?' Vitulus said, appearing at his prefect's shoulder. Felicius just had time to register a huge cut on his senior centurion's right cheek, to clock how his left shoulder seemed to sit a little lower than the right, that his left arm hung uselessly by his side. There was no time for sympathy.

'I've no idea,' Felicius said, 'but get the men back in line. Now.'

He walked out of the ranks, sure the horn had come from the south or east. Were there more enemy out there? Another party fresh from their boats, ready to finish the job their comrades had started?

The enemy had stopped fleeing, he noticed. They were two hundred paces away, huddled together in a circle. They were leaderless, beaten, their indecision clear.

'Well, if they're not expecting company...' Felicius mused, before the horn sounded once more.

To the south, in the distance, a standard appeared.

Then another, and another. A line of men with red shields, sunlight glistening off helmets and mail. There was a cry of 'Roma!' and then a thundering charge into the bewildered Germans.

Felicius allowed himself a smile before slumping down onto the turf, exhausted. His men were safe. The Second Legion had come.

6

'Dead?' Felicius said incredulously.

'That's the rumour, anyway,' Clementius said, standing with his back to the parapet. They were three hours out of battle. Felicius still had blood on his hands and face, but he had shed his armour and wore just a plain blue tunic. Clementius, the Second Legion's commander, was still in full armour.

'When?'

'Couple of weeks ago, when the raiding began in earnest. The Dux took a ship over to Gaul to try and make contact with the emperor and his court.'

'He couldn't have just sent a messenger?'

'We did. We sent three ships, but none of them returned. That's when the chief said he'd go himself.'

'So you're telling me the Dux, the supreme military commander of this island, sent three ships to Gaul to make contact with the emperor, and when none of those ships returned, he decided to go himself?'

'Yep.'

'Fuck,' Felicius said, looking out across the flat green waters of the Narrow Sea. Didn't seem there was much else to say.

Felicius had marched the length of the island, hoping to make contact with the one man who held the power to change the fortune of Rome's future in this most western province. The Dux Fullofaudes had always proven himself to be an astute man in a crisis, and gods knew there had been enough of them in the past few years. There was not a spring that passed without there being disruption on the Wall or raids from the Scotti in the west, but rarer had been the raids from across the Narrow Sea, with the fleet based along Britannia's east coast and Gaul's west coast doing a reasonable job of keeping the marauding Saxons and Franks at bay.

'I can't believe he would have gone himself,' Felicius continued, speaking to himself as much as Clementius. 'I've never known Fullofaudes to abandon his post like that before.'

'He received a message, shortly before he made his decision. I don't know what it said or who it was from, but when he tossed it in a brazier, he was white as snow,' Clementius said in a quiet voice. 'I don't know what's going on here, but whatever it is, it's bad.'

Felicius nodded. Looking at the prefect, judging the foreboding expression he saw on his colleague's face, he decided to take him into his confidence. He spoke of what he knew, what he had seen and heard in the north. Clementius was silent when he finished. Felicius saw the shiver of fear run down the other man's spine.

'What of Nectaridus? Surely he at least stayed?' Felicius said after a while.

The comes maritime tractus Nectaridus was in command of the fleet that guarded the Narrow Sea. He too had been commended by even the emperor himself for the fine work he had done keeping the sea clear of pirates.

'He left on the second ship to depart from here. He arrived by sea, through the channel from Regulbium on the east coast, a few days after we sent the first ship west. Said he'd seen the ship go down, two enemy vessels boarding at the same time.'

'Gods give me strength,' Felicius muttered. 'So

now you and I are meant to recover the island by ourselves?'

'Don't seem to remember you complaining about my lads earlier on today,' Clementius rebuffed, seemingly finding some of his former strength.

The Second Legion had made short work of finishing off the Franks. In little over an hour, they had the beaten survivors rounded up and duly executed. Felicius had enquired whether it would be worth keeping them as prisoners, but Clementius had said he had no room to keep them and no food to feed them. Death it was. Clementius had not bothered with the complexities of hangings or crucifixions, just sent a century of his men in amongst the wolves to butcher them where they stood. No one had tried to fight back; it seemed their bravery had deserted them the moment their commander fell in battle.

Clementius himself was something from a bygone era. He wore a bronzed cuirass under a red cloak; his helmet was polished steel trimmed with bronze. He appeared to base himself on the statues of Caesar that were to be found decaying around the empire, and Felicius wondered at a man who fussed over his own appearance as much as Clementius clearly did. His bald head was a perfect round, his nose flat and wide, making his dark eyes appear as if they were set too far apart.

Felicius by contrast put very little stock in what he looked like, or what he wore. His straw-coloured hair was as wild and untamed as it had been in his youth, his armour and helmet the same as his men's. He knew that if a stranger approached the two men now, they would automatically think Clementius his superior, when in fact they held the same rank. But that was just another thing that endeared Felicius to his men.

Felicius had that rare quality in an officer, one seemingly lacking in these times: he actually gave a shit about his men. The Fourth Cohort were kitted out with the best mail Felicius could get his hands on. Their swords were well made and sharp, and stocks of spears were maintained, so the soldiers didn't have to worry about re-using ones damaged in battle.

The Second Legion, in comparison, were a rag tag bunch in broken and ill-fitting kit. No one century had matching mail; some of the men were wearing armour Felicius thought their grandfathers must have gone to war in. Their swords were a mismatch in lengths and styles, some men still using the short swords that Felicius thought had gone out of commission in the time of Marcus Aurelius. Clementius, Felicius surmised, was every inch the modern officer, caring only for himself and not his men, and Felicius thought less of him for it.

'So, what are you planning to do?' he asked Clementius.

'Do?' the prefect said, eyebrow arched. 'You've told me yourself what it is we are up against. I've had no contact from any of the other units based in the area. For all I know they're dead or deserted. No, colleague, I do not plan to do anything.'

'So you will just sit here behind your high walls and wait for help?' Felicius would have struck the man if he had not been relying on his help.

He hit the wall in anger instead, realising that the walls were themselves part of the problem. Rome had always been an aggressor, an invader, always on the attack. As the years went by and the coffers in Rome dwindled, and emperors became more and more fascinated with killing each other than the barbarians that threatened to overwhelm their borders, something changed.

In a bygone era, when men such as Augustus, Hadrian, Aurelius, and Severus ruled, there would have been no need to build such fine stonework so deep in Roman territory. Fortresses were for the frontiers, for the far north overlooking the Caledonians, the west keeping an eye on Hibernia and the ever-wild Scotti. But here, in the southeast of the province, surrounded by friendly territory, the very idea would have been dismissed as a waste of resources.

And yet here they were, sitting safe and sound behind high stone walls, because Rome could no longer guarantee the Narrow Sea – a sea Rome called her own – would always be safe and free from pirates. Fortresses such as these could be found along the southern and eastern coasts of Britannia now, as well as the western coast of Gaul. It was another admission of Rome's slow fall of power, her rotting decay. The empire was slowly but surely falling in on itself, the system rotten at its very core. And there seemed to be no way of stopping it.

'What do you expect me to do?' Clementius snapped, bringing Felicius around from his reverie.

'How many men do you command?'

'A thousand, give or take. Though that's including the men we lost saving your arse today.'

'And how many ships?' Felicius continued, ignoring the thinly barbed jibe from his colleague.

'Just three remaining. Two are scaphae exploratoriae, small ships, used for scouting. The other is our last remaining warship, a bireme.'

'Is it seaworthy?'

'It is,' Clementius said with a sniff. Felicius thought once more of the poor state of the men of the Second legion and tried to think of a reason why the prefect would have kept his ships in better condition than his men, coming up short.

'The bireme has a captain? A crew?'

'It does,' Clementius said shortly, not liking where the conversation was going.

'Let me take it to Bononia, see what I can learn.'

Clementius scoffed. 'What makes you think you will succeed when better men, sailors, have failed?'

'Nothing at all,' Felicius said with a shrug. 'I just seem to be the only man here with the heart left to try.'

Clementius reddened in anger, and Felicius braced himself for the inevitable backlash. It didn't come.

'You'd need the permission of the governor.'

'Priscus?' Governor Priscus ruled the southern-most province in Britannia, Britannia Prima.

'That's the man. I'll have a rider go to Londinium first thing. If he's still alive, I'll get your permission.' With that, Clementius walked away down the stairs and was lost in shadow. Felicius stood in the weakening light of the sun a while longer, wondering at his colleague. Maybe he had been wrong to judge the man. They had no idea what it was, or who it was, they were fighting, but they were in a war nonetheless. Felicius and Victorinus would need all the allies they could get. Once more he thought of the letter of transfer, the bland smile on his commander's face when he'd handed it over. Everyone had thought him finished, shipped off to an early retirement in this backwater of a province. He'd been determined to prove them all wrong when he first set foot on British soil. Somewhere along the way though, whether it was meeting his wife or holding his daughter for the first time, he seemed to have lost some of that ambition, that drive. Now seemed as good a time as any to find it once more. He wiped his nose with his hand and then remembered he was still plastered in blood. With a sigh, he rose to his feet. He needed to check on his men.

* * *

Two days later, Felicius stood on the quayside, one step ahead of the rising sun. Permission from Governor Priscus had been given mercifully quickly, limiting the time the prefect had to consider the folly of his path.

He knew nothing of sea warfare. Briefly, during his

time with the western field army fighting the Ala-manni on the Rhine, he had witnessed the ships of the Rhine flotilla do battle with their German counter-parts. But those ships had been small and light, river craft being very different vessels to the one that awaited him now.

The bireme was vast, sitting in the shallow water. A dark shadow in the purple haze of pre-dawn. Felicius stood and watched as the gathering light revealed the secrets it had been hiding.

The ship was manned by eighty oarsmen, who sat beneath the deck almost one atop the other, two banks of twenty oars to each side. Felicius thought it a dim existence, devoid of light and fresh air. Clementius had told him the previous evening that the Roman biremes were faster, stronger and far superior to anything the Germans could put to sea. He wondered then how so many had come to be sunk by inferior ships.

The first red rays of dawn crept over the eastern horizon, light spilling onto the still, grey water. Felicius could see two more ships now, sitting at anchor further out in the wide channel that cut the mainland off from the island of Tanatus, a small and sparsely populated patch of land in the southeast of Britannia.

The ships were smaller than the bireme, their

hulls painted a blue grey to help them blend in with the water beneath them. Their sails were the same colour, and even the crew wore blue. Again, Clementius had bragged to him the previous evening that all this made the ships virtually undetectable out on the open sea, that they could creep up on the enemy and be upwind of them before they knew they were even there.

Again, Felicius had silently wondered how the fleet had lost so many of these ships if they were as superior as Clementius made out. He hadn't the heart or the courage to question his colleague on this, as he would be putting his life into the hands of these ships and the brave men that crewed them.

He had forty of his men behind him, a half century under the command of Vitulus, his senior centurion. Felicius had originally intended on leaving the man behind in charge of the rest of the cohort, due to the very likely circumstance they would have to sally out from Rutupiae and fight off another band of raiders. Not to mention the man had needed his left shoulder popping back into place after the battle against the Germani. Vitulus, though, had been enraged at the prospect of being left behind. Touched by his loyalty, and secretly relieved that he would have the man beside him, Felicius had changed his mind, leaving the cohort under the command of one of his other centurions.

'Are you sure about this?' Vitulus said behind him.

Felicius turned, shrugged. 'Someone's got to do something.'

'But does it have to be you?'

'Not scared of a little water, are you, Centurion?' Felicius said with a half-smile. 'I seem to remember telling you to stay here with the men. Offer's still open if you've lost your bottle.'

Vitulus reddened and rolled his shoulder. He winced at the pain and Felicius's half-smile split into a broad grin. 'I know, I know! Nothing scares the formidable centurion Vitulus, slayer of a thousand foes!' He laughed, heard the men behind his centurion snigger. Vitulus was famous throughout the cohort for his prowess in the wrestling ring and on the battlefield. He'd challenge anyone to a fight, swords or fists; made little difference to him.

Vitulus might have replied but before he got the opportunity, there was a cacophony of noise from the waiting bireme and a bare-chested man jumped from the ship onto the quay, making his way towards the waiting soldiers at a jog.

'Prefect Felicius,' the man said, offering a salute. 'I'm Captain Fidelis. Are you and your men ready to depart? Just that I'm eager to be away before the tide drops.'

Felicius smiled and held out a hand. The two men shook and Felicius thought it was like shaking a brick, the skin of the captain's hand was so rough.

'How long will it take us to reach Bononia?' Felicius asked, picking up a saddle bag he had hastily filled with a few possessions the evening before.

'We'll be there by sunset, Neptune willing.' Fidelis fell into step beside Felicius and the two men walked down the quay to the ship, boarding via a wooden plank lowered from the side of the vessel. The ship's crew stared silently at the small column of soldiers as they boarded, a grim suspicion twinkling in their eyes. Sailors and soldiers were not famed for getting along.

Felicius stood to the side and watched on as his men made their way uncertainly aboard the ship. 'Does your ship have a name, Captain?' Felicius asked Fidelis, more for the need for aimless conversation to quash his growing nerves than anything else.

'She's not been given one yet, she was only finished last week. It's customary for the crew to give her a name on her maiden voyage, so I guess we'll have one by the time we reach Bononia.'

'You mean this ship hasn't sailed yet?'

'No, sir,' Fidelis said, shaking his head. 'With the

speed in which our ships have been sunk recently, the lads in Rutupiae have been building as fast as they could to get more of our ships out on the water.'

'I didn't know they built boats here?' Felicius said, frowning back at the fortress of Rutupiae, taking in the high stone walls, but seeing no evidence of a ship-yard anywhere.

'This one's the first,' Fidelis said in an annoyingly chirpy voice. 'Shall we find out how they've done, sir?'

* * *

The sky was a blue bowl overhead, the sun a scorching orange. Felicius sweated in the thick blue woollen tunic he and his men had been required to wear. He stood at the prow of the ship, rocking easily with the motion, the salt spray stiffening the skin on his face. To his surprise he found he was enjoying the experience of being out at sea. There was a certain tranquillity to be found away from the hustle and bustle of the life as a unit commander in the Roman army.

If he were still in Rutupiae he would be parading his men, checking the condition of their kit after their recent battle. After that he would visit the men in hos-pital, raise their spirits with a word or two in each man's ear, then he would see to the funeral funds of the men who had not been so lucky.

Each day was a monotony of routine, of giving orders and following them up. Here, in the middle of the Narrow Sea, those constant duties and worries were as far away as the distant specks of land to the east and west. Behind them, to the west, was Britannia, a place he had come to know as home for the last five years. Ahead of him was Gaul. Felicius felt a sense of returning as he looked into the distant blackness that marked out the land. When he had departed Gaul for Britannia, it had seemed to him that he was leaving the empire behind to a certain degree. From the western shores of Gaul, one could walk uninterrupted right the way through the Roman empire and end up at the gates of Persia, if you were inclined to, anyway.

Felicius had never felt such an inclination, but there was some sort of odd comfort in knowing that if you wanted to, you could. Once he had departed for Britannia, he had felt the sea as some sort of wall, separating him from the empire he had served so loyally all his adult life. 'Out of the loop,' is what he had heard his father-in-law say on many occasions. 'Backwater province,' was another of the old man's favourite sayings. Not that he would be saying anything any more.

His thoughts turned sour as he relived finding the old man's body. The writing in blood on the wall. Valentia. He still had no real idea what was happening on the island, or how it could be stopped. He tried to think of another example of different groups of people from outside the empire joining forces and attacking Rome, but came up short. Sure, there had been countless occasions when the Germans had banded together and caused havoc on the Rhine and Danube frontiers. But their alliances tended to be short-lived, their chiefs much preferring fighting among themselves than actually making war with the empire.

How was he going to explain all this when he reached Bononia? He had a sealed letter from the governor which he was sure gave as detailed an outline of the crisis as the man could manage. His only hope was that that letter, coupled with his verbal report, would be enough.

Closing his eyes, he prayed. He was never really sure what god he prayed to these days; he just closed his eyes and mumbled some words. He didn't bother to dedicate them to any particular deity. Ostensibly, he was a Christian. But that was only because his parents had been Christians, and they had just assumed he would be taking up their religion. No one had ever actually asked him what he believed in. On balance, he supposed he was. He liked the idea of worshipping the old gods, as they were mostly known these days. Jupiter best and greatest; Juno, mother of the empire. Mars, God of war; Mithras, the secret warrior cult. The list went on. Trouble was, he could not bring himself to believe in any of them. The more the pagan worshippers amongst his friends spoke of them, the more they sounded like children's bedtime stories.

His friend Victorinus was a pagan, he knew, and Felicius always felt a sense of embarrassment when the tribune kissed his fingers and raised them in salute to Sol Invictus, the rising sun. Not that he would ever actually challenge someone on their beliefs. He sincerely hoped that the days of religious persecution were behind them.

Thinking of his friend led down a path that ended with his wife and daughter, and he prayed to a nameless god once more for their safety. Had he done the right thing leaving them in the north? He assured himself he had. Wasn't like their march south had gone smoothly. But would they be any safer up there? With bands of ravaging barbarians marauding the land? He ground his teeth in frustration. There was nothing he could do to change the past now.

'Fuck this for a laugh,' Vitulus spat behind him. Felicius turned to find his senior centurion gripping the rail as if it were the last jug of wine in Britannia. His eyes were red, skin a pale green.

'First time at sea, Centurion?' he said in a light voice.

Vitulus found himself unable to reply, busy as he was emptying his bowels of the dregs of bile that had so far escaped his retching. 'With respect, sir,' he managed to croak out once the deed was done, 'fuck you.'

'Sounds like someone's going to be on latrines for a while,' Fidelis said through a wolfish grin, strolling easily down the deck.

'A fine idea, Captain,' Felicius said, before a small laugh escaped his lips as Vitulus once more threw his head over the railing and vomited into the sea.

'Not too much longer now, sir,' Fidelis said. 'If the wind and weather hold, we'll make landing in a couple of hours.'

'Glad to hear it. I assume the new ship is holding up well?'

'Couple of minor leaks down below but nothing we can't handle. It's perfectly normal, with newly built ships,' Fidelis said in a reassuring tone, seeing the concern written on the prefect's frown.

'And no sign of the enemy?'

'No, nothing yet. I've a look out placed atop the main mast, I'm sure you've noticed. The lad has the best eyes on this ship; anything stirs, he'll give us plenty of warning.'

Felicius looked up at the mast, seeing for the first time the fair-haired youth, perched precariously on a wooden beam. He seemed to be playing with a metallic disc, holding it up to the sun so it caught the light. 'What's he doing?' Felicius asked, pointing up.

Fidelis cursed. He moved away from the prefect, called up to the youth and unleashed such a barrage of abuse that Felicius felt Vitulus next to him take a mental note for the next time one of his men pissed him off.

Felicius gave Fidelis a wry smile as the captain walked back, apologising. 'A lot of your crew seem to be of German origin,' he said after a while. It had been nagging him all morning. The men who crewed the still unnamed ship spoke in their mother tongue whilst they worked. Felicius could not help but feel uncomfortable at the fact that his life was in the hands of men who shared blood bonds and kinship with the people who would be stalking these waters, looking for a fresh target to sink.

'I wouldn't let that worry you, sir. How many German contingents do we have in the western field army? Ten? Fifteen if you count the cavalry squadrons.

They serve Rome out of their own free will, same as the men who man our ships.'

That was true enough, Felicius conceded. There had been units of Germans serving with the field army that had fought the Alamanni, when he had been serving on the Rhine. It hadn't bothered him at the time; he didn't think he'd given it a second thought. But everything seemed so different right now. There were bands of Germans, Scotti and Caledonians all on Roman turf, raping Roman women, killing Roman children, burning Roman settlements. He didn't think he'd ever known Rome to seem so weak and powerless in all his years of service. How hard would it be for a spy to sneak past the Rhine? Declare himself an outlaw from his people and sign himself up for twenty-five years' service to the empire?

He looked once more to the top of the mast, to the fair-haired young man keeping watch up there. *All our lives are in your hands.* Once again, he saw the sailor raise the small metallic disc, the sunlight gleaming as it reflected off its surface. Was this just some kid fooling around? Or was he a traitor, guiding the sea wolves in for a feast?

Valentia. If the last few weeks had taught him anything, it was that anything was possible. And no one was to be trusted.

7

'Sail! Due north!' the lookout called, and immediately all was chaos on deck.

The ship was carving a path west through the chop, the waves being forcibly parted by the hull. Felicius and his soldiers bounced and swayed, gripping hold of whatever was closest. Vitulus had emptied the last of the bile from his stomach and was still hunched over at the prow, sweating and shivering, refusing all offers of water, claiming he'd seen enough of that to last him a lifetime.

'How far off?' Fidelis bellowed to the youth atop the mast, pushing men from his path as he bounded his way to the ship's rail.

'About a mile off. They're upwind of us, closing fast.'

Felicius looked north, the sun high in the sky behind him. He didn't need to squint, and yet all he could see was the white-topped waves rolling in their easy motion. He'd always had the impression you could see for miles when out at sea. Apparently, he could see less than one.

'So that ship gets within a mile of us, upwind, before that lad notices he's there?' Vitulus said quietly in Felicius's ear.

'Hmmm,' was the prefect's only reply. He had given up looking for the enemy ship; it would appear soon enough. His gaze flickered between the men of the crew. He estimated their number to be twenty-five. Silently, he cursed himself for not counting them earlier. 'I want the men ready to fight in five minutes.'

'Aye, I'm on it. But who are we fighting?'

'Follow my lead.'

He went to walk off towards Fidelis but Vitulus called him back before he'd made five paces. 'Do the men wear mail?'

Felicius considered this a moment. 'Can any of them swim?'

'Not that I know of.'

'Then tell them to put it on. Won't make any difference if they go over.'

He walked across the deck, his head facing forwards, eyes shifting in all directions. The crew seemed
in no panic that there was an impending threat.
Trouble was, Fidelis and the men of the Fourth were
so gripped by the appearance of the ship that no one
else had stopped for a heartbeat to notice. The
lookout on the mast still perched easily. Felicius
thought he even saw the man share a smile and wink
with another sailor on deck, who pulled a rope to
loosen the main sail.

'Tighten that rope, you fool!' Fidelis screamed.
'They'll catch us soon enough as it is. We don't need
you idiots making it easier for them!'

Felicius stood alone in the centre of the deck,
feeling the rhythm of the ship run through him. Below, a drum beat out the strokes and the rowers
strained at their stations, knowing now that they
rowed for their lives.

He loosened his sword from its scabbard, taking
comfort from the feel of the heavy pommel in his
palm. Still his eyes flickered over the crew, none of
whom showed the slightest hint of worry that they
were soon to be attacked.

'Are your men ready?' Fidelis asked him. The captain seemed to have transformed into a different person since the sail had been spotted. His weather-beaten face was a plum red, sheened in sweat. Lank hair stuck to his scalp as if it were sculpted in place.

'My lads will do their part,' Felicius said quietly. 'Will yours?'

'Will mine? What sort of question—'

'Look around you, Captain,' Felicius said in the same low tone, but with enough authority to quieten him. 'Do your men seem rushed? Uncertain? There is an enemy bearing down on us, and these sailors seem to still be enjoying a carefree trip out at sea in the sun.'

Fidelis joined the prefect in silent observation. Felicius knew the man would find it hard to accept that his men would mutiny. He had probably served with a lot of them before, maybe even recruited a few himself. To him it would be impossible that they were none other than they seemed – good honest men serving the empire much the same as him.

Trouble with being an honest man was you assumed everyone around you was too. Fidelis was a sound sailor, no doubt; knew the sea better than the back of his own hand. But he was no great judge of men, and that fact was slowly dawning on him now, Felicius could see it in his dumbfounded expression.

'Your man atop the mast has been waving a

metallic disc at the sun all morning. How far do you think that light reflects across the sea? A mile, two? Another one of your lads just took the wind out of the main sail as we are supposed to be fleeing from the enemy. That the action of a man desperate not to be caught?'

'Neptune's cock,' Fidelis muttered. He trembled now, had grown redder, and in the right light Felicius was sure he would have seen steam rising from that damp hair. 'What do we do?'

'How many sailors are there aboard this ship?'

'Twenty-three, not including me, and the men below deck.'

'How many from across the Rhine?'

'Eighteen,' Fidelis said, not having to think on it. 'Most of them only signed up a few months back, last time I was over in Bononia. Thought it was a bit odd, to be honest. We'd struggled to get enough men on the water for ten years now, then all of a sudden—'

'A whole crew's worth turns up at once,' Felicius finished.

'Was too good an opportunity to turn them away. Ship damn well nearly sank on the way back to Rutupiae, what with all the extra weight on board. Was only in one of the scout ships.'

'We're going to have to kill them, Captain, and fast.

I'm going to alert Vitulus, get your man off that mast and round up any loyal men you still have, but quietly.'

They moved apart, Felicius feeling self-conscious as he tried to avoid eye contact with every sailor he passed. 'Over here, lads, got a quick job for you,' he heard Fidelis call to three of his men, before the captain summoned the lookout down from his perch.

'Are the men ready?' Felicius said to Vitulus. The centurion nodded. 'We're going to take out the crew first, Fidelis has got some of the lads he believes to still be loyal down below deck. Every sailor still up top dies.'

'We'll follow your lead, sir.'

Felicius looked north. The approaching ship was visible now, gaining fast. It had blue sails and the hull was painted the same colour. He noted with interest that the barbarians seemed to be copying the Roman tactic of camouflaging their ships with the sea, then he wondered for a moment who had in fact copied who. Rome had never been renowned for her prowess on the waves.

Fidelis had returned back on deck and was fitting in place a leather breastplate, a giant single-headed axe resting against his torso. The two men locked eyes and Felicius nodded, then he turned and picked his first target.

The lookout was down from the mast, openly staring at the incoming ship with a half grin on his face and a glint in his eye. 'You should arm yourself, brother,' Felicius said, standing easily beside him.

'Why would I do that, Prefect? I do not plan on fighting today,' he said in heavily accented Latin.

'You will not defend yourself when they attack?'

'It is my hope that I shall not need to. I am not their enemy.'

'Is that why you spent the morning signalling them from the mast?' Felicius said, tugging free the dagger from its sheath at his back.

The lookout stood a head shorter than Felicius, a wiry frame under his baggy blue tunic. His hair was a light brown, wild and long, blowing freely in the wind that assaulted them from the north. He was thin faced, his nose long. Felicius thought him not dissimilar to a hawk, and thought his position as lookout to be fitting. He waited a heartbeat longer before brandishing the knife, taking pleasure in the moment the glint of triumph dulled in the man's blue eyes.

One roll of his shoulder later and he had the blade buried deep in the lookout's guts. Twisting, he used his left hand to push the man backwards. Ten quick strides brought them to the ship's rail and there Felicius stabbed him once more, before throwing the body overboard. The lookout didn't so much as squeal.

'Get 'em, boys!' Felicius roared, and his men responded with a cry of their own. They had spent all morning in an uncertain silence on deck, adjusting themselves to the roll of the sea, trying not to watch as their centurion emptied his breakfast into the dark water below. Now all that tension was released and the forty men charged with gusto into the stunned sailors, and the day ran red.

'Well, that's the first objective complete,' Felicius said to Fidelis as he wiped clean his knife on the hem of his cloak.

'Not sure how we're meant to finish the journey once we've dealt with this lot,' the captain said, gesturing to the German ship, a growing presence now.

'Let us worry about that after. I've never fought at sea. Where do you want my men?' Felicius wasn't too proud to submit himself to the sailor. He outranked Fidelis and knew too well there were colleagues of his who would ignore the captain's advice in this situation and follow the course of action they thought best. Felicius, though, had a wife and daughter to return to and was more than happy to follow a more experienced man's lead.

'They'll hit us to the north side. Their ram will aim for the centre of the ship so split your men into two groups and have them attack from either side when they do.'

'We will not try and defend this ship?'

'No, Prefect,' Fidelis said with a grimace. 'Once the ship is rammed, she will be lost. Our only hope is to board their ship in turn and take that.'

'And our rowers?'

'Will be released from their benches at the last moment. They will form our reserve.'

Felicius spared a thought for those poor men below deck. They were not slaves but free men paid a wage to row across the sea. How would he feel if he were one of them now? Knowing there was an enemy in sight but not knowing where they were. It took courage, to carry on in your duties, trusting your life to your superiors. His respect for them grew.

Vitulus and the men of the Fourth had finished throwing the last of the traitorous crew overboard, and the ship left a red trail in its wake. 'Have half the men with you at the prow, I'll take the rest with me to the stern. Fidelis says the ship will be lost once the enemy ram us, so our job is to board the other ship and take it as quickly as we can.'

Vitulus saluted, passing down the order, and twenty men followed him to the front of the ship. Felicius watched a moment. His men shared jokes and checked each other's helmets and armour. As always the prefect felt the weight of guilt that crushed him every time he had to plunge his men into battle. How many would die today?

'Prepare to be rammed!' Fidelis screamed over the keel of the wind, and then Felicius had time to think no more, as all around him was chaos.

* * *

'Archers!' Felicius called, throwing up his shield as two arrows buried themselves in the linden board.

He rocked on the deck, the sea seemingly growing excited at the sight of impending battle, the waves growing in their anticipation, as if they reached higher, straining to see more of the action.

Felicius risked a glance over the rim of his shield and saw the enemy vessel, not fifty yards off now, and all along her deck were men armed with spears and bows, sunlight glinting from their helmets.

He adjusted his footing as the deck rolled beneath

him. The wind seemed to sharpen, the tang of salt grew heavier, and he squinted as it began to sting his eyes. 'Brace!' came the call from somewhere to his left, and before he could readjust his vision, there was a mighty crack that could have been a thunderclap, and Felicius was pitched from his feet, thrown backwards. He flew for a second before hitting the deck with a crash.

'Fuck,' he managed to croak out, sucking in air as his lungs screamed in protest. He staggered to his feet, mail weighing him down. His vision was blurred, hearing clouded. He staggered like a drunk and when the deck lurched beneath him once more, he fell flat on his belly, his head thumping so hard against the wood his helmet fell off and rolled away.

He lay still a second, letting his senses return to him. He had one of those blissful seconds, like when you stub your toe and you stand there, just waiting for the pain to kick in, and then it does and you're cursing, hopping, wondering if you're ever going to be able to face walking again.

That was what hit him, once the blissful second had passed, but it was a pain that intense all over his body. 'Fuck this,' he groaned, letting the pain wash over him. His lungs burned; ribs protested with every breath. He tried to raise himself up and his arms screamed at him to stop. He ignored them.

Into a sitting position, head throbbing but clear, he took in the carnage around him. Where once had stood the proud mainmast of the newly crafted boat there was now a carved wolf head, and behind it the prow of another ship. Fidelis had not been joking when he said the ship would be finished once rammed; it was split almost entirely in two.

His men were in disarray, some standing, others crawling, some lying still as corpses. They needed help. They needed their leader. With a roar he rose to his feet, immediately discovering his left leg was in worse shape than his right, the old wound in his thigh burning with every step. His sword still sat at his waist, and he drew it now, stooping to snatch up his helmet and plant it back on his sweat-soaked head. Using his sword as a crutch, he propelled himself to his men, shouting orders to those in any state to hear them.

In a few heartbeats he had ten men lined up behind him. None looked particularly ready for battle, but they would have to do. Vitulus and the others were lost to sight behind the enemy ship. He hoped they had fared better. 'We need to board that ship,' he called, pointing to the wolf's head with his sword.

'This ship is done for. Our only hope now is to take the enemy's vessel and finish our journey on her.'

'ROMA VICTRIX,' his men began to chant, and Felicius gave them a grin. There really were no better soldiers in the empire. They moved forwards together, a few more of the broken men who had lain on the deck finding their wind and their courage and joining the advance. Surely it had been as bad for the men on the enemy ship? Felicius thought as they approached. They would have been thrown about too, would be up there, nursing sore heads and broken bones. Speed was the key here; he just hoped he and his men had recovered quick enough.

There was no movement from above as they reached the snarling wolf. Felicius ran a hand down the carving, marvelling how something so beautiful could be so destructive. A rope hung down next to it, seemingly come loose in the collision. Felicius pulled hard on it twice, checking it was secure, before replacing his sword in its scabbard and beginning to climb. 'Follow me, quietly,' he hissed to the man behind him.

It was just ten pulls up the rope, but his arms were still heavy from the earlier impact, and even without that he thought he would have struggled with the weight of his mail. On the fifth he regretted giving the order to put it on, but with a few more strains he managed to grasp the ship's rail. He peered cautiously over the top, seeing a scene that was pleasingly as chaotic as the one he had just left.

Men lay strewn across the deck, swords and spears scattered where they had fallen from flailing hands. Vitulus must have been attacking from the ship's far side as all the enemy left on their feet were concentrating their efforts over there. Two archers loosed arrows in quick succession, men threw spears, and a bearded man in full mail who Felicius quickly surmised was their leader shouted commands and made expansive hand gestures.

Slowly as he could, Felicius lowered himself onto the enemy deck and freed his blade once more. He crouched down, heart thumping as he waited for his men to join him. One by one the men from the Fourth grouped around their prefect. He counted them off, the thirteenth man giving him a nod to say he was the last in line. He had thirteen men; before him were up to thirty enemy.

But the thirty enemy had still not noticed their ship had been boarded. This was where Roman discipline and organisation would have made the difference. Even Felicius, with his limited knowledge of sea warfare, would have had men stationed around the deck, on the lookout for potential incursions.

None of his men had shields – they would have been unmanageable on the rope climb – so Felicius quickly decided that a swift charge would be the order of the day. He gave his men one last look before turning and heading off across the enemy deck, still at a half crouch. He aimed himself for the enemy leader, who stood five paces behind his men, waving a sword in anger as his men rained missiles down on Vitulus and his men.

Felicius adjusted the grip on his sword with a sweaty palm and raised the blade. Still silent, he waited until he was three paces behind the German before aiming a stab at the exposed skin on the back of the man's neck. As the sword tip burst through skin and ground on bone, Felicius let out a howl at the burning pain that ripped through his shoulder. Two handed, he forced the blade in deeper until he felt the snap of the neck, and the man dropped soundlessly to the deck.

'ROMA!' he roared, raising his bloodied sword to the heavens. Around him, his men echoed his cry and darted forwards, each man slaying an enemy before they could react. For the first time he felt the sway of the deck on the enemy ship and reminded himself his friends were sinking the other side of the rail. He forced his way forwards, blocking a thrust with a spear with the flat of his blade, before stepping inside his assailant's reach and hacking at an arm. The spear fell to the deck, and its owner slumped to his knees. Felicius finished the man with a thrust to the heart.

He found a length of rope coiled by the ship's rail. He tied one end to the rail and threw the rest over the side. Peering over, he could see Vitulus looking back through a square of shields. He had ordered his men to form the tortoise formation as the missiles rained down upon them. Felicius was delighted to see most of the twenty men he had left with his centurion were still standing.

'Well, come on then!' he called, gesturing to the rope. Turning back to the deck, he saw with glee his men had pushed the Germans back towards the rear of their own ship. There was a lull in the fighting, the enemy regrouping, digging deep to find their courage. It is no easy thing to do, once the first spray of blood has misted the air, to find yourself on the back foot and have the strength of character to quash the natural instinct of retreat.

These men, though, had nowhere to retreat to. They had rammed their target, splitting its hull, and now the Roman ship was sinking slowly to the dark depths of the Narrow Sea. Their only route to survival lay in victory. Felicius felt, rather than saw, a disturbance in the air just above his head and immediately lowered himself into a crouch. As he did there was a twang off the side of his helmet and an arrow dropped to the deck, its iron head snapping from the shaft. *They're not beaten yet,* he thought.

Vitulus dropped to the deck beside him, and one by one the rest of the men from the Fourth followed. 'Quite something, eh?' the centurion said, wiping blood from his forehead.

'Like being on the end of a cavalry charge. Worse, actually. You all right?'

'I'll live. You lose many?' Vitulus said, gesturing to the men Felicius had boarded with.

'Seven still on our ship, didn't have time to see if they were still breathing. You?'

'One dead, huge chunk of wood split his neck open. Let's get this shit finished, sir. I want my feet back on dry land.'

'Couldn't agree more. Come on then, let us get it done.'

The men of the Fourth moved at a run, giving the

enemy less chance to loose more missiles. The battle was over in a matter of heartbeats.

Felicius wiped blood and sweat from his face, cleaning the blade of his sword on the tunic of a dead enemy. The deck was clear of enemies now, the bodies thrown over the side. Fidelis and a few of his men had gone below deck and released the imprisoned rowers from their chains. These men now stood squinting in the sunlight, bone thin and skin as pale as snow. Felicius wondered when they had last been freed from their chains. 'Can we sail this ship?' he asked the captain, who had been talking in broken German to one of the freed slaves.

'Aye, these lads will help us, on the promise that they will be free to return home once we make land.'

'Will they?' Felicius asked, unsure whether their freedom was something Fidelis had the power to grant.

'Aye, they will. They'll be put under guard and escorted back across the border, but they are fine with that. If I can tell the powers that be in Bononia that they have assisted us, they won't begrudge them their freedom.'

Felicius wondered what sort of freedom it would be, alone in the wildlands of Germania. These men had ended up slaves for a reason. He doubted they had homes to return to. But their fate was not his concern. 'Will we still make landfall before sundown?'

The nameless Roman bireme would forever remain as such. She had sunk to the depths at an alarming pace when the German wolf ship had reversed oars and backed out of the wreckage. She was now being rowed by free Romans, who had complained bitterly at the state of conditions below deck. Fidelis had promised them all a week off and a bonus once they reached Bononia, though, and that seemed to have calmed their complaints.

'Perhaps, with the wind on our side. I'll need some of your lads to help on deck though.'

'You'll have them,' Felicius said. He walked away from the captain and stood alone for a while. Seemed strange to think it was only that morning he had set off from Rutupiae. He thought once more of his wife and daughter, and hoped they were safe in the small farmhouse with Sarai and her boys. Victorinus would have got them there, no trouble, he reassured himself. He wondered what his old friend was up to now. The areani were a laughing stock, a rag tag bunch of drunks and rejects, and now, perhaps the only loyal force left at Rome's disposal in northern Britannia.

Once more, he marvelled at the lengths someone had gone to, setting so many different tribes loose on the island. Who had the resource to fund this? The contacts to set it up? The burning ambition to see it through? The wind buffeted him as he stood, the ship rocking to the waves' rhythm, and just for a moment, he thought he heard a voice on the breeze.

Valentia.

8

It had been three weeks since Victorinus had said goodbye to Felicius at the crossroads on the southern road. Since then, he felt as if the days had blurred together.

After leaving the farmhouse and saying goodbye to his children, he, Cassius and Pastor had ridden north then east, riding by night and hiding by day. The journey had taken twice as long as he'd thought. The roads were still crowded with refugees, mothers holding murdered children, families fleeing with nothing but the clothes on their backs. But Victorinus had also seen armed men riding amongst them, searching every wagon, stopping every hooded figure.

They were looking for someone, or a group of people, and Victorinus did not get the impression they were friendly troops looking to help the local people. Travelling cross-country, eventually they found themselves back on the Wall, finding Halfhand and the others at the fort of Condercum, the third fort inland from the Narrow Sea.

It stood on a hilltop, with gates south of the Wall facing onto the road from the east and west. It was square in shape, and unlike most of the other forts along the Wall, it still seemed to be in good condition.

Halfhand was standing on the parapet above the western-facing gate when Victorinus and his two companions had ridden up the hill. He gave them a smile and a wave before saying something inaudible to a dark-skinned man standing beside him. The gate was opened, and Victorinus rode through into a cobbled courtyard. Here, for the first time in what seemed an age, the tribune saw what seemed to be an orderly Roman fort, running efficiently.

There were two granaries, standing on stone stilts a foot or so off the ground. An armed guard stood at the entrance to each one; it was not just rodents, after all, that tried to steal grain when they thought no one else was looking. Next to them, smoke rose lazily from

the rooftop of a bakery. Victorinus had not eaten a
proper meal in days, and the aroma of baking bread
was as welcome to his nostrils as a flask of red wine
would have been to his growing anxiety.

An armoury and blacksmiths stood joined together on the fort's southern wall, once more there
were armed guards stationed at the entrance to both.
Victorinus hoped there would be enough kit in there
to equip an army. All he'd need then was soldiers to
equip.

To his left, along the western wall, was a large stable. The stench of hay and horse manure was overpowering as he moved away from the bakery at a
canter, before dismounting at the stable door,
throwing the reins to a waiting slave.

'Salve, brother!' Halfhand called as he clambered
down the stairs from the parapet two at a time. 'Am I
glad to see you.'

'You too, old friend,' Victorinus said into the fabric
of Halfhand's tunic as the men hugged.

'How did you fare at the farm?' Halfhand was one
of the few men who knew of Victorinus's family and
his marital struggles. Over the years the two men had
so often swapped sob stories over a jug of wine that
there wasn't much each man did not know about the
other.

'You know how it is,' Victorinus said in a small voice. His hand automatically reached for the pouch at his waist, where it found the small wooden horse his son had given him. Absently, he stroked the horse, leaving it in the pouch. 'How about you?' he said, clearing the emotion from his voice. 'What news?'

'All in good time, sir. I think you should meet our hosts. We went east, as you ordered, made it all the way to Segedunum, but there was no one there to talk to. We took the northern road back, along the Wall, and when we came to Condercum, we found Decurion Abel Felix and his men.' Halfhand stepped aside and the dark-skinned man from atop the wall came into view.

He was tall and slim, hazel eyes beneath a balding scalp, the remnants of his black hair dancing on the breeze. 'Tribune,' Felix said, saluting. 'Welcome to Condercum, sir. Myself and the Ala I Hispanorum Asturum are at your command.'

Victorinus was momentarily stunned. Not in his wildest dreams had he imagined he would find a single century of men still loyal to Rome in the north. Every fort and milecastle he had passed on his way from his home had been deserted. To find a full cavalry wing still ready to serve was a relief beyond words. 'How many men do you have, Decurion?' he eventually managed to stammer out.

'We're under strength, sir, as all of us are these days. But I still have three hundred and eighty men, fully equipped with a mount and packhorse. If you order us to ride out tomorrow, we'd have enough rations for two weeks.'

Victorinus could have wept. 'Do you know, Decurion, I think you might just be my favourite person on this island.'

Felix smiled, showing two rows of neat, white teeth. 'I'll try not to take that personally,' Halfhand muttered, not that his superior was listening.

* * *

So it was that the Ala I Hispanorum Asturum rode out from Condercum the following day. The cavalry wing had been formed in the Asturian region of Hispania a hundred or so years before, though to Victorinus the only things that seemed to be linking them back to their routes these days were their name and their commander.

The ranks were mostly filled with local men, trained to wield a spear from horseback at a young age. Some of the men seemed to have the sunbeaten skin of Felix, though Victorinus thought some of this must have been inherited from their fathers or grandfathers, who had been shipped to the northeast of Britannia many years ago.

'It is true, Tribune,' Felix said as they walked their horses west, 'many of my men are the descendants of those who first served under our banner.' He gestured to the dragon banner that swam through the thick summer air. 'The men who originally travelled to this island mostly stayed here upon retirement. They met local women, bought a small patch of land, and lived out their lives growing what crops they could in the lands they'd spent their youths defending. Most do not speak my language, or have any real knowledge of Hispania. Though I have a few that crossed the Narrow Sea just to fight under the same banner their forebears did.'

They rode with the rising sun on their backs. The weather was warm and sticky, despite the rain that had fallen the night before. The grassland around them sparkled with morning dew, and the trees and plants were full of the colours of summer. Breathing in deep, Victorinus could make out the smell of wet grass on a warm day, despite the overpowering odour of horse sweat and leather. It was a scent that brought him joy and reminded him of being in the far wilderness of the north, surrounded by nothing but wild countryside. It was where he had always felt happiest, his natural territory, and was one of the reasons why he had chosen to lead the men on this route.

They were travelling north of the Wall, over un-kept fields and through nestles of brambles and bushes. Victorinus did not trust the road that ran from east to west on the Wall's southern side. Felix was sus-picious about the loyalty of too many of the troops stationed there, and there were bound to be spies lurking at the milecastles that dogged the road, lying in wait, ready to report the movement of troops to one of the many bands of invaders roaming free across the land. They had ridden north from Condercum, riding for an hour so to be out of sight of watchful lookouts along the Wall.

'Feels wrong, does it not, to feel like an invading enemy on home turf,' Victorinus said to no one in par-ticular.

He had spoken long into the night with Halfhand and Felix, the patter of rain hammering the tiled roofs covering their voices from prying ears as they shared information. Halfhand had discovered nothing new. He had ridden offroad to Segedunum, staying away from all major towns and settlements. They had hidden from two raiding parties of Saxons, skirted a large band of Caledonians and arrived at the fortress to find it empty, the gates to the north and south swinging in the wind.

'Everything had been burned,' Halfhand had said. 'The granary and armoury were empty, no sign of a struggle.'

'You think it was our lads?' Victorinus had asked.

'Aye. Probably took all they could carry, burned what they couldn't and fucked off.'

'But why?' Victorinus spoke into the flames of a flickering fire. 'Why just decide to revolt now?'

Felix spoke next. He had been a decurion of the Spanish horse for fifteen years, serving under the same prefect for the entirety of his service. One day, not two months ago, the prefect – a bald and brash Pannonian – had announced to his officers he was leading his ala of cavalry into a rebellion against Rome, and that there would be coin and plunder for all who joined him. Fifty men had elected to join the prefect, men who had travelled from the Danube borders with the prefect when he had taken up the command. The rest had stayed, and the officers had appointed Felix as their temporary commander, until another senior officer could be appointed.

'Must have been a shock,' Victorinus remarked.

'Yes, of course. Porcius had always been a good

commander, diligent in his duties and fiercely loyal to Rome. I thought when Valentinian ascended to the throne he would be delighted to have a fellow Pannonian as ruler of the west, and his brother, of course, ruling in the east. But he always seemed indifferent about our emperor, reluctant to speak about him, very disengaged when we renewed our oaths every year.' It was common practice for all military units to renew their oaths of loyalty to the emperor at the beginning of every campaigning season, even if everyone knew troops' loyalty changed with the wind these days. Long gone were the days of Augustus, Hadrian or Aurelius, these pioneers who had helped shape Rome into the immortal power that was now nothing more than a memory.

'He had a friend, Porcius, some high-ranking senator who owned a villa, not far from the fort. He had been going there more and more before his desertion. He too is a Pannonian, I believe.'

'You know this man's name?' Victorinus asked, shifting through his memories, trying to recall a Pannonian senator at one of the many governors' banquets he had attended with Felicius.

'No, I never knew. Again, Porcius would never speak of him, and I was his junior officer. It was not my place to ask.'

Victorinus cursed his past self, for what must be the thousandth time. Wasn't it bad enough that the drink had robbed him of his wife and children? Now it was keeping a vital clue hidden from his sight.

'Where is this villa?'

'I'm not sure exactly, though the prefect always rode east when he left the fortress.'

'How long would he be gone when he went and visited?'

'Seven days? Eight?' Felix said uncertainly. 'I know it seems odd now, with all that has happened, but I never thought much of it at the time.'

'I understand,' Victorinus said, thinking that he would have felt the same indifference if his commander decided to take a little vacation every now and again, especially in times of peace. Discipline among the highfliers of society wasn't what it once was, which was in turn how Rome found herself in messes such as this.

'He could have gone anywhere in that timeframe,' Victorinus added, talking more to himself than the other two. 'We don't know if he stayed with this man for one night or three. Don't be hard on yourself, Felix, you've done nothing wrong.'

The decurion spoke of what he had seen over the past weeks. The fires on every horizon, the bands of roaming warriors stalking the roads. He had not seen any large forces of Caledonians though, which Victorinus found interesting. That told him the Caledonian advance must have been mainly in the centre of the Wall. Maybe they – whoever 'they' were – had not been so certain all of the garrison troops in the forts along the Wall would fold or turn. The more he thought about it the more certain he became they would find more loyal troops in the north.

It was true enough that there were insufficient men left in the northernmost province to deal with a threat on this scale, but surely there would be enough to form a small army? An army that could fight in the shadows, hit the enemy in swift, deadly raids and slow them down, at least until Felicius returned to the island with a relief force.

Victorinus had heard nothing from his friend since their parting. He thought of him numerous times a day, wondering if he could have made it to the south coast, and then over to Gaul. It was a tall ask for any force. But Victorinus had no idea how far south this rebellion had spread. Just because the north was in chaos did not mean the south was too. Britannia was a big island, one that had taken Rome years to garner control of. No, it would not be lost so easily.

His plan was to ride to the fort of Vindobala. Halfhand had sent Drost and Severus ahead to scout it out. It had been deserted when the areani had ridden south what felt like years ago, after they had encountered the first fire and Pastor had nearly got himself killed.

Victorinus was still not sure what to think of Pastor. Twice over the last week he had noticed the lad stalking around the camp when he thought the others were all asleep, paying no attention to the goings on around him as a good lookout should. He would whisper to himself, ineligible breaths on the wind, and once Victorinus had seen him huddled by the campfire, dipping a quill in ink and scrawling on parchment. He hadn't known the boy could write; he should have. So far, he'd kept his concerns to himself. It had been, after all, weeks since he'd last succumbed to the bottom of a wine cup, and his nerves were tingling on edge. The sane part of him knew too well he could be experiencing paranoia, his brain telling him a good drink would calm him down.

He did not want to make himself look weak or fearful in front of his men, even Halfhand, a man he knew was his man through and through. Still had his pride, after all. So for now he kept his concerns to himself, and Pastor even closer.

The lad rode at his right shoulder now, draped in

his yellow cloak despite the rising heat. He reminded himself that Pastor was a boy still, and his life up to this point had been anything but fun. He raised his hat a nudge and turned, giving Pastor a smile. 'You good?' he asked casually.

'I'm fine,' Pastor replied, his wide eyes growing in surprise.

'Slept like a baby last night, this one did. I was certain some god or other was going to pop down from the heavens and tell him to stop fucking snoring,' Cassius piped up, a cheeky grin fixed to his hairless face.

'Well, it took me a while to nod off,' Pastor replied. 'Your fucking hair illuminating the room and all!'

Victorinus chuckled and lowered his hat, leaving the youths to their fun. Life had been hard and strange in the last few weeks, and he would wager they hadn't seen the worst of it yet. Let them have their fun.

He rode in silence a while, absently stroking the wooden horse that he couldn't remember removing from his pouch. He daydreamed of a Britannia free from rebellion, at peace with their northern neighbours. Where he could spend more time at his farmhouse, treat Sarai like a queen, dote on his children and mourn the one he'd lost.

Just a fantasy, of course. In the real world, he'd already lost them all.

The sun had risen in the clear blue sky, the morning dew as much a myth as his happy family when Halfhand, Drost and Severus rode into view. Victorinus was reminded of how ungainly Severus seemed on a horse. He had often seen the man swaying on foot as if he'd had a liquid breakfast, something Severus said he was unable to stop doing, since he had spent the majority of his life aboard a ship. The bald ex-sailor rode with his legs fanned out to either side of his mount's flanks, so you could see daylight between his dark trousers and the leather of his saddle. When he dismounted, he did so with a grimace, and Victorinus once more mused what trouble this man could have got himself into on the Rhine frontier to suddenly run to the far north of the empire.

'Fort's still empty,' Halfhand said simply. 'Rode through to the road on the southern side. I rode east for a mile then turned back. The lads did the same to the west. Didn't see a soul.'

'Any smoke?' Felix asked, nudging his horse forwards so he was alongside Victorinus. He too had seen the vast columns of black smoke over the horizon, though he had refrained from sending men out to investigate. Victorinus had pondered whether to call

the man out for his perceived cowardness, but Victorinus needed him much more than Felix needed the
tribune, so for now, he had held his peace.

'Few drifts to the southeast, but not the same den-
sity to which it was before. Reckon it was a barn or a
house, not another one of those V things.'

Victorinus grunted, adjusting the position of his
hat. His fingers itched with the need for wine, the uncertainty of what they would find when they crossed
back to the south.

'Just had a thought, boss,' Severus said, once more
swaying on his feet.

'All on your own?' Victorinus said, sarcasm oozing
as he fought to quash his nerves.

'Well, it's just that there's never been a better time
to take the fight to the northerners, has there? What
with them all being in the south.'

A pause of silence, in which Felix scoffed a laugh,
Halfhand rolled his eyes and Drost looked set to burst
with rage.

'What a wonderful idea,' Victorinus said. Gods, he
needed wine. 'We could offer them a trade, couldn't
we? They can keep the lands south of the Wall, you
know, the lands our ancestors fought and died to conquer. They can have the tin in the mines, the cities
we've built and farms we've toiled. And in return, we

can take the unspoiled wilderness, the mountainous terrain, the unfarmable fields of moss and bog. They can wear our fine armour and march under our proud standards, trade with our fellow citizens with our coin once they've tired of having it away with our wives. And we can fight to survive the harsh winters, struggle to grow food and resort to eating each other once we've run out of horses.'

Pastor had his head buried in Cassius's shoulder, his shoulders rolling in mirth. Drost was not sure who had offended him more, his brother in the areani or his tribune. He looked ready to bury them both.

'Was just a thought,' Severus said with a shrug.

'What a loss to the Navy you continue to be,' Victorinus said with a shake of the head. Gods, he could use a drink.

'So, what is your plan, Tribune?' Felix asked.

'I need to get to Coria, where our headquarters are stationed.'

'You think you will find answers there?'

Victorinus shrugged. 'I don't know to be honest, but we've found out sod all on our own. I've had no contact with anyone apart from yourself and my friend Felicius since this started. Maybe my commander will have some answers.'

'Are there more of you, in the areani?'

Halfhand gave a derisive snort. 'Have you heard much about the areani since you came to Britannia?' Victorinus asked.

Felix shrugged. 'You are scouts, tasked with keeping an eye on the Caledonians. I had never had dealings with one of your number until your man showed up at my fort.'

'Odd, don't you think? That you could serve here for, what, ten years? And not meet the men responsible for keeping you up to date of the movements of the people you are supposed to be defending that fort from?'

'Can't say I've ever given it much thought.'

'There are more of us, to answer your question. Not as many as there should be but, like most active units across the empire, we have struggled for men.'

'And you have the reputation for being a bunch of drunks and outcasts,' Felix added.

'Yeah, that too.'

'So, we ride for Coria?'

'Aye.' Victorinus nodded. 'You will still accompany us?'

'Of course,' Felix said, a sly grin spreading slowly across his face. 'I would love nothing more than to ride to war with a bunch of drunks and outcasts.'

* * *

As it happened, their journey south was peaceful and uneventful. The sun continued to scorch them from its perch in the deep blue sky. They passed through fields ripe with crops and fruit, helping themselves to whatever they could carry, unchallenged by long-departed farmers.

The roads were clear now; the local populace had fled well to the south. Victorinus had scouts out in every direction, but the horizon stayed clear of dust clouds or woodsmoke, two clear signs that there were raiders in the area.

Coria was a small town, by Roman standards, anyway. A clutch of houses lined the road as they made their way under the north gate of the fort, passing through into the town beyond. Stationed at a crossroads, with the main military road running north to south out of the town's southern gate, the main road connecting the east and west began here and ended at Luguvalium in the west.

It was here that the supplies of coal and tin mined in the northern towns of Britannia were stored and sold. Cartloads of product came through, evident in the debris that lined the side of the road. The air was rich with the tang of woodsmoke and industry. Many a man who moved to allow the riders to pass had faces blackened by coal or squinted in the fine sunlight. Victorinus thought they had spent too much of their lives below ground.

They made their way through a bustling market, the smells as common to them all as the lice under their mail. Merchants hustled with the populace over herbs and spices, oils and meat. Slaves darted between stalls, slips of parchment in their hands. A pottery was open for business at the rear of the market square; here, two women were having a blazing row, it seemed over the purchase of one particular product, but Victorinus did not slow to find out.

One conspicuous absence was the soldiers that should have been on patrol. In any town across the empire there would always be a half century of men at least on duty, ensuring nothing got out of hand. Here, it seemed, there was nothing to stop the people doing what they wanted.

'I sense we shall not find what you seek here,' Felix said to Victorinus. They rode two abreast on the cobbled road, the two officers leading the way. Felix had left his men outside the fort, letting their mounts drink their fill from the river that ran east to west on the edge of the town. Victorinus had been unwilling to let the men even enter the fort, he was so uncertain at what they would find. Paranoia still dominated his every thought, and if he took one hand off the reins, he knew it would be trembling with the need for wine.

He needed his wits about him today, perhaps today more than any other he had survived thus far. They rode straight through the town, the air becoming clearer as the buildings became more sporadic. On the southern edge of the town, they halted at a pair of iron gates, flanked by whitewashed stone walls.

'What is this place?' Felix asked. 'It does not look like an official building.'

'Because it isn't,' Victorinus said simply. He dismounted; the others followed his lead.

'It might be best, Decurion, if you wait outside. I'm not sure how this is going to play out.' Victorinus didn't take his eyes from the gates as he spoke. He saw movement on the wall to his right, the glint of a helmet reflecting the sun's glare.

'And if it goes badly? How will I know?'

'If we're not out in an hour, assume it has gone badly. Pastor, Cassius, you wait with the decurion. Halfhand, Severus, Drost, you're with me.'

He walked towards the gate, leaving his horse with Felix and the others. He looked back at her before moving on. Odd, what giving a name to something could do. He'd never much cared for his mounts before, but this one, Amor, had come to mean something to him. Maybe she reminded him of his son? Now was not the time to dwell on it.

Two armoured figures appeared beyond the gate, both resplendent in chain mail and polished helmets. They had swords at their hips and spears in their hands, but neither carried a shield. Little point in lugging around a shield when you had high brick walls and iron barred gates to hide behind.

'State your name and business,' the man to Victorinus's left said.

'Tribune Sixtus Victorinus, here to report to the prefect of notaries, Secundus.' Victorinus studied the two men as he spoke. The man to his left, the speaker, was of medium height and build. There was no sign of any hair poking from beneath his helmet, his face clean shaven. He had a sharp, pointed nose and thin, pale lips. He had a certain stillness to him; an undrilled quality only veteran officers seem to possess.

His companion was taller and broader, and the shabby grey hair beneath his helmet matched his beard. His nose was wide and flat, and the knuckles on the hand that wielded a spear were lined with white scars.

'What business do you have with the prefect?' the

smaller man said, again speaking without moving an inch.

'In case you hadn't noticed, soldier, the province is overrun with rebels. I am here to seek counsel with my superior.' Victorinus stared at the smaller man. There was something familiar about him, something the tribune could not put his finger on. The prefect, Secundus, always had guards on the door, men who had served their time in the military and wanted a fairly easy payday to keep the money lenders at bay until they reached their winter years. But it was not here he recognised the man from. Gods, he needed a drink. His nerves were in tatters.

'Wait here, I will check whether the prefect is at home.' Which was another way of saying he was going to check if the prefect actually wanted to give Victorinus and his men a minute of his time. Wouldn't have been the first time the bastard had said no.

As it was, their wait was short-lived. The gates were opened with a squeal and Victorinus, Halfhand, Drost and Severus walked through into a large courtyard. At the door to the villa they were relieved of their weapons, standard practice when greeting one of the most senior men in Britannia.

They walked through a light and airy vestibule, through a reception room decorated with elaborate mosaics. A small pool sat in the middle of the chamber, an open skylight above it. Victorinus never had worked out why the cream of society insisted on having this in their homes, especially on this rain-swept island. Surely they got wet enough as it was?

Moving through a corridor which ended in a walkway under a portico, surrounding a small square garden complete with a water feature and four apple trees. Third door on the right and their escort stopped, knocking twice before it opened. 'Just you, Tribune, your men can wait in the kitchen. We'll see them fed and watered.'

'Very kind,' Victorinus said, nodding to his men. He hoped he would see them later. He entered a spacious library, two candelabras shining against the far wall despite there being plenty of light. Shelves filled with scrolls and tablets lined the wall to his right, a large desk, open shuttered window behind it, to his left.

'Tribune,' a slight figure said from behind the desk. He rose to his feet without seeming to get taller, a slip of a figure in a light blue toga. He was fifty if he was a day, the thinning grey hair on his head less evident than the hair protruding from his nose and ears. His narrow eyes were dark, his mouth seemingly too big for his face. He walked around the desk and took

Victorinus's hand, which the tribune thought he had never done before.

'Domine,' Victorinus said with a nod of deference. He may have despised the man, but rank was rank when you served the empire.

'You know I'd half believed the rumours when I was first told,' Secundus said, looking up at Victorinus with a haughty expression. His nose had a purple tinge, his pale cheek flushed red. Victorinus knew an addict when he saw one; he was one, after all.

'Rumours?'

'Yes. Regarding your death,' Secundus said, moving past Victorinus to a small round table, on it a jug of wine and two cups. Secundus poured himself some wine, left the other cup empty, and regarded the tribune as he sipped. 'I prayed for your soul.'

I'm sure you did, you turd. Victorinus breathed in deep, exhaling slowly. He would have loved to have said something so impotent to his commanding officer; with a cup or two of red in him he probably would have. But he was sober and conscious of the armed men who stood on guard the other side of the door behind him. 'Well, I thank you for your prayers.'

Secundus walked slowly back to his desk, the jug of wine coming with him. He took his seat, not gesturing for Victorinus to take the one facing him. He spoke once more, his light, scratchy tone sounding the way a rat would if it could speak. 'There have been some changes to the chain in command in the area. I'm sure you have noticed.'

'Changes?' Victorinus said. He was too stunned to do anything other than repeat that word.

'Yes, changes. We are under new leadership. No longer do we serve an emperor far away, who does not give a second thought to those of us that he has abandoned to the far reaches of the world. We are at the centre of the wheel that spins our fate, masters of our destiny once more! Doesn't that give you a thrill, Tribune?'

For a moment, Victorinus flapped like a fish out of water. He was shocked to his core. He had known, of course, that his commanding officer was rotten. Over the years, Victorinus had seen the man abuse his power time and time again. He had used the agentus in rebus to spy on his political enemies, men who had done nothing wrong other than to have the nerve to disagree with him. He had accused them of crimes they did not commit, had his agents testify against them in court, watched on in silent glee as they were executed or exiled.

Secundus represented everything Victorinus despised about the 'cream'. Power hungry, greedy, selfish. He cared nothing for the people who served him. Victorinus had lost count of the number of times he had needed to chase his superior for his and his men's monthly wages. There was money at his villa, there was never a shortage of that, it was just that the prefect could not be bothered to pay him. He was a man with no military standing or experience, but here he was, a commander of armed men.

'There are barbarians within our borders.' Victorinus spoke quietly, but he oozed menace. 'People have been killed, families torn apart, children abducted. Pirates from Germania have stolen food from communities, Caledonians from across the Wall are stealing our children. Starving people roam our roads, desperately seeking salvation from our soldiers. But our soldiers are not in their forts, are they? They are not out taking the fight to the enemy; they are not pushing them back over the Wall or into the sea. They have been paid to flee, to abandon the people they are sworn to serve.' He didn't know this; he was fishing. But the gleam of triumph in Secundus's eyes told him he'd hooked his line well.

He simmered, barely keeping his rage in check. He should have known this worm would have been up in it to his eyeballs. Through the soldiers he commanded and the spies in the agentus in rebus, he was one of the most powerful men on the island, if not the most.

'A necessary evil, I'm afraid. But our troops have not fled, I'll have you know. They are simply regrouping, readying their strength, so that together they can reclaim the province. Under the command of our new leader, of course.'

His head swam. He felt the sweat beading on his forehead and the dampness of his tunic as it clung to his back. This wasn't happening, couldn't be happening. 'What is Valentia?' Victorinus asked.

'Valentia is freedom!' Secundus said with a wave of his arm. 'It is justice, equality, a new order! Valentia, dear Tribune, is our new home.'

Without realising, Victorinus moved his hand to the pouch at his waist and stroked the wooden horse his son had given him. 'Why are you telling me this?' he said in a hoarse whisper. He was thinking about his family now, of Sarai and his boys. The men he had met on the road, the leader in the cavalry helmet.

And then it struck him. The guard at the gate, the stillness that seemed to exude from him. He knew where he had seen that man before.

In a moment, he had free the dagger he kept stuffed down the side of his boot. With a snarl, he moved towards Secundus. He would kill the man and be damned with the consequences. He took three steps and saw the expression of the prefect change from one of haughty arrogance to fear, his eyes widening behind his bulbous nose.

And then he saw nothing but stars. He sank to his knees, tried to scream but he could make no noise. The dagger dropped from a numb hand. The last thing he remembered was a pulsing pain on the back of his head.

9

He woke to a rank taste in a dry mouth, a tongue that felt like leather and a pulsing pain in his head. He groaned, tried to roll over and found his hands manacled to a metal chain. The chain ran down to manacled feet, then carried on, into a stone wall at his back.

Struggling to a sitting position, he found his tunic soiled. He cursed. Bad enough to be stupid enough to get himself captured, let alone pissing himself in the process. With a surge of panic, he remembered his men. Halfhand, Drost and Severus. What had happened to them?

'Mornin', Chief,' a voice said, somewhere in the murky light.

Squinting, Victorinus shuffled forwards as far as

he could. For the first time he took in his surroundings. He appeared to be in some sort of dungeon. The floor was cold flagstones, the only light from a brazier that flickered the other side of the iron bars that caged him.

'Halfhand?' he managed to croak out. His throat burned when he tried to speak, his numb tongue refusing to follow his brain's commands.

'Aye, it's me. Got Severus and Drost in here with me.' The other two muttered their hellos, though neither managed to muster much enthusiasm.

'The fuck's going on, boss?' Halfhand said.

'Damned if I know,' Victorinus replied. He tried to rub his sore head but his manacles wouldn't stretch that far. His wrists caught on the metal that encased them and he gritted his teeth against the pain.

'Assuming that prick Secundus has thrown his lot in with the rebellion?'

'Yeah, something like that.' Victorinus felt dizzy. His vision blurred, the flickering light of the brazier causing him to sway. 'Should have seen it coming, I suppose.' He craved water, longed for a long drink from a cold stream. The irony wasn't lost on him, the wine dependant who had scorned people who preferred water to wine now willing to beg the next person he saw for a cup of the clear liquid.

'We need a plan, sir.' Drost this time. Victorinus opened his eyes. It was only when he did that he realised he'd been holding them closed.

'You three get roughed up?'

'Nah, not really. One minute we're tucking into a bit of cold meat and a jug of the good stuff, next we're surrounded by six men with swords out. Starting a ruck didn't seem the sensible thing to do.'

'Fair enough.' His head rolled again. He wondered if this was what it was like to be at sea. All that water, not a happy thought.

'What happened to you, anyway?' Severus piped up. Victorinus forced himself to keep still. Squinting, he could make out his three companions in a cell opposite. They had straw beds and a bucket to piss in; he hadn't been awarded such luxury.

He tried to think what Secundus had said to him, before the white light had taken him. Valentia, a new beginning. Something along those lines. His broken brain tried to put together the pieces but he couldn't get them to form the right picture.

'He's been in on this since the start,' Victorinus said slowly. 'Whoever the man is behind this, he must be a friend of Secundus. That or he promised Secundus so much coin he wasn't able to say no.'

'Never trust the cream,' Halfhand scoffed.

'Ain't that the truth. Not that there's much we can do about it from in here.' Victorinus tried to reach the pouch at his waist and felt a moment of panic when he realised it was missing. Amor. Suddenly getting his hands back on that wooden horse seemed like the most important thing in his world. 'How long was I out for?' he asked.

'Three or four hours, I reckon,' Halfhand said. 'Be dark out now.'

'What do you think the others did when we didn't come back?'

'Felix has nearly four hundred horses with him. If Secundus thinks he can march up to the fort and overpower him, he'll be in for a bit of a shock.'

'I hope they got away. Should have told him to run south if we didn't come back, hook up with Felicius.'

'How d'you think he's getting on?' Halfhand asked.

'Damn sight better than us I hope.' Victorinus rolled his neck, felt some of the feeling come back into his body. He had the beginnings of pins and needles in his left leg, the tingling sensation growing higher as the blood tried to force itself around his wrecked body.

'Don't suppose any of you have any tools?' he asked with more optimism than he felt.

Halfhand and Drost shook their heads. Severus,

though, shimmied around the cell floor until he could get a manacled hand beneath his tunic. 'Got a knife,' he said.

'Fuck me,' Halfhand said softly, shaking his head like a disappointed parent. 'You had that in your tunic all this time?'

'Yeah?' Severus said with a sorry shrug. 'Was wondering when the right time was to let you guys know.'

'What a continued loss to the Navy you are,' Victorinus said with a sardonic laugh. 'Get the fuck out of your manacles and help the rest of us.'

After some more cursing, a lot of shuffling around, a few near misses and two full-blown arguments that would have ended in violence had Halfhand and Severus not been in chains, the three men in the other cell were free. Drost took responsibility for picking the lock on the iron gate, and did so with far less of the above. A few moments later and Victorinus was out of his cage, head like a hungover bear and legs as wobbly as a newborn calf.

'Where exactly are we?' Victorinus asked as they stood in the corridor, the light from the brazier growing dimmer by the second.

'We were taken from the kitchen, down a small corridor which led to the door at the top of the stairs,' Drost said. He had found an axe propped up against the wall at the bottom of the stairs and now whirled it around in a circle, limbering up his arms.

'How many soldiers do you think there are up there?'

'One way to find out, Chief,' Halfhand said with a shrug.

'So four of us, one knife and one axe, against what is in all probability a small army.'

'What are we waiting for?' Severus said, a manic grin fixed to a sweat-soaked face.

They climbed the stairs. Wasn't long, twelve steps only, but Victorinus felt his legs grow heavier with every one. His head pulsed, the rhythm of the pain in sync with the beat of his heart. His hands searched for the absent pouch at his waist. All he could think about was getting it back, holding Amor once more. His son would never forgive him if he didn't bring the toy back.

Drost took the lead; he had the axe, after all. Victorinus assumed the door atop the stairs would be locked, but when Drost gave the handle a squeeze it opened without complaint. It was dark, the corridor and its bare white walls glowing in the light of another brazier. They paused as Drost peered from behind the door, his head turning left and right. There was no sound. Victorinus dared not breathe.

'All clear,' Drost said, moving out from behind the door. The others followed, Victorinus happy to be led as he alone had no clue where they were. He longed to get a message to Felix and his cavalry, or even to just know they were safe. To do that, though, he would first have to break out of here.

'Which way?' he hissed to Halfhand. Annoyance grew in him as his three companions just stood still in the corridor.

Halfhand shrugged. 'Ain't me that gives the orders around here.'

Victorinus sighed. 'Back towards the kitchen, then.'

They moved at a creep, the flagstones silent beneath carefully planted feet. They rounded a corner and the garden Victorinus had seen that afternoon came into sight, hiding amongst the shadows.

A sound from a doorway to their right and they all froze. Victorinus itched for a blade, not that he was a famed swordsman. But if he was going to die, he'd rather go down fighting than being whipped like a dog. The sound died away and collectively the men let loose their unspent breath. Victorinus assumed these rooms were for the slaves and maybe the soldiers. Secundus would sleep at the front of the house, away from the hustle and bustle of the kitchen.

Ten more paces down the porticoed corridor and they reached the door for the kitchen. There was no handle on this, just a swing door, typical for a busy room that was used to seeing people pop in and out all times of the day or night. They paused outside, Victorinus studying the pool of light that crept through the base of the door, checking for movement within.

He was about to order Drost to burst in when a voice spoke. 'How long are we leaving that rabble down in the dungeon?' a man said. He had a high-pitched, sing-song tone, and immediately Victorinus thought the man sounded like Cassius. He built a picture of the man, in Cassius's image. Short and slim, flowing blond hair and a certain femininity to his looks. Pale eyes and soft skin, an unlined face unused to the sharp edge of a shaving blade. It couldn't possibly be Cassius though; the thought was ludicrous.

'Until the boss says so,' another replied, and instantly Victorinus knew who this was. It was the man in the cavalry mask on the road, the same man who had stood guard at the gates of this very house earlier on today. The same man who had likely clubbed him around the back of the head and given him the immovable headache that stalked his every step.

Rage built within him. This man had threatened

his wife, his children. He knew too well he had been far from a perfect husband, would never be the doting father his children would mourn when he'd be dead and buried. Might be too late to put any of that right now, might be a burned bridge too far.

But there was one thing he could do. He snatched the axe from Drost and kicked the door so hard it burst free of its hinges and hit the tiled floor with a crash. Stepping in, he saw a flash of blond hair as it ducked out a door to the rear, but he paid it little attention as the other man in the room rose and freed his sword in one smooth motion.

'I got the runner!' Severus shouted, and he barged through the kitchen, upending a stool and scattering the remains of someone's dinner as he barrelled into a wooden table.

'You,' Victorinus said as the rear door swung shut. 'It was you on the road, wearing the cavalry mask, you who threatened my family.'

'You're in deeper than you can handle, Tribune,' the man said. He was stoically calm, a steady hand holding an unwavering blade. 'Leave now, and maybe you will escape with your life. But know this, drunkard. You take one more step towards me and your family will pay for your mistakes with their lives. Already had to bury one little boy, haven't you? What was it that happened to him? Oh yes, died of a fever whilst you were out whoring with your sad little mates.'

The sword moved from his left hand to his right, the blade catching the light as it moved. The man's eyes never wavered, fixed on Victorinus. 'You will not hurt my family,' he growled.

'Oh no, not me, mate. But my men will. They have their orders should anything out of the ordinary happen to me or the prefect. See, the boss knows you're not quite the useless drunk you pretend to be. Knows you've got a bit of backbone. He knew you wouldn't fall in with the rest of us. Those men you came across north of the Wall were meant to kill you.'

'I hope you're better with that than they were with theirs.' Victorinus pointed his axe at the man's sword. Victorinus was aware of Halfhand and Drost behind him, forcing their way into the room. Half-hand moved past Victorinus, found a metal pan hanging from a hook in the wall. Drost bunched his fists and rolled his shoulders, making his already im-pressive physique seem bigger than it was. Victorinus felt his heart warm then, stood a little straighter. Would have been easy to let this whoreson taunt him into some reckless lunge, watch in despair as the axe bit nothing but air and then, off balance, be able to do nothing about the sword point licking out to take his life.

But he did have a bit about him, had been around the block. And he had his friends with him. 'They were amateurs,' the man scoffed. 'Good for nothing but dying, so it turned out anyway. Played their part though, got the first fire going. That was all we needed them for.'

Victorinus had so many questions. So much of what was happening made no sense. He wanted to know who was behind this, who could hold such a grudge against the empire. But he knew he would get no answers here. 'I grow tired of your voice,' he said, moving further into the room. The kitchen was large, as bestowed a grand villa such as this. There was a worktop to his right, a cutting board and a knife on top, next to the remains of a loaf of bread. He eyed the knife briefly. Drost followed his gaze and reached out to pick it up.

'Now, come on, lads,' the man said. 'Three against one is hardly fair, is it?'

'It took three of you to threaten my wife,' Victorinus said.

'To be fair, she's ferocious. It'll take at least four of my lads to gut her, I reckon.' The man sniffed, then offered Victorinus a slow smirk.

'Who are you?'

'Me? Oh, I'm nobody, just an enrolment number on a scrap of parchment in the grand history of Rome's mighty legions.' The man wore mail under a long-sleeved tunic, and bronzed greaves covered his shins. Victorinus realised he was dressed differently to the other soldiers in the province. This man had served with the field army; it was only them, after all, who got the most up-to-date kit. Even his sword looked new; the bone on the pommel still shone in the soft light of the braziers. Victorinus's own, wherever that was, was dull and dented, much like the blade, now he thought of it.

'So you served with the western field army. Did your time holding back the barbarians across the Rhine and Danube. And then, what, thought instead of retirement you'd pop over to the most distant border in the west and earn yourself some easy coin?'

The man smirked again.

Keep him talking, Victorinus thought. 'No, you were sent here. Your master, whoever that may be, sent you, and some like-minded souls with you, over here to sow the seeds of rebellion. You've been in on this since the start, haven't you?'

'My lips are sealed,' the man said, though the smirk remained.

'They will be soon. For good. So, who is it? This man who would bring the island to its knees?'

'To its knees?' the man scoffed. 'Look around you, friend. Can't you see we already are? I'd wager you've never left this rain-sodden place, but let me tell you, brother, it doesn't get any prettier across the Narrow Sea. Everywhere you go the roads are in disrepair, the troops are undermanned and under paid. Officers at every station are trying to scam what coin they can from under their superiors' nose. You know how it is, bet you've done your fair bit yourself. Money needed for equipment, for supplies. The money arrives but the promised goods never do. Who gets the blame? The emperor, the governor. They aren't even aware they're getting scammed. The system's rotten, the empire's broken, soon to be ground to dust forever.'

'And what will you do? What will this Valentia of yours bring to the people that Rome cannot?'

Halfhand was edging around the wall to Victorinus's left, Drost moving further to the right, away from his tribune. Victorinus knew what they were about. They would encircle this fool, make sure any way he turned he'd be faced by an armed man – if you count a saucepan as a weapon, anyway.

'Justice! Freedom! A right for every man to have a say in their destiny! We will make the world anew, tear apart the old regime and build a new one from its ashes.'

It was Victorinus's turn to smirk. 'Sounds very much like you're just going to overthrow the emperor and replace him with the same thing. Been done before, brother, quite a few times actually. You should read some history.'

Halfhand was almost at the man's right shoulder now, the saucepan hanging low by his side.

'I don't expect you to understand, Tribune. You who spends your life in the company of the savages north of the Wall. What do you know of the world? Of the struggles of the people who try to survive under our corrupt regime? Soon Rome will be nothing more than a memory. Valentia will rise and the people will rejoice!'

With a movement so sudden Victorinus had no time to react, the man lunged across the kitchen, his sword point licking out faster than a viper's tongue, and the tribune just had time to picture the faces of his wife and boys before he was sent flying into the worktop to his right.

Hands hit his shoulder and he flew across the kitchen, hitting the wooden top with a thump, his ribs digging into the edge of the counter. Rebounding back into the melee, he barged into the back of Drost, who had been quick enough to react to the man's sudden attack, and sent his friend hurtling out of the reaching blade's path. Victorinus then thumped into the back of Halfhand, who had also tried to get his commander out of harm's way, and he fell into their attacker. They crashed together, forced into a tight embrace. Together they tumbled and smashed into the table, sending it flying across the room before both men collapsed to the flagstone floor.

Sword and saucepan clanged on the floor before making a break for freedom. Victorinus still stood, winded, lungs burning with every breath. Whether Drost or Halfhand had saved his life or not, far as he saw it the two of them owed him at least a couple of new ribs. Staggering, hunched over, right hand still gripping the axe, left hand wrapped around his torso, he ambled towards the two men now grappling on the floor. Drost beat him to them and aimed a savage kick at the back of their enemy's head. The man grunted at the pain but didn't relinquish his grip, locked as it was around Halfhand's neck.

There was blood on grey tiles, and Victorinus didn't know if any was Halfhand's, but when he got a glimpse of his friend's face, his skin was pale, his eyes a jaundice yellow. He didn't seem to have the energy to fight the man off and Victorinus panicked. Halfhand was one of the few people in the world he would be prepared to risk his life for, he could not let him down.

Drost kicked the man on the head again, and this time he relinquished his grip on Halfhand. The areani scout rolled away, and the panic in Victorinus rose as he saw the blood on his tunic. He had been stabbed in the torso, high on his left side. *That blow had been meant for me.* Victorinus had seen enough wounds to know when one was fatal and this one was bleeding badly.

He forced himself to snatch his eyes away from Halfhand to the commotion to his right. Drost had his knife held above the man's face but was unable to force it down any further. The soldier had hold of Drost's arm and was using all of his strength to keep him at bay. Victorinus took two steps and lifted the axe above his head, before arcing it down in a savage blow, the blade striking the nameless man on the top of the head. Blood erupted from the wound, then some other stuff Victorinus would have struggled to name.

The fight was over, the axe stuck hard in the dead man's head. Victorinus bent over double, breathing hard, sweat pouring off him. The ribs on the right side of his torso still burned. He knew the pain would grow worse as the adrenalin wore off. Drost still had hold of his knife. He seemed unable to take his eyes from the axe and the lumps of brain and bone that surrounded it.

'Ugh,' Halfhand grunted, behind Victorinus now. The tribune spun on the spot and lowered himself to his knees.

'Oh, my brother,' he said gently, taking his friend by the hand. His fingers rubbed the stubbed scars of Halfhand's left hand. 'I'm so sorry.'

'Not... your... fault,' Halfhand whispered between shallow breaths. His teeth were gritted, his eyes distant, pupils shrinking. 'Promise me... you'll finish this.'

'I promise. I promise you I will.'

Drost walked to Halfhand's other side. He didn't lower himself as Victorinus had done, he just stood there, looking dumbfounded at the dying man on the floor. 'I'll give you two some privacy,' he said after a moment's silence, which was filled with nothing but Halfhand's shallow breathing. 'Goodbye, Halfhand.' He nodded before leaving the kitchen to keep watch in the corridor.

'What am I going to do without you?' Victorinus said, tears carving rivets down his cheeks. 'You are the best friend anyone ever had, you know that?'

'No, I'm not. If I had been... I would have stopped you drinking... and whoring all the damn time... and told you to go home... to that lovely family of yours.'

Victorinus smiled, a sad smile full of bitterness and regret. 'I would not have listened.'

'It's not... too late... for you... and Sarai.'

'I think it is, brother. I made my bed, now I must lie in it.'

'You must... go to them.'

'I will,' Victorinus said, reaching out a hand and stroking his friend's hair. 'Be at peace now, old friend. You have fought for long enough.'

Victorinus thought he might slip away then, but he fought on, his shallow breaths bubbling blood. He became aware of noises out in the corridor, hobnailed boots ringing off the flagstones. Drost burst back through the door, wide eyed and animated.

'We've got to go!' he said as he clattered past them, not sparing Halfhand a glance. 'Soldiers, lots of the bastards!'

'Give me a sword... prop me up,' Halfhand wheezed.

'No!'

'Do it... I'm a dead man... either way... rather go down... fighting.'

Drost turned from his position at the rear door of the kitchen. It was only then Victorinus remembered

Severus had gone running off that way. And then he remembered the flash of blond hair he had been chasing. Nodding, he reached behind him for the sword that had dealt the death blow to his friend, the blood on the blade still wet. He heaved Halfhand up to a sitting position, propping him up against the overturned table. 'I'll never forget you, brother,' he choked out, trying and failing to keep his voice in check.

'Go,' Halfhand whispered, giving his commander one last smile.

They left. The door opened onto another corridor, another brazier lighting the end of the passage. Once at the end they had the option of left or right, and Victorinus paused for a moment to try and get his bearings. To his left the passage curved round and he pictured the outline of the villa in his mind. 'Go right,' he said, setting off straight after Drost.

As they reached the gardens at the side of the house, they heard screaming and a clash of iron behind them. Halfhand, loyal to the end. There would be a time to mourn, a time to remember. But now, they just had to run.

'Where do you think Severus got to?' Drost asked as they reached the wall.

Victorinus didn't answer. He had no answers, not now.

Not when his heart was broken.

10

The sun seemed to shine a little brighter this side of the Narrow Sea. The air was thicker, the breeze less prominent, and instead of bringing with it a refreshing blow of sea air, it carried nothing but more thick heat.

Felicius stood outside the headquarters of the Navy base in Bononia. His tunic clung to his back, and his blond mane of hair was lank and dull, clinging to his scalp. He should have been dressed in full battle regalia, given the status of the man he was waiting to see. But truth be told he didn't think he could handle the weight of his mail right now.

He had fought in Gaul before, of course. Many a time he had regaled to Victorinus stories of battles won under this furnace of a sun. Spoke with pride at the fitness of the men he commanded, how they had prevailed where lesser men would have succumbed.

But by all the gods, he couldn't remember it ever being this hot. Or had his years in Britannia softened him? Maybe he should ask to be posted back out east. He could return to Egypt or Syria, remind himself of what proper soldiering was. He knew he wouldn't though, knew how well that would go down if he presented the suggestion to Lucia.

He thought of his wife and daughter then. He had abandoned them at a small farmstead in a province wracked with rebellion. Lucia had just lost her father, saw his corpse in all its grizzled glory. The body still gave Felicius nightmares, the writing in blood on the wall above the governor. *Valentia.* There was still something else that disturbed him, something he had not been able to bring himself to properly address. Lucia had seemed terrified upon finding her father's body. Julius Narcissus, governor of Flavia Caesariensis, had died a bad death. They had found his body in his sleeping quarters, throat slit, bloodied knife still clutched in a numb hand.

But that had not been the disturbing part. As well as the blood on the wall, there had been a V burnt into the governor's chest. Felicius had been sure his wife had detected some sort of meaning in this. She should have been numb with the shock, distraught with grief at losing her father so unexpectantly. But she hadn't been.

Grieving, sure. She had wept over her father's body in the manner any daughter would have done. But there had been something else. The stench of terror overpowering the tang of blood. There was something, something she knew that he didn't, and he hadn't had the heart to press her for details. That had been a mistake, a weakness in him that he would need to iron out were he to turn his career around. No one was above suspicion, no one was to be given any special dispensation, even if that person had given life to your only child.

He'd not been able to hide his disappointment at being told his wife had given birth to a girl and not a boy. He'd felt guilty for it, even as the soft frown played over his face; he knew he was not behaving as a husband should. Lucia had lain on the birthing bed, bloodied sheets cleared away before he had been allowed into the chamber. Marcelina snuggled to her breast; Lucia had shed tears of joy as she introduced their daughter to her father.

Sure, he'd managed a smile eventually, even lowered himself down to kiss the child on her head. But all the while he'd been jealously thinking of his friend Victorinus, and the sons he and Sarai managed to produce with ease. He had never voiced this, would never dare. And as Marcelina had grown, he had come to love her with all his heart. But a son, an heir, a man to carry his name when he was nothing more than a memory, was something he coveted more than anything else.

Shaking his head to free himself from that chain of thought, he refocused on the immediate future and why he was standing where he was. He knew he would be expected to provide answers. He was here to make a report, but all he had to offer was speculation and rumour. Britannia was aflame, overrun by bands of barbarians, and the army appeared to have either defected or abandoned their posts. He imagined how well that was going to go down, then remembered the ship he had been travelling on, sinking into the sea. *Yes*, he thought, *it's going to go down about as well as that.*

'Prefect?' a feminine voice said behind him. Turning, Felicius was surprised to find a man, a eunuch, he assumed. The man was short and run to fat, bald as a baby with soft, delicate skin. Felicius walked towards him and was hit with a wall of fragrance so strong it could have masked the stench of a rotting body.

Maybe it was; the eunuch was wrapped in fine-looking, thick, dark robes. He must have been roasting. 'He's ready for you now,' the eunuch said in his sing-song voice.

Felicius followed him into the coolness of a summer villa. High stone ceilings had succeeded in keeping the worst of the heat at bay, and two slaves stood in opposite corners of the reception room, wafting giant fans, which blew a gentle and welcome breeze across the vast open space. Looking around, Felicius, a man married into high society, well accustomed to the luxuries the highborn surrounded themselves with, stood in awe.

The walls were covered in beautiful paintings, depicting triumphant generals from the glory days of old. Julius Caesar seated on a golden throne, a barbarian warlord kneeling at his feet. Felicius stared at the painting, trying to remember the barbarian's name. The man had united the tribes of Gaul against Caesar and his legions. But that had not been enough to stop the great man.

'Vercingetorix,' a voice said from an open doorway. Turning, Felicius found himself locking eyes with a man in his early fifties. He wore his greying hair cut short in the military style; his brown eyes blended with his sun-kissed skin. His nose was short and pinched, above thin, dry lips. He was of average height, a slim body still clinging to youth, maintained by a militant routine, despite his advancing years.

'Domine.' Felicius saluted, standing to attention.

'At ease, Prefect. It is good to see you. How long has it been? Four years?'

'Five, Domine.' *Five years since you cast me out from your army.*

'Britannia has done you good, it seems. You look well. How's the leg? Really? That's good to hear. Come, let us retire to my study, I shall have refreshment brought.'

He followed in silence to a well-lit study. There was less finery on show here; it was minimalistic, a place of work and nothing else. There was a table with two wooden stools, some shelving against a plain wall, an armour stand in the corner, complete with a bronzed cuirass.

Valerius Jovinus, Magister Militum of the western empire, right hand of Emperor Valentinian, smiled as a slave brought in a jug of cooled wine, two cups and a platter of fruit. Jovinus poured the wine and gestured to the food. 'Help yourself, old friend.'

'Thank you, Domine,' Felicius said, reaching out to grab an apple.

'Let's dispense with the formalities, Gaius, no one

is on parade here. I heard you took a wife, had a daughter, I trust they are well?'

'Yes, sir, Lucia, daughter of Governor Narcissus. She and my daughter Marcelina are well, thank you.' He hoped that was true.

'Glad to hear it. A man should be married. There is, after all, nothing more important than family.'

'Yes, sir,' Felicius replied, trying to remember if the famed general himself was married.

'Though you have not braved the pirates of the Narrow Sea to talk of such things,' Jovinus said, a half-smile on his lined face. 'What news from Britannia?'

Felicius took a long draught of wine before he spoke. He talked for what felt an age, feeling a sense of release as he spoke freely of the happenings in Rome's most remote posting. He talked of fire and death, of rebellion and treachery. He felt exhausted when he was done, as if speaking of the horrific bloodshed was more tiresome than actually shedding the blood.

'So that is why I have come to you, sir. We need men in Britannia, as soon as possible. The people are scared, they have nowhere to run, no one to protect them. We need a leader, a man to lead us to glory. We need you, sir.'

Jovinus was silent a while, chewing his tongue in

thought. Then he leant forward on his stool and spoke to Felicius in a low tone. 'Valentia, you say.'

'Yes, sir. Seems to be some sort of code word, or rallying cry. Whatever it is, or means, it appears to be the cause that the rebels are rallying to.'

Another period of silence. Jovinus narrowed his eyes as he stared at the prefect. Felicius felt as if he was being weighed, measured, his worth being calculated like a slab of meat on the butcher's table.

'Does the name Lupus Valentinus mean anything to you, Prefect?'

'Lupus Valentinus?' Felicius copied, rolling the name around on his tongue. 'No, sir, not heard of him before. Who is he?'

'Maybe he was before your time,' Jovinus said with a shrug. 'He is, was, a senator. Served with the western field army for a few years. Pannonian by birth, he is the brother of some lawyer in Rome, who has a certain influence over our emperor.'

'Influence?'

'The man has apparently been invaluable in quelling the recent religious unrest in the city. These new Christian factions pop up all the time, seems there is one in particular growing more popular by the day. There is peace on the streets of Rome for now though.'

'There are different factions of Christianity? I thought the main religious disputes were between the emperor and the senate?' Felicius blew out his cheeks in amazement. Once more, he was thankful he had managed to keep himself distant from religion and the fanatics that poisoned the minds of the people around them.

'Britannia really is a backwater, isn't it? Yes, as you know the empire is mostly Christian these days, but most of the senators, myself included, still worship the old gods. Christianity, though, is a different beast entirely. Factions have begun to emerge; new churches spring up from nowhere with priests and bishops all presenting their own visions of God. It is tiresome, and troublesome. If the emperor backs the wrong horse, then he will lose a lot more than a bad day at the races. It is a distraction, and a very unwelcome one.'

Jovinus drained his cup and poured both men more wine. He selected a fig from the tray on the table and chewed it, his eyes once more narrowing. 'But I digress. Britannia is the issue here, and Lupus Valentinus is very much at the heart of it.'

'He is the man responsible for the uprising?'

'He is. He was outlawed from court two years ago, for crimes I will not repeat here. His original sentence was death; it was only his brother's intervention to Valentinian that spared his life.'

Felicius sucked in air as he took the information in. What could the man have done that was so bad he had been sentenced to death? Jovinus himself had been lucky to avoid the same fate a few years earlier, Felicius remembered.

Jovinus chuckled. 'I can read you like a book, old friend.'

'Sir?' Felicius said with as much innocence as he could muster. He had never been a good liar.

'You are thinking that I myself was lucky to be spared execution after I was named imperator by my troops in the field.'

Felicius contemplated denying it, then saw there was little point. He had not long been posted to Britannia when word first spread that the emperor Jovian had wanted to replace Jovinus with one of his own men. It had not gone down well with the field army, particularly as Jovinus had just won a great victory on the Rhine front. 'That news did reach us up on the Wall,' he admitted.

'It is true enough, so no reason why it shouldn't have. The army proclaimed me emperor after a great victory on the Rhine, though luckily for me I had the nous to calm them and bring the officers back to their senses before it got out of hand. Then I made legs to the emperor Jovian and prostrated myself at his feet. Relations between the two of us were... a bit cold, shall we say, for a while. But he died and Valentinian made his bid for the purple. I did nothing to contest it; in fact, I threw my full support behind him. He is a good man; he trusts me and leaves me to run the army as I see fit. That, old friend, is the limit of my ambitions.'

Felicius smiled. He liked the man, despite the fact it had been Jovinus who had exiled him to Britannia in the first place. He had served under Jovinus on the Rhine and Danube borders. The general was a career soldier, a born tactician and an able, if not particularly charismatic, leader of men. He thought Jovinus would have hated being emperor. The fact that there had been two in the last seven years alone should have been enough to warn off most potential suitors to the purple. Being head of an unstable state did not come with a pension and a plot of land, just an inevitable knife in the back.

'So, this Valentinus, he was exiled to Britannia?'

'Yes. Flavia Caesariensis was chosen because your father-in-law, Julius Narcissus, was known to the emperor and of proven loyalty. There were enough troops in the area to keep an eye on him, and he was close enough to the Caledonians north of the Wall that they might just get lucky on one of their raids and kill him for us. Sadly, we seem to have underestimated the man.'

Felicius was momentarily stunned. He gulped wine from his cup. It was all he could do to stop himself going on a rant that could end with his dismissal from his post. For all the respect the general seemed to hold him in, he didn't think he would survive a full-on verbal assault on the man.

'Gaius, whatever you have to say just spit it out. If you get any redder, I'm worried you may explode.'

'Sir,' he began, before taking a couple of breaths to control himself. 'There are Saxons and Franks raiding down the east coast. There are Scotti raiding the west, and what appears to be the entire population of adult males from Caledonia killing at will south of the Wall. Our troops have deserted their stations. From what I hear some are even fighting with the enemy. People are being killed, food stolen, farms destroyed. It will take years for the island to recover from this. Financially it may never be the same again. And yet you sit here and speak mildly of underestimating this Valentinus! How could he do this? Where did he get the coin to bring so many people to his banner?'

It was a shock to Felicius to discover he was now

standing up, leaning over the wooden desk, white-tipped knuckles pressing hard on the surface. He was also out of breath, and there was a commotion at the door behind him, two armed men bursting through, spear tips pointed at him, suggesting he may have slightly raised his voice.

'Peace, dear Gaius, peace. Leave us,' he said to the soldiers. 'There is no trouble here.'

Felicius sat back down, hands trembling. Jovinus poured him more wine and he drank greedily. 'I'm sorry,' he said once his heart had returned to its normal steady beat. 'It has been a trying couple of weeks.'

'And you have lost men. I know that feeling all too well, Gaius. But I want to assure you, help is on the way.'

'The emperor will dispatch the field army?' Felicius said in hope.

'Part of it, yes. We are weeks away from a major conflict with the Alamanni. I'm sure you remember them.'

Felicius did. They were a ferocious tribe bordering the Rhine and Danube. He himself had fought in countless battles and skirmishes against them. They were formidable opponents, a creditable threat to stability within the empire.

'I have been given a month to clear the sea of pirates. I have just one week left, though the work is almost done. Fidelis tells me I have you in part to thank for that.'

'Fighting at sea is something I have no wish to repeat,' Felicius said, thinking of the battle he had fought just a few days before. 'I'm just glad your men didn't attack us as we made for Bononia, I was sure some eager lookout would see the Frankish ship and we would be rammed by allies.'

'Fidelis knows his business, and he got you here just fine. I read in his report that eighteen of his crew were killed before the fighting even started. Was there any proof they were in collusion with the enemy?'

Felicius explained about the lookout signalling the enemy ship and then his insistence he would not be the one fighting.

'Then you know the problems we are having with manpower presently,' Jovinus said. Felicius nodded.

'I know it is the same everywhere, so spare me the sob story, Prefect. But the Navy bases on the west coast of Gaul are our best hope of keeping the Narrow Sea free from pirates. We must do what we can to protect them.'

'So who will come and rescue Britannia?' Felicius asked.

'Not I, I'm afraid. The emperor wants me in place to deal with the Alamanni. But we have an able man leading the relief force. The comes rei militaris Flavius Theodosius, a man you may have come across before, has been appointed to the task. He is a commander of considerable experience, and we have released detachments of the Heruli, the Batavi and the Iovii to quash this rebellion. Some two thousand men in total. They will see the job done, Prefect.'

Felicius didn't think two thousand men sounded like much of an army. Britannia was huge, had taken Rome years to conquer and decades to stabilise. And that was with an army more than ten times the size of the one the emperor Valentinian had seen fit to send across the Narrow Sea. But that was not the most pressing question on his mind.

'How long have you known about this, Valentinus?'

Jovinus shuffled on his seat. He clasped his hands together and swallowed before speaking. 'We have been aware for a while that he might be up to no good. We had orders sent to the prefect of notaries in Flavia Caesariensis, asked him to use his agents in the north to find out what they could and report back to us. The report came back squeaky clean. Nothing untoward seemed to be happening;

the notary was satisfied his men had done their job well.'

Felicius knew there was a 'but' coming before the general had taken a breath.

'But,' he continued at last, 'it would appear that the notary in question, a man by the name of Secundus, is either much worse at his job than we thought, or more likely, he is in league with Valentinus and was feeding us duff information.'

Felicius nodded. He knew, of course, that Secundus was head of the agentus in rebus, as well as Victorinus's unit, the miles areani. For a brief moment he panicked, his mind working through wild scenarios where his old friend was part of the conspiracy all along. He thought once more of Lucia and Marcelina, staying with his friend's family. *No*, he said to himself, *there is no way Victorinus is a traitor*.

'So how has this man come by the funds required to do this?' Felicius asked. 'Think about it, sir. He has got armies from three different countries to come together in rebellion. He has paid off the troops on the Wall, bribed at least one senior official in Britannia, and that's before we get to the small stuff, such as the German sailors on the ship just waiting to betray us. How, sir? How does someone do this?'

Jovinus gave the prefect a sad smile and small

shrug. 'That I don't fully know. How he got the money I can speculate, but again, it is not my place to say. As to how he does the rest, well, I think our history is full of determined, charismatic men who would stop at nothing to achieve ultimate power, would you not agree? I saw you studying the painting of Caesar out there.' He gestured past the door. 'How did he persuade his legions to turn on Rome and fight the senate? Should they not have laid down their weapons and handed him over?'

'But he was their leader,' Felicius found himself saying. 'He led them to victory for ten years, from the south of Gaul to the shores of Britannia! How could they break a bond like that?'

'How could they indeed. Now, Valentinus may not have done that. He hasn't had the time or the resource yet. But he does have a vision, and I'd wager he can sell it well. That is how this happens, old friend. Sure, there will have been deals brokered with Saxon chiefs, bribes offered to the tribes of the west and those north of the Wall – not that they would have required much encouragement for a season of free reign in the south. But as to how he got the Roman troops to leave their posts, how he got officials such as Secundus on side, that all started with a vision.'

'But you had heard the word Valentia before to-day,' Felicius said.

'I had,' Jovinus said with a small nod. 'As I said, Gaius, it all starts with a vision. This one in particular seems to have spread like wildfire.'

Felicius knew there was more to it, knew too he would not get all the answers he wanted. Jovinus was one of the most powerful men in the west. He stood at the shoulder of an emperor and had the rare privilege of being privy to some of the most innermost secrets of the empire. Felicius on the other hand was nothing more than a prefect. There were a hundred or more of him in the western empire alone. He was of little importance, nothing more than a pawn on the board, and he could be replaced in a heartbeat.

'So, when does this Theodosius sail?' he said at last.

'Next month, right after the ceremony.'

'Ceremony?'

'Gods, Britannia really is the end of the earth, isn't it? Come, let us take a stroll around the garden and I shall fill you in on all you have missed.'

11

AUGUST, AD 367

The comes rei militaris Flavius Theodosius arrived at Bononia with little fanfare and less fuss. His troops were already there, had been in place for two weeks, and even before the general had dismounted, he was hounding an unfortunately positioned aide, asking why the men had not already begun to be shipped across the Narrow Sea.

'We should be taking action, man! What is the delay?'

The aide looked around, finding his colleagues shrunken into the shadows. 'You... You, sir. We were waiting for you.'

The general sighed, slapping his leg in frustration.

'It will take four trips to get all our men and provisions across, yes?'

The aide gulped then nodded.

'So why would you wait for me to arrive when we could have at least shipped some of the men and equipment across by now?'

He got no answer, the aide deciding his question was probably rhetorical.

'Gods, man! Are the ships ready? Yes? Then let us begin loading!'

Felicius watched the exchange with a half-smile dancing beneath his beard. He had heard many things about Theodosius, and it was amusing to see the descriptions of the man brought to life in front of him. The prefect had endured a frustrating three-week wait at Bononia. Dismayed at the delay, he too had questioned the general's aides and clerks as they began to arrive, imploring them to be proactive in getting as many men and equipment over to Britannia before the general arrived. His words had fallen on deaf ears.

So he had exercised and socialised, keeping his body battle ready and learning everything he could about the men he would be marching to save Britannia with. Jovinus had fulfilled his obligations to the emperor Valentinian and was now back in eastern Gaul, preparing the western field army for a late summer campaign against the Alamanni over the Rhine. He had spent the rest of the day with Felicius after their meeting, filling the prefect in on the happenings of the world beyond Britannia's shores.

The emperor had been ill. This was not the first time in recent years Valentinian had fallen ill with either a fever or a bout of sickness, and the last one had taken some time to shift. Worried for his long-term health, and the instability his death would bring to the empire, Valentinian had promoted his eight-year-old son Gratian to the rank of Augustus, giving the boy all the honours he himself enjoyed. That had been the reason for Theodosius's delay; as a senior commander in the army and a member of the senate, he had been expected to attend the ceremony.

Felicius had riled at the news when he had been told. He thought it typical of the politics of the empire. Attending a ceremony for an eight-year-old child was now more of a priority than preserving the lives of the people the eight-year-old was now expected to rule over.

'But who will it be that saves these people?' Jovinus had countered.

'The army, of course,' Felicius replied.

'And those men must swear fealty to their emperor before they leave the field army.'

'The child won't be emperor, not until his father has passed. It's not as if an eight-year-old boy will be deciding our fates any time soon.'

Felicius had kicked the ground in frustration.

'I understand your concerns, Prefect, I do. But think too of Theodosius. Position and favour are everything at court, and the general has not always had an easy relationship with Valentinian. He needs the emperor onside if he is going to be successful in Britannia.'

'Poor Theodosius,' Felicius muttered, but he left his arguments there. Nothing he said would make the slightest bit of difference.

But now Theodosius had arrived at Gaul's western shore, summer had full hold on the land and Bononia was a furnace. Felicius actually found himself looking forward to the journey over the Narrow Sea, if only for the prospect of a breeze.

Theodosius dismounted his horse, throwing the reins to a waiting slave. He wore just a plain short-sleeved tunic with no trousers, sandals on his feet and a brown leather belt around his waist. His thinning hair was cut short, a red scalp showing beneath. 'Domine,' Felicius said as the general approached. He saluted and then stood to attention.

'And you are?' the general said, squinting in the strong sunlight as he looked up at Felicius.

'Prefect Gaius Felicius, sir, commander of the Fourth Cohort of Gauls.'

'Ah, you are the man who braved the seas to bring us word of the rebellion. Well met, Prefect. Jovinus has told me good things about you and your men. I look forward to working with you.'

'Thank you, sir.' Felicius flushed slightly at the praise. Everything he had heard of Theodosius indicated that the man was as hard as iron. Praise from such a man would undoubtedly be hard to come by. He was pleased they seemed to be getting off on the right foot. 'I am eager to get back to Rutupiae and my men, sir.'

'I'd wager you are. Why did you not tell these fools to begin boarding the second the ships were ready?' Theodosius said, motioning to the clutch of clerks and aides behind him.

'I did, sir,' Felicius said without hesitation. 'My suggestions were not listened to.'

'Is that right?' Theodosius muttered. He turned back to the men in question and began haranguing them once more. Felicius tried and failed to conceal the smirk that grew across his face. The general was not a tall man, nor was he particularly well built, but he had a presence like no other Felicius had ever met. Jovinus had always possessed a rather mild character, always calm, and Felicius could not recall him losing his temper with anyone. If he was the calm of the summer sea, then Theodosius was a winter storm. He could see why the emperor would want two very different men as his senior commanders in the army. When seeking guidance on military matters, Felicius knew receiving advice from different points of view was beneficial.

'Right,' the general said after he had finished his verbal assault. 'Where can I get some wine?'

* * *

The return voyage proved to be far more uneventful than the one over to Gaul, much to Felicius and his men's relief. Vitulus had still not reconciled to the losses they had taken in the sea battle and eyed every sailor on the ship suspiciously until they reached Rutupiae.

Fidelis had been an unwilling passenger on another man's ship, his scrutinous eye seemingly disapproving of every turn of the steering oar and raising of the sail. 'We'd have been back in half the time if I'd have been in command,' he said as they disembarked, just loud enough for the captain of the ship to hear him.

Felicius was greeted by Clementius and one of his centurions, both men sporting fresh cuts on their faces and hands. 'I know legionaries and auxiliaries aren't famed for getting along, but really, gentlemen, I've only been gone a few weeks.'

His joke brought a wry smile from the two officers, before Clementius filled him in on their exploits. 'We had word of a Saxon band roaming a day's march to the east. Your centurion and I decided we'd had enough of sitting pretty behind our high walls, so we marched out and stuck it to them.'

'Any losses?' Felicius asked anxiously.

'Five dead from the Fourth, sir,' the centurion said. 'Clementius lost a few more.'

'We routed them, though, killed the bastards to the last man and burnt two ships. A good day's work, if you ask me.'

Felicius had spent the remainder of the day or-ganising marching camps to be constructed for the field army. The Heruli and Batavi were the first men to disembark, so much to their fury, this task fell to them.

'You have made yourself an unpopular man, Pre-fect,' a voice said behind Felicius as he lent against the battlement of Rutupiae's northern wall, watching the men work in the last of the sunlight.

Felicius rubbed his tired eyes and turned to see a young man in a resplendent green tunic smiling at him. He was of middle height and slenderly built, a clean-shaven face and waft of perfume giving an effeminate impression. 'It is not the job of a commander to be popular, just to be obeyed,' he said through a thin smile. 'Apologies, but you look familiar, have we met?' Felicius thought he had been introduced to all the commanders in Theodosius's army, but it appeared there was one he had missed.

'Forgive me, Prefect, we have not. I am Theodosius, son of the comes rei militaris Theodosius. I hold no official rank in this army. I'm merely here as an observer.' He offered a small bow before extending out a hand, which Felicius ensured he shook firmly.

The prefect paused for a moment, unsure how to address the general's son. Theodosius held no military rank, but he was from a family of senatorial class. Should he address the young man as sir, or was he the senior man of the two? 'Most people call me Theo, if that helps,' the young man said, an easy smile spreading across his face.

'Theo it is.' Felicius returned the smile, feeling a genuine warmth towards the young man, who seemed very different to his father. 'Who did you sail over with?'

'I came with the Heruli. I've been spending as much time with them as I can since we left the main army for Britannia. Father wants me to learn as much about the common soldiery as I can.'

Felicius nodded. 'Time well spent, I'm sure. You're looking for a career in the military?'

Theo shrugged. He leaned on the parapet next to Felicius and said, 'I guess? My father is pushing me to. I don't know what else I'll do, so...' He shrugged again.

Felicius studied the younger man. For a moment he allowed himself to wonder what it must be like to grow up in the shadow of a man such as Theodosius. The general was not an old man yet, still at the height of his power. Life could not have been easy at times for Theo, carrying the weight of a father's expectation on his back.

'The army is a good place for a man,' he said after a while, suddenly wanting to reassure the younger man. 'It forges you into something better than you were.'

'Unless you get killed, of course,' Theo said, the smile returning to his face.

They stood in silence a while, an easy companionship growing between them, despite the fact they had just met. Below them came the sounds of men at work, of timber being cut and dragged, hammered into the earth. Men shouted and horses whinnied in protest. Fine specks of wood dust spiralled into the orange sky, and Felicius felt as if he were witnessing the calm before the storm. If the men down there thought life was hard now, they would soon realise how wrong they were. Down there were men who would die crying for their mothers. Men who would die from wounds whilst they were convincing themselves they would live. Men who would die from wounds they never saw coming. War was a harsh mistress, a relentless beast with a constant thirst for blood. War was what these men knew; war was their job. But no soldier ever went into battle ready to die, no matter how brave, no matter how strong.

Felicius became aware of a commotion on the plain below, to the east. A band of Heruli warriors were hurtling abuse at the nearest men from the Batavi, and as he watched on, Felicius saw one man hurl a spade and another jump the ditch that separated them and throw a punch. Then all hell broke loose.

'Gods above,' Felicius said, pushing himself away from the wall and heading for the stairs. 'I'd better go and sort this out.'

'Wait, I'll come with you,' Theo said as he hurried after the prefect. The two men made their way down the steps, through the open gate and out into the plain. They skipped past men stripped to the waist, spades arcing up and down as officers shouted encouragement at their backs, everyone keen to have the work complete before sundown.

Felicius cursed his armour as he ran. Everyone told you the merits of good mail when you joined the army; no one ever told you the downside. Moving fast was near on impossible; every twist or turn rubbed your torso, and if you didn't have two layers of tunics on underneath it would rub your skin raw. Then there was the constant maintenance, always worse in the winter months, when there was not enough spit in a cohort of men to get the damn thing to shine on parade. But there was the off chance the bloody thing would save your life one day. Sometimes you just had to take the rough with the smooth.

Lungs heaving now, he reached the eastern edge of the half-built fort where a group of Batavi were exchanging blows with a few Heruli warriors. Three centurions stood around the group, two with their vine sticks already bloody, but it seemed even three officers at their most persuasive was not enough to put a stop to this fight.

'What is the meaning of this?' he called in a breathless tone that carried no further than three feet from his mouth. No one seemed to notice his arrival. A Batavi warrior, clad in a red tunic, had a black-clad Heruli in a neck lock. Next to them, two men rolled around on the mud, a dust cloud pluming around them. 'Why have you not put a stop to this?' Felicius demanded of the nearest centurion.

The man just shrugged. 'Not like we haven't tried, sir,' he said, holding up his blood-slicked vine stick.

Felicius cursed. Freeing his sword, he gripped it by the flat edge of the blade and hammered the pommel down on the head of the nearest warrior, who fell to the ground without so much as a grunt.

His opponent roared in delight before seeing Felicius approach him. He raised his hands in defence but it did nothing to stop the pommel striking again; two blows and another man was eating dust.

'I said ENOUGH!' The fighting stopped then, sparring men moving away from one another, eyeing the prefect warily.

'What in the gods names is going on here? Have you forgotten we are all on the same side?' He moved amongst the men. There were eight left standing, three were badly cut, the rest stood panting. 'I want the men responsible for starting this ruckus on latrines for the next month,' he said to the onlooking centurions, each looking as guilty as the men being punished.

'The thing is, sir...' one of them started and then trailed off, his eyes seeking out one of the Heruli warriors.

Felicius followed the man's gaze and found himself locking eyes with a man in his middle twenties. He had long raven hair and dark eyes. His face was splattered in dried mud and blood, a small clump of earth stuck in his beard. 'Name and rank, soldier.' Felicius reversed his sword as he spoke, pointing the tip of the blade at the man's neck.

The man smiled, revealing two rows of yellowing teeth, at least two missing from the top row. 'I do not answer to you,' he said, then spat blood on the floor.

'You fucking well do,' Felicius growled. 'I am a prefect of Rome, an officer in the army of the comes rei militaris Theodosius, and you will give me the proper respect due.'

Once more the man grinned, a sardonic grin that left Felicius wondering if there was something he didn't know. And then he got his answer.

'Ah, Felicius, I see you have met my cousin. May I introduce Flavius Maximus, son of my father's older brother.' Felicius turned around just in time to catch

Theo's grimace as the young man saw the sword point at his cousin's throat.

'Cousin?' Felicius said incredulously.

'That's right, sir,' Maximus said, proffering a small, ironic bow. 'Not sure my uncle will take too much of a shining to you when I tell him you had a sword to my neck.'

'I'm not sure your uncle will take to kindly to you, Maximus, when he discovers the reason why the prefect had to do so.'

They all turned, Felicius frowning as he did so. General Theodosius sat atop a fine white stallion. His left hand held the reins whilst his right sat lightly on his hip. 'Fighting with the common soldiery again, are you?' He sighed and dismounted, throwing the reins to one of the centurions, each looking like they'd rather be putting down the rebellion on their own than be standing in front of their general in a situation such as this.

'Uncle,' Maximus said, his tone instantly changing. 'I thought you weren't sailing until tomorrow.'

'Yes, that's what everyone thought,' Theodosius said, squaring up to his nephew. 'But that's the thing about rebellions such as this; you can't quite be sure who you can trust. After all, the dear prefect here had to fight off a whole crew on a Roman ship on his way over to Gaul, isn't that right, Felicius?'

Felicius nodded, stunned that the general knew of this. He hadn't told him. 'So when a general cannot even trust his own troops, I find it better to keep certain things in my closest circle.' Every man in earshot was instantly aware that Maximus was clearly not in the general's closest circle.

'Why are you here, nephew?'

'You wanted me to accompany you to Britannia, sir,' Maximus said, eyes on his feet now.

'Yes, but that isn't what I asked, is it, you fool. Why are you here? Fighting with the men I have been appointed to lead?'

There was a pause of silence in which Maximus went as red as the setting sun.

'When will you learn how to behave as a man of your breeding should? We are an example to the men we lead, at all times. Did your father teach you nothing?'

Felicius didn't know where to look and so took a particular interest in the forming clouds overhead. Far as he was concerned, there was a time and a place for hard conversations such as this, and this wasn't it. He would never give one of his officers a dressing down in front of their men; it didn't set the right example.

Maximus made to reply but the general cut him off. 'Do not waste your breath, you insolent pup. We march out at daybreak; we can talk on the road.'

Daybreak? Felicius scowled. What was the point in having the men build these defensive positions if they were only going to be here a night? He felt a prick of irritation crawl over his skin. 'The defences will be needed for the remainder of the army that will make the crossing tomorrow,' Theodosius said, addressing Felicius as if he had read the prefect's mind. 'Plus, if things do not go as planned and we end up in retreat then we will need somewhere to fall back to.'

'We will not wait for the rest of the army, sir?' Theo asked of his father.

'No, my son. I plan to march for Londinium. It is the largest town in the south and I hope the governor there will have some more up-to-date intelligence for us. I have already written to him outlining as much. Plus, we need more provisions and carts to carry them. Any more questions?' he asked, rotating his head around so he looked each man in the eye. 'Good, now get these walls built so the men can get some rest. We march with the rising sun.'

Felicius waited until the general had mounted his horse and ridden away before scowling at Maximus and nodding to Theo and making his way back into

Rutupiae himself. Thoughts were caged in his mind. He rolled them around, played with them, but did not open the lock and set them free. Overall, he was satisfied with his efforts in the last weeks. It had proven a good move to head to Gaul himself. Jovinus had cleared the sea of pirates and he reasoned they should expect to encounter fewer bands of Saxons and Franks on their march north.

He was with an army, an army that would grow even stronger when the detachment from the Iovii landed the following day. Some two thousand men had been shipped to the empire's most western backwater to retake the land in the name of the emperor. Couple them with Felicius's own men and those of the Second Legion, and they were a force to be reckoned with.

Felicius knew his history well, especially when it came to the Roman military. This army of theirs he knew would have been nothing special back in the glory days. Rome once commanded nearly half a million men at arms; he doubted they had a tenth of that these days. But if their armies were shrinking in numbers then so were their enemies, thanks to the hard work of their forebears. Yes, he reassured himself. Rome had stood on the edge of defeat before, and had prevailed. She would this time.

His thoughts carried his feet to his quarters without him realising. One of his men stood guard at his door and he sent the man off to find Vitulus and ordered him to tell his centurion to come with wine. He took a seat at the small desk in his room and flattened out a piece of parchment. He needed to send word to Sixtus. He had so much to say for a moment he wondered where to start. Valentinus? The field army? Surely, he thought, Victorinus must have worked some of this out for himself by now? A lot of people wrote his friend off as nothing but a drunk, but Felicius knew him for what he was. He was brave and intelligent, fearless when he needed to be.

There might be an army ready to march in the south, but Felicius knew his old friend could well be the one who would strike the death blow to the enemy. He wrote, a candle flickering on the desk the only light. He'd covered three sheets and was just signing off with his name when Vitulus knocked on the door and poked his head around. The centurion smiled, producing a jug and two glasses from behind his back, and he stepped inside. 'How is it that you earn twice as much as me and I'm always expected to provide the wine?' he said as he closed the door behind him.

12

A glint of silver in the darkness above him and he brought his sword up in an arc and parried the blow that would have taken his head. Stepping towards his opponent, he lowered his blade and shoved him hard with his right shoulder, sending the man spiralling over a table. Turning, he was just in time to see a spear whistling towards him. He ducked and rolled, landing heavily on his left shoulder, and the spear clattering off the wall behind him.

Wincing at the pain in his shoulder, he rose, wishing for a moment he wasn't carrying the weight of his mail, then thanked the gods he was as a sword scraped down his side. He bellowed in pain and rage, hacked with his own blade and felt it bite into flesh.

There was a spurt of blood, hot on his face, and he grinned, lost in the battle joy, as he stabbed down at the fallen man, cutting short his agonised cries.

'Sir, we need to leave!' a voice said, somewhere off to his left, but he ignored it and pushed himself further into the fray. An axe appeared in his eye line, blade coming for him. He cut at the shaft of the axe with his sword and it cleaved into the wood. He tried to wrench it free but it was stuck fast, and the axe and its owner came back with it. He kicked the axe man in the groin, wrenched the weapon from his palm and hurled both axe and sword across the chamber. Freeing his dagger from his waist, he stabbed the axe man three times in the torso and threw him to the floor.

Heaving in air, he watched in savage joy as the battle carried on around him. Two grappling men off to his right knocked over a brazier, and flaming coals spilled to the floor, the rushes lighting in an instant. 'We really need to leave, sir!'

'Not until I have my answers!' Victorinus spat. He wiped blood from his face with the sleeve of his mail, but all he achieved was to spread more across his skin. He reached for a jug of wine on a nearby table and drank greedily, feeling the liquor invigorate him further. He wondered why he'd ever stopped drinking.

The wine made him feel good, untouchable, like the commander of warriors he knew he could be, the man he used to be. There was a thought, caught at the back of his mind, a nagging doubt that maybe what he was doing was wrong. A picture of a face plastered itself behind his eyelids, a young boy, holding up a wooden horse. This gave him pause for a moment. He knew that boy; at least, he thought he did. And the horse; the horse held some special importance... but he couldn't place it.

Quashing the nagging doubt, he snatched up a spear that lay discarded on the floor and threw it at the first person he saw. The spear took the man high in the chest and he fell down with a shocked intake of breath. 'Victorinus, we must leave, NOW!' Felix was at his side, a bloodied blade in his hand.

'Not until I have my answers,' Victorinus roared again, bloodshot eyes blazing into the decurion.

'You will get no answers here, my friend. Nor will you find them in the bottom of a wine jug. We have to leave; you need to sleep.'

'I need to kill!'

'I'm sorry, sir, but this is for your own good.' Felix backed away and Victorinus staggered around, confused. And then there was a blinding pain in the back of his head and he was forced down to his knees. He collapsed to the floor, his hazy vision just making out the dancing flames of a growing fire.

Not this again, he thought as he slipped from consciousness. And why is the world on fire?

* * *

The sun was shining when he woke. The blinding light sent a lance of pain tearing through his head, and before he could stop himself, he vomited bile down his tunic. 'Bastards,' he muttered, trying and failing to rise to a sitting position.

'I did tell you this would happen,' a voice said, somewhere off to his right.

'Bastards,' he croaked again, this time succeeding to sit up He opened his eyes a touch. Once more the daylight offended him, but he persevered. 'Why would you do that?' he hissed in pain as he touched his pulsing head with a tentative hand.

'Because you were drunk and out of control, for the tenth time in the last two weeks.' It was Felix who spoke. He rested against the stump of a long-felled tree, sipping water from a skin.

'So you're saying I had four days off? Doesn't sound so bad to me. You should have seen me back in the day, just ask Halfhand—'

He stopped short. The reason why he had drunk himself to oblivion ten times in the last two weeks resurfaced in his mind, crushing him once more. One of the reasons, anyway. He sank back to the ground.

'I know this has been hard for you,' Felix said, lowering himself to a crouch and offering Victorinus the water skin, 'but you have to pull yourself together. You have men relying on you to lead us through this. I have committed myself to you and your cause, my men too. I will not allow you to let us down.'

It had been nearly three weeks since Halfhand had sacrificed himself at the villa, allowing Victorinus and Drost to escape. It took a day more for the two men to hook up with Felix and his cavalry detachment, who had taken themselves off to a nearby forest and bunkered down.

The prefect of notaries, Secundus, had sent a detachment of soldiers out after Felix and his riders, but they had not succeeded in finding them in the forest. Victorinus had been numbed to find Cassius not with Felix and his men when he found them. He had not truly believed it was the young man's voice he'd heard in that kitchen, that the crop of blond hair he'd seen must have belonged to someone else.

But Cassius was missing, Severus too. Pastor, though, had shown up. Two days after Victorinus had reunited with the Ala Hispanorum, they had been riding hard for the west, Victorinus desperate to reach his family before Secundus could. Pastor had been waiting at a junction on the road, his head badly bruised, left arm broken.

'We ran when the soldiers started streaming out of the villa,' he'd said through cracked lips. 'Cassius told me to follow him, and I did. Didn't really notice where we were going for the first few minutes, then I realised we had lost the decurion and his men. That's when he turned on me, knocked me from my horse and beat me, left me for dead.'

Victorinus knew he was lying; might as well have been written in ink on his face. How could Cassius have ridden off with Pastor and been in the kitchen when Victorinus and the others burst through the door? Didn't add up.

Felix had told Victorinus he hadn't seen the two youths since just after the tribune had parted from him. The two areani men had said they were off to get supplies and the next thing Felix knew, he was having to order his men out of the city in a fast retreat.

There was an old saying Victorinus had remembered a tribal chief telling him once, when he was visiting an allied village north of the Wall. 'Keep your friends close, and your enemies closer,' the chief had said when explaining why he had allowed the son of a rival to marry his daughter.

Victorinus remembered the lesson and cut Felix short when the decurion went to challenge Pastor. 'The lad's been through enough.'

The tribune rose unsteadily to his feet, unsure whether the pain in his head was due to the blow he'd received or the wine he'd drunk. Figured it was a bit of both, and moved off to relieve himself by a nearby tree. As he walked back, his hand reached for the pouch at his belt and he was once more struck by a crushing loss. Remembering those first few days after losing Halfhand.

He'd not been able to retrieve the pouch whilst escaping Secundus's villa. After finding Pastor on the road, they had made haste for the farmstead, Victorinus desperate to set eyes on his wife and sons.

They were gone.

The door to his home was smashed off its hinges, the kitchen table upended, a pot of stew, destined to never be eaten, sat over a burnt-out fire. Of his family, or Felicius's, there was no sign.

'What sort of husband are you? What sort of father?' Amata had screamed at him as he left his home, Publius struggling to hold his wife back. 'You weren't here when little Leo died. You didn't see the damage it did to Sarai, to Maurus! And now they're gone, taken! What are you going to do? When are you finally going to step up?'

Victorinus had seen Delphina in the doorway to their home, the girl, tears in her eyes, hugging herself as she watched her mother rage.

'She is worried for our daughter,' Publius said when Amata had finally tired of her rage. 'What would we have done if those men had taken her?'

'How many men were there? Did you see what standard they rode under?' Victorinus asked.

'There were eight of them. The leader was the same man as before, in the cavalry mask.'

Victorinus recoiled as if Publius had struck him. 'That isn't possible, I put an axe in that man's head.'

Publius's eyes widened. 'I can only tell you what I saw, Sixtus. Looked to be the same man to me, had the same manner about him. Plus, he had the tattoo on his right arm.'

'Tattoo?'

'The V on the right arm. All the men had it. Same as when they came before. What's going on, Sixtus?'

Victorinus closed his eyes and tried to think. He had not noticed the tattoo on any of the men he had fought so far. How could he have missed something so obvious? 'I don't know, old friend. I have to go; I have to find my family.'

'I wish you luck, brother.' Publius touched Victorinus's arm as he spoke, and the small gesture nearly brought the tribune to tears.

It was that night Victorinus fell off the wagon. They were on the road, travelling back east, as they had no clue where else to go, when they came across a lively tavern in a small settlement. Victorinus had taken himself inside and ordered a jug of wine, then proceeded to drink himself senseless. He was on his third jug when he noticed a man at the bar with a V tattooed on his right arm.

Victorinus watched as the man ordered four jugs and took them back to a table of another five men, all with the same tattoo. He'd killed them all.

Two weeks of hunting taverns for men with the same tattoo had brought many more nights of hard drinking and many more bodies to bury the next morning. But still he was no further to discovering more about Valentia. It seemed to be some sort of sect, with men ready to die rather than reveal what they knew.

He slumped back down to the ground. They were back in the forest, five or so miles northeast from Secundus's heavily fortified villa. They lit no fires, and had made a camp so deep amongst the trees that no one had discovered their presence yet, but it was just a matter of time. He thought of Felicius as he sat there, his head still pounding like a smithy's hammer. How could he tell his friend he had failed to protect his wife and daughter? *What sort of husband are you? What sort of father?* Indeed. What sort of friend.

He had received no communication from Felicius since his friend had set off for the south, and he doubted there would be any way he could receive any now. How would Felicius know where to find him? His thoughts grew darker as he sat there, the warmth of the sun basking down on him through a gap in the canopy above.

'How's the head?' a voice said behind him.

Victorinus turned slowly – turning quickly just wasn't an option for him right now – and looked up, into a beaming Drost. 'It was you who did this to me, wasn't it?'

Drost shrugged. 'You would have ended up a drooling mess on the floor either way. I just sped it up a little, that's all.'

'Did Felix tell you to do it?' It concerned him that Felix might have begun to hold sway over his men.

'He suggested it might be the best course of action.

Quite enjoyed it, if I'm being honest.' He shrugged again, then resumed grinning.

'One day, I'm going to gut you like a fish.'

'I don't think you know how to gut a fish.'

He had it right there, Victorinus had to give it to him.

He held out a hand and the Caledonian lifted him to his feet. He swayed for a moment, and realised what it must be like to be out at sea, not that he'd ever been aboard a boat. 'So, what's the plan, Chief?' Drost asked.

'Plan?'

'Yeah, plan. You're the chief, you come up with the plan. Just wondered if you'd thought of anything yet?'

'Thought of anything?' Victorinus repeated again, his head pounding harder now. 'Drost, I am a recovering alcoholic who has been off the wagon for two straight weeks. Couple that with the fact that some cunt knocked me out cold last night, I don't quite feel ready to form a plan just yet.'

Drost's slow grin turned into a snigger and despite the weight Victorinus carried on his shoulders, he found himself chuckling too. He breathed in deep, a small smile still dancing on his lips. Drost was right. He needed a plan, needed to do something other than get drunk and lay waste to the first tavern he came across. He was just composing his thoughts when Pastor raised the alarm.

'Rider! Approaching from the south,' the youth called, scurrying through the trees.

Victorinus scowled at the boy. His bruises had faded, though his arm was still bandaged and in a sling. Pastor had a reckoning coming soon, they all knew it. But until then he would suck in all the air he could. 'Does he have a shield? A symbol?' Victorinus asked.

Pastor shook his head. 'Nothing.'

Felix kicked into gear, giving quiet orders for his men to form up around Victorinus. The tribune stayed in the clearing, enjoying the heat of the sun. Whoever it was that had come looking for him would not find him hiding in the shadows. He had grown tired of that.

'Shields!' Felix called as the rider rode into view. He appeared to be a young man, sitting easy in his saddle as the horse picked its way over the forest undergrowth. Felix's men left their mounts tethered, but stood in three ranks, shields facing the newcomer.

The man paused when he saw the wall of shields awaiting him in the sunlight. 'I am seeking the tribune Sixtus Victorinus of the miles areani,' he called. 'I bring word from the prefect Gaius Felicius.'

Victorinus walked through the files of shields, showing his face to the newcomer. The rider dismounted and saluted, but was wary of approaching so many armed men. 'You recognise me?' Victorinus asked.

'Aye, sir. I serve under the prefect in the Fourth. Seen you around Vindolanda often enough.'

Victorinus nodded, his mind still not made up. Felicius had five hundred men under his command; it was not surprising Victorinus did not recognise this one man. 'How do I know you come from the prefect? You are an enemy spy for all I know.' Silently, he cursed himself and Felicius for not forming some sort of code word for exchanging communications. But, like a great many other things that had happened in the last months, there was little he could do about that now.

The rider reddened slightly, studied his boots a moment and then raised his head to speak. 'The prefect said if I were challenged, I was to give you the following message.'

Victorinus raised an eyebrow and waited a moment. 'Well? I ain't getting any younger over here.'

'He told me to say you're a drunken fool and the only reason you joined the areani is because the army wouldn't have you.' Instinctively, the rider stepped back, a hand going to the sword at his waist.

Victorinus was speechless for a moment. Drost burst into laughter behind him, quickly followed by the other men in earshot. When the cacophony had calmed, Victorinus approached the rider and held out a hand. 'The message, soldier,' he said.

'Here you are, sir. And I'm sorry, sir, I'm sure the prefect didn't mean it.'

'A joke between two friends, think nothing of it. How did you find us?'

'People are talking about you all over the north, sir. They're saying you and your men are rooting out the traitors under cover of night, burning the taverns and whorehouses the enemy are using as their bases.'

Felix clapped Victorinus on the shoulder. 'We're famous!'

An icy spike of fear trickled down Victorinus's spine. If they were being spoken of, then someone had told this man where to find them, and that did not sit well with the tribune. 'Who told you we are in this forest?' he asked.

'The owner of the inn I stayed in last night. Just a waystation on the road, really. He said you and your men have been here for the last few weeks, but the enemy haven't been able to flush you out yet. I've been on the road for three weeks; thought I might as well try my luck. As it happened, only took me a few hours to track you down.'

'Thank you, soldier. Felix here will see you and your mount are fed and rested. I will have a reply for the prefect. I will send for you when I am ready. You have done well.'

With that he turned away, half his mind already desperate to uncover the details of the message from his friend. His eyes sought out Pastor as he walked into the shade. The youth was sharing a joke with one of Felix's men and must have felt eyes on him as he turned and met Victorinus's gaze. The tribune did not look away. How could they be famous throughout the province? How could everyone know where they had made camp? Someone was talking; someone was getting messages out. Victorinus knew who his coin was on.

13

The night crept upon them like a thief in the dark. Silent as a cat, graceful as a swallow's dive. The shadows grew as the sun waned in the west, the sky a mass of orange, blotted with purple bruises. The forest drummed to a different beat, owls called out above, mice scurried through the undergrowth, the wind whispered through the trees.

Victorinus lay as silent as stone, eyes closed, ears alive to the forest around him. They had no tents. Every man slept out in the open, grateful it was the height of summer and not the depths of winter. Rolled in his cloak, the tribune waited, prepared to wait all night if he needed to.

Sentries patrolled the perimeter, their handovers concluded without the blare of trumpets and resetting of clocks, which would have been standard procedure in a barracks. Out here they had to be silent. They were invaders to their own land, outnumbered and under resourced. Cunning was their most fearsome weapon.

Opening his eyes a touch at the sound of whispered voices, Victorinus saw two helmeted silhouettes in the near distance, spear tips glinting from the light of the rising moon. He closed his eyes once more, ignoring the guards as they whispered a brief handover. The movement he was waiting for would come from behind him, if it came at all.

He had stayed sober today, his mind so focused on what he must do he had barely missed the drink. Though he knew from recent experience it was a wagon much easier to fall off than get back on.

Felicius's letter had been both brief and informative. He was back on the island with an army, moving north. The emperor had sent an experienced general to cleanse Britannia, and by the end of summer they would have victory. Men had clambered around the tribune, desperate for details. Victorinus had given them none, saying only they were riding south and east at daybreak. Word had spread round the camp like wildfire.

His thoughts drifted to his family, as they always did when he had some time to himself. He prayed to the gods they were still alive, that he would still be able to save them. That afternoon he had written a reply to his friend Felicius. It was the hardest letter he'd ever had to write. How do you tell a man that his wife and daughter are missing? What was there you could say to soften the blow? He hadn't tried to in the end, didn't have the words. He just promised he would get them back. It was a promise he intended to fulfil or die trying.

A slight rustle in the undergrowth behind him brought him back to the task in hand. It was followed by the sound of a cloak unfurling, a disturbance in the air as a figure rose from the ground. He couldn't make out the footfall at first, but with a pang of nerves he heard the gentle slap of boots on mud. They were getting nearer.

Before he knew it, the soft tread reached him, and he sensed a figure looming above, felt the man's nerves through his shallow breaths. Victorinus tried to keep his own even, his eyes closed but not scrunched shut. He wasn't sure if the figure would be able to make out his face in the darkness, but he didn't want to take any risks.

After what felt like an age, the figure moved off to the south, his gentle footfall almost silent on the forest floor. Almost, but not silent enough. Victorinus counted to thirty and slowly eased himself out of his cloak. He rose to a crouch, turning his head to the left and the right, surveying the land around him.

Moonlight pierced holes through the forest canopy. It was in one of these pools of light Victorinus saw the figure moving. The silhouette stopped and turned back, but appeared to not see the tribune squatting in the darkness. When the figure moved off, Victorinus did too. He pondered for a moment if he should wake Drost. He had a sudden longing to roll back the weeks and start this sorry mess over again. He had enjoyed his time working with the five men in his little squad for the areani. None of them had been perfect, and he had suspected for a while that a couple of them were not all they had seemed. But they had been his men, and he would have shed blood for any one of them.

He sighed as he moved past Drost, leaving the Caledonian snoring in his cloak. Irony was, a few months ago Drost would have been the one he'd have wagered would turn out to be a traitor. Funny feeling, thinking you've weighed the measure of someone, only to find out they had been stuffing their pockets with rocks.

He snuck through the forest, his prey always in his sights. They were moving away from the track, deeper into the wilderness, and Victorinus wondered if his target knew where they were going, had trodden this path before. A twig snapped beneath his boot and Victorinus hunched behind the nearest tree. He could not see his prey now, but he knew they had stopped, had turned back, frantic eyes scanning the darkness for movement.

He counted to fifty in his head, slow breaths calming his racing heart. Slowly, ever so slowly, he eased himself from behind the tree. It was darker here, the canopy above putting up a stronger shield and keeping the moonlight at bay. He cursed himself for stepping on the twig, but a voice of reason whispered to him that he could not keep his eyes on two things at once. Halfhand would have ghosted through the trees, would have had naked iron at his quarry's throat without the man knowing he was even there. But Victorinus was not Halfhand. He was heavy footed, bigger built, more suited for tavern brawls than night-time espionage.

He squinted from behind the tree, worrying the

light in his eyes would betray his presence. He had removed his armour before bedding down for the night, left his sword there too, though his dagger was strapped to his waist. Was that a mistake? Too late to worry about that now.

His quarry had stopped, a frantic head shifting from left to right as wide eyes scanned the dark. There was plenty of wildlife making a home under these trees; could have been anything that made the noise. Victorinus watched as his prey considered those thoughts. He imagined the other man comforting himself with them, wearing them like armour. After another scan, the prey moved off into the forest.

Victorinus reckoned he'd followed for an hour before the figure stopped beneath a giant ash tree. Lowering himself to his knees, immersed in the darkness, Victorinus watched and waited. He was as sure as sure could be that the figure was here to meet someone, and he had a good idea who that person was. But he had to be sure, be certain, before acting.

After a short wait he heard a whistle, then another. The first was pitched low, the second high. Victorinus closed his eyes and listened. He didn't know why you could hear better with your eyes closed, but from his experience it was a fact. The whistle was answered from the figure he had followed here, and holding his breath, head bowed, eyes closed, Victorinus heard footsteps approach the ash tree.

They came from his right, so the west, and that was important to remember. A man stepped into a puddle of moonlight. Eyes open now, Victorinus saw a hood lowered, a shock of blond hair like fire in the blue-tinged haze. Two figures embraced and whispered softly to each other, close as lovers. Victorinus could not make out what was being said, but he couldn't risk getting any closer. He reasoned he didn't need to; this was all the proof he'd needed.

He hesitated a moment longer, fingers curling the hilt of his dagger. He thought of Sarai, pictured Maurus, wide eyed, giving him his prized toy. He cursed the two men, swearing his vengeance. Then, giving them one last look, he slunk back through the forest, a murderous glint in his eye, fury in his heart.

* * *

Dawn was cresting in the east when the men mounted their steeds, ready to depart. The forest was peaceful, the sun bringing colour to the world, spears of red and orange piercing the canopy above. It was warm already, Victorinus feeling the first beads of sweat break the skin on his brow as he checked the harness on

Amor's saddle. He whistled to himself as he did. He had woken with a clear head – even the pain from the blow Drost had struck him had receded – and he breathed in deep, savouring the scent of the woods.

'You seem brighter this morning, Chief!' Drost called. The Caledonian himself seemed unusually cheery. He sat atop a fallen tree, checking the blade of his axe. Victorinus assumed it was the prospect of using it that had the man in such high spirits.

Victorinus didn't respond, just walked over to his man and said in a low voice, 'Stay close to me today.'

'Gods, you're not planning on getting wasted again, are you?'

'No, but good one. I'm not sure what's going to happen, to be honest. But something will.'

Drost paused, his eyes scrunching as he thought. 'What was in the letter from Felicius? What do you know?'

'Not much more than you. But I have my suspicions. Today we find out where my family are. Today we find out what happened to Severus.'

Drost unconsciously looked to Pastor, who was making a show of trying to mount one handed, his left arm still hanging useless in a sling. 'Where did you go last night?' he said suddenly. 'I saw you leave the camp and head south.'

Victorinus too was looking at Pastor. The youth looked tired this morning, like he'd barely slept. His eyes were red rimmed and every movement was sluggish. 'You'll find out later. Like I said, just stay close to me.'

'You know you can trust me, don't you, Chief?' Drost said with a severity Victorinus had rarely heard in the man. 'I know you haven't always, and I know it must have seemed suspicious, me arriving from the north, wanting to join the men paid to spy on my own people. I have my reasons, and they're my own. But Halfhand and Severus were my friends too, and if it is Cassius that caused their deaths, and that one' – he jerked his head in Pastor's direction – 'is in on it too, I'll see them both dead.'

Victorinus held the Caledonian's eye for a moment, seeing if his gaze was matched. It was. It was true the tribune had been suspicious of the dark-haired youth who'd appeared from the wilderness; who wouldn't have been? But right now, Drost was the only man he had complete trust in. Felix had done nothing to hint he may not be what he seemed, but Victorinus had not been around the man long enough to get the full measure of him. Drost, however, was his brother of the areani, and he would break down walls to see his brothers safe.

'I trust you, Drost. I haven't always, and I'll be the first to admit that. But right now, I do, and I need you to watch my back and keep that axe ready. And maybe not use it on me today, eh?'

Felix rode abreast with Victorinus as they left their makeshift camp, leaving nothing but a couple of smouldering fires in their wake. 'I had scouts out south and east this morning. They say there's a path through the woodland but it's narrow. We could only ride two abreast.'

Victorinus shrugged. 'We're not going southeast, Felix.'

The decurion frowned; he turned his dark eyes to look on the tribune. 'You lied to me? You do not trust me?'

'I trust you, brother, rest assured. I had to lie to everyone, to hide the truth from one.'

Felix turned on his mount. His eyes automatically sought out Pastor. Turning back, he spoke in a low voice. 'One of my men woke me in the night, said he was on watch and saw you follow a cloaked figure out of camp, heading south. Care to tell me what you were up to?'

'Not yet, and I am sorry. I don't mean to keep anything from you, Felix. You and your men have proven yourselves to be invaluable; the courage and loyalty of your unit does you credit. But today I will find out where my wife and children are, and to do that I need surprise.'

Felix nodded. The Spaniard had seen first-hand the pain the tribune had gone through. Victorinus had allowed himself to be dragged down into the depths of Hades, and now he was trying to reach out towards the light. 'Whatever you need, we are with you, sir. What news did the messenger bring?'

Victorinus turned again, making sure he could not be overheard. 'There is an army in the south, landed a couple of weeks ago. Two thousand or so men from the western field army, under the command of a General Theodosius. They are marching north. The emperor is aware of the rebellion and a man called Lupus Valentinus, who is supposedly behind it. Seems he is a senator, was exiled to Britannia a few years ago. That's what I know.'

'Valentinus,' Felix said. 'Guess we know where Valentia came from then.'

'Not exactly subtle, is it?' Victorinus chuckled. 'I don't know what the man did to deserve exile. I don't know how he has managed to pull this charade off. But from what I can make out he is nothing more than a usurper. His Valentia will be Rome in all but name, with himself as emperor.'

There was the sound of hoofbeats on the forest floor behind them. Victorinus turned to see Pastor making his way to the head of the column. His left arm was across his chest, his right holding the reins. 'Sir, where are we going? I thought we were going south and east?'

Victorinus smiled. 'Change of plan,' he said simply.

Pastor momentarily blubbered like a fish out of water, before eventually finding the words he sought. 'Why were we not told?'

'I thought everyone had been told, no? Felix, you knew about the new direction, right?'

'Aye, sir, of course.' Felix made a show of rubbing his face, to cover his smile if nothing else.

'There you are, young Pastor. You must have been rolled up in your cloak last night when we spread the word. How else would you have not heard? You were with us all night, weren't you?'

Pastor flushed a shade of red. 'Of course.'

'Why don't you ride ahead with the scouts. You seem like you could do with a ride to breathe some life into you.' Pastor nodded and rode off, trailing the two men Felix had tasked with scouting their route.

'What will you do with him?' Felix asked.

Victorinus shrugged. 'Haven't decided yet. Though

I'd wager a month's coin he'll lead us to Cassius at some point on the journey.'

'So, we leave him be?'

'Aye, for now.'

The two men rode in silence for a while, the rustle of the forest providing the background noise. 'So where are we going?' Felix asked after a time.

'I spent last night thinking on this,' Victorinus said. He had removed a loaf of bread from the pack on his saddle and was struggling to chew it. The bread was far from fresh.

'Where would you go if you were hoarding an army and didn't want to be noticed?'

Felix thought a moment. 'You'd need a big fort. It would need to be somewhere secluded, preferably away from the road, but close enough that you could make a run for it if needed. You'd also want it to be defendable...' The decurion trailed off. He looked at Victorinus, his dark eyes widening. 'Epiacum?'

Victorinus smiled and nodded. 'Can't think of anywhere better in the north. It's a big fort, easily big enough to fit five or six hundred men, enough space around it to camp a couple of thousand more. It's away from the two major roads in the north. The only way you can get there by road is the direct link to Fort Magna on the Wall.'

'There are lead mines there, are there not? Isn't that the only reason the fort is there?'

'Correct. I've no idea how you mine for lead, so I don't know if they're using the mines as defences. It also has a range of defensive ditches around the walls. Would be a right bastard to try and assault.'

'Is that what we are going to do?' Felix had an air of caution in his tone.

'Gods no! How do you think our few hundred cavalry would fare? No, it won't be us doing the assaulting, we'll leave that to the field army when it gets here.' Victorinus was suddenly struck with visions of Maurus, his eldest son, forced to work in the lead mine. He imagined a pitch-black pit, a boy with a leather satchel filled with lumps of lead strung over his bony shoulders. A man with a whip stalking his every step, ready to punish the boy for every misstep. Maybe he would assault it after all.

'And when will the field army get here?'

'I don't know. But some things are becoming clearer to me now. The fires, the pirates, the Scotti in the west and the Caledonians from the north; they're not part of the plan, as such.' Felix raised an eyebrow at him, was about to speak before Victorinus cut him off. 'They are the distraction. We're meant to be going after them, to put a stop to whatever it is they're doing.'

'All the while giving time for this Valentinus to build his army,' Felix finished.

'Exactly! That is why there are no soldiers at the Wall, or in the many forts across the north of Britannia. They haven't abandoned their posts for no reason, or taken Valentinus's coins to disappear into the night – well, most of them haven't, anyway. They've grouped up with him, formed their own army. And that army is the plan. That army will be the one to "cleanse" Britannia of the invaders. They will make themselves the heroes, and the local populace will worship them.'

'And this Valentinus will drape himself in purple.'

'Aye. Constantine was first acclaimed emperor in Eboracum, did you know that?'

'That depends which Constantine you're speaking of.'

'The Constantine, the man who marched from Britannia to Rome, to the far east and back again, and re-conquered the world anew. The man who built Constantinople, a city said to be greater than even Rome itself. He saw the empire for what it was, nothing more than a crumbling tower, ready to collapse as soon as someone removed one more brick.'

'Maybe Valentinus sees the same thing he did?'

'No. Constantine did not invite barbarians into his domain. Did not sit and do nothing as women were raped, children captured for slaves. He had many faults, no doubt, but deep down he had the empire's best interests at heart. At least a close second to his own, anyway. What we are dealing with here is very different, and it must be stopped at all costs.'

Felix smiled. 'It is good to see you like this, Tribune.'

'Like what?'

'So passionate and fired up. Sober, too. You do not have to sell me the idea of riding south to save an empire. I ride with you to save your wife and children. If we can save Rome at the same time, then that is nothing more than a bonus.' The decurion reached across from his saddle and slapped Victorinus on the back. The tribune briefly pondered if he should rebuke his subordinate for such a move, for it was not how a junior officer should behave towards his commander. But he reasoned that the commander should not be getting drunk for two straight weeks and starting fights in every tavern he came across. Then he realised he hadn't thought about wine once that morning, and a slow smile spread across his face.

'Thank you, Felix. I am so glad I found you. I've done a lot of wrong in my life, mainly to Sarai and my boys. Believe me when I say I would gladly give my life to get them back unhurt. But I won't let you and your men do the same. Now is the time for reason, not emotion. We scout out Epiacum, see what we can learn about the army we are to face. Then we make for Felicius and the field army marching north. Together, we shall put an end to this.'

They were out of the forest now, the sun beating down on lush green fields. There was no breeze, and Victorinus sweated freely. He wished he could ride without his mail on, but doing so at a time of war would be foolish. Every man had helmets, shields and weapons at the ready. They would not be caught off guard.

One of the scouts came galloping back along the track towards them, dust swirling in torrents around him. He was pointing off to his right, Victorinus's left. The tribune followed the scout's outstretched hand and saw a thin dust cloud over the treetops. He grinned. There was an army out there somewhere, desperately seeking the quarry they were told would be leaving the forest in that direction.

Pastor had stopped his horse on the side of the track, his eyes fixed on the dust cloud. Victorinus slapped him hard on the back as Amor trotted past.

'Good job I decided on a change of course! We'd have stumbled right into that lot otherwise.'

He chuckled to himself as Pastor fixed him with a look somewhere between fear and confusion. Today was a good day, he thought to himself. The sun was shining, he had good men around him, and he was riding to save his family. Oh, and an empire too.

14

'Hercules! Hercules! Hercules!' the men of the Batavi chanted as they locked shields for the third time that morning. Storm clouds rolled like angry waves over-head, bolts of lightning striking through them, as if the gods too wanted them dead.

Felicius was being driven mad by the tinny sound of rain hammering his helmet. He stood with the men of the Fourth Cohort of Gauls, lined up as a reserve behind the three deep ranks of Batavi to their front.

They were three days north of Londinium, fol-lowing the arterial road that bled life into the island. In truth, Felicius wasn't sure exactly where they were; the rain and constant fighting had slowed the army down. General Theodosius had a little over three thousand men under his command now, with the Second legion being the first of the southern forces to accept his command.

But for every ally they welcomed into their column, two more enemies sprung from the wilderness.

'Gods damn these barbarians!' Theodosius riled. He was astride his white stallion, the beast biting at the bit to be let loose and spread its legs. Horses were always skittish in battle, even the ones that had received the best training. Felicius thought them not dissimilar to men in that way. The prefect would much rather be in the front line with the Batavi than standing and watching them at work, efficient as they were. Theodosius approached battle in much the same manner he approached the rest of his life – with little fuss and less fanfare. He rode without a host of retainers in his wake, just a horn blower following his prowling horse. Felicius felt his admiration for the man grow by the day. He needed no reassurance, had none of the insecurities Felicius had seen in high-ranking men before, who had the need to surround themselves with arse lickers at all hours of the day. He simply went about his business the only way he knew how.

The enemy had appeared on a hilltop, not two hours ago, barring the way north. They had chosen their spot well, holding the high ground, with wood-land to their left flank and a lake to their right. There was seemingly no way around them.

'Through them we shall go!' Theodosius had called as he ordered the Batavi forward. They were the freshest troops, having not fought the day before. The Heruli had led the column then, Flavius Maximus leading them. Four times the march had to be halted to clear the road of invaders. Two parties of Saxons, one of Franks and even a few hundred Caledonians. Felicius had known fear then, a sinking sensation in the depths of his bowels. How could the Caledonians have reached so far south? Not in his wildest dreams had he thought the northern savages would have done much more than steal what they could from the northern province and run back to the safety of the mountains. He fretted all through the previous night. If they had come this far south then what were they going to find the further north they travelled? He feared for his wife, his daughter. Too long he had been away. Every day was a toil, a labour to survive, just to get back to them.

'Ready spears!' the general screamed, and Felicius snapped from his reverie, shaking his head and re-moving his helmet, the sting of the rain bringing him back to his senses. The Batavi were panting hard now, their initial rush of adrenalin wearing thin. They were fighting what appeared to be a horde of Franks. They presented a wall of multicoloured round shields, iron helmets and booted feet the only evidence men stood behind them. That and the dead bodies that littered the ground between the two armies.

The Batavi raised their shields once more, men panting, squinting through the rain. The howling wind was a southerly gale, sweeping the rain into their faces. Theodosius flicked his wrist to the horn blower, who sounded the advance once more. The Batavi trudged uphill, shields level, shoulders hunched. A few of the Franks lost their discipline and left their line, streaming down the road in a frenzy. They were quickly cut down. Centurions called the step as they approached the Frankish shield wall, and then as one they sprung forward, spears snaking out through gaps in the shields, striking at flesh and bone.

'Let me join them, Father,' Theo pleaded for the second time that morning. 'They need a leader.'

The youth was bareheaded, clad in mail, sword bared, though he stood far from the fighting. Felicius had come to like the general's son in the weeks since they had met. He was inquisitive, stern, a wise head on a young body. He sensed the man would go far, if he stayed alive.

'Gods, boy, are you so determined to die?' Theodosius sighed, tiring of the repetitive conversation. He looked from his son to the raging battle to his front, his lips twitching as he thought. 'They do look as though they could use a little pick me up,' he said, to himself as much as the men around him. 'Prefect Felicius.' He turned back to the men of the Fourth. 'You shall accompany my son and see he returns in one piece. Theo, you shall assume command of the Batavi for the remainder of the battle, but you will heed the advice of Prefect Felicius and Centurion Ketill.' Theo smiled and nodded. Felicius winced. He understood all too well what was expected of him. Not only was he responsible for the wellbeing of the general's son, he was also effectively being given command of the Batavi, even if he was to command through Theo.

He fitted his helmet back in place, pushing back his soaking hair out of his eyes. Once the straps were tied, he hefted his shield and drew his sword. 'Vitulus, you have the Fourth. Stay close to the general.'

The centurion nodded, but even over the cacophony of the battle he could hear Theodosius cackle. 'I am not so old that I need a babysitter, Prefect!' Felicius turned back to see Theodosius patting the hilt of the sword at his waist. Both men smiled.

The short run up the hill was a torture in itself. His

rain-soaked kit weighed twice as much as usual, and his calves were on fire when he reached the rear ranks of the Batavi, his left thigh burning with the familiar pain.

'Domine, Prefect.' Senior Centurion Ketill, commander of the Batavi force, nodded a greeting.

'Centurion, my father has ordered me to take command of the battle, with yourself and the prefect here to assist me.' Theo spoke well, and Felicius felt his admiration for the young man grow. He too knew his place, understood his limits. He would not be too proud to ask for help, or to listen to the advice of veterans who made their coin in war.

Ketill grinned, a horrible, blood-splattered grin that would have put the fear of the gods in Felicius had they been fighting on opposite sides. 'About time the old man let you off the leash! What are your orders, sir?'

Theo breathed in deep, his dark eyes taking in the battle before him, raging not twenty paces away. 'Reinforce our flanks, push hard on both sides and bottle them up. I would think they will see the futility of continuing the fight before too long.'

There was a brief moment of uncertainty as Theo looked, wide eyed, at the two experienced military men standing either side of him. Felicius smiled and nodded. Ketill did the same. 'A fine plan, sir. I recommend I hold the centre with the first century, who are already fighting there. The men will have to stand fast whilst their comrades push forwards.'

Felicius nodded again, relieved it would be him who had the unenviable task of holding a thinned line. 'No, I shall do that myself,' Theo said, causing Felicius to groan inside. 'I need to prove myself in battle. Now seems as good a time as any.'

Ketill issued orders and moved off to the right flank. Felicius checked his helmet once more, before checking the straps on Theo and tugging at his mail. 'Keep your shield high, knees bent. Don't show the bastards an inch of flesh, you hear me?'

Theo didn't reply, just nodded. Felicius could see the younger man had paled, and his tongue circled his lips repetitively, fingers twitching on the hilt of his sword. It is no easy thing to enter the line of battle for the first time. War is a great leveller, and all men, highborn or low, are made equal as the shields clash and the blood flows. Felicius could remember all too well his own debut in the theatre of death. He tried to recall what the men around him had said to him at the time.

They eased through the Batavi until they stood in the front rank. Ketill had ordered the men back a few paces, and there was another lull in the battle. 'Plant your feet well, and keep your eyes moving. Battles are not decided by heroes; that's just for the songs. They're decided by the men who keep their wits about them, lost by the men who don't.'

Soldiers nodded as Felicius spoke. One even went as far as to clap Theo on the back. 'You'll do fine, lad,' the soldier said. Felicius was about to turn and rebuke the man when, with a roar, the left and right flanks of the Batavi surged forwards as one, and another cry of 'Hercules!' filled the air.

The wind seemed to pick up pace. It drove at their faces, rain like icy spears as it struck at his face. 'With me! At the walk!' Theo called, his voice shrill in the gale. They moved forwards, shields touching. 'Hercules! Hercules! Hercules!' the men around them chanted, building themselves up for another dice with fate.

Ahead of them, the flanks collided with a mighty bang. Most of the men had lost their long ash spears now, and swords were drawn, the iron dull in the colourless air. Five paces away and Felicius sucked in a lungful of air, tasting blood and sweat. Three paces and he snarled, all conscious thought losing him. He was there to kill, to hack and swipe, to take the life of any man that came near him. It was the life he knew, what he had been trained for, what he thrived on. He sprang forwards on aching legs to cover the last patch of ground. The road beneath his boots was slick with blood, dead men still lying where they'd fallen. An axe appeared over the rim of his shield and he raised the linden board so his adversary couldn't hook his curved blade over the top. Driving the shield forwards, he lunged low, his sword plunging into his enemy's thigh. The man screamed, a high-pitched wail, and fell to the cobbles with a thud. Felicius stepped forwards, almost on top of him, and saw the look of terror in the man's blue eyes before he swiped at an exposed throat with his sword, taking his first life of the day.

Snapping his head back up, he glanced to his right, just in time to see Theo block a sword blow with his shield, then return with a lunge of his own. The blow caught the Frank on his mail, which held, but the attack drove the man backwards into his friends behind him. Slipping on the blood-soaked cobbles as he tried to regain his footing, the swordman fell flat on his face, and Theo hacked at the back of the man's neck.

'Good kill! Now eyes up!' Felicius called, already marking his next target.

A bearded man with no shield and a spear

charged him, leaving Felicius no time to get out of the way. He raised his shield and caught the spear on the boss, the impact causing a jarring pain to rip through his left arm from wrist to shoulder. He winced, lowered his shield a touch and was stunned when the spear cut the air, inches from his face. The man was quicker than he looked. Felicius licked out with his sword, a blow he didn't expect to make contact, but it bought him a couple of seconds to recover himself. Bringing his shield back up, he raised it slightly higher than was wise and saw the Frank look down at his exposed legs. *Well, come on then.*

The spearman took the bait and lunged low. Felicius rammed his shield down, catching the spear just past the blade and trapping it against the cobbles. His right arm already in motion, he hit the spearman on the side of the head with his sword, and the man dropped to his knees, stunned. Half a step back gave Felicius all the space he needed to stab his would-be killer hard in the chest, the sword punching through mail and tearing flesh.

And then there was one less man to hurt his wife and daughter. 'Hold now! Hold now!' he roared, forgetting the pretence that Theo was giving the orders. He couldn't see the men on the flanks, had no idea if they were pushing on as planned. He had to trust in Ketill and his men.

Ducking behind his shield, he leant into it, taking the pressure of the man the other side doing the same. Theo was holding his ground. As Felicius watched, he claimed another kill, a blind lunge over his shield robbing an enemy of an eye. For a time, they huffed and panted, pushing and cursing over the shields, the rain falling on them all the while. The clash of iron could be heard on the flanks, the roars of victory, the anguished screams of the wounded. It was impossible to know what was happening.

And then there was a new sound, hobnailed boots grating on the road, the signal to advance sounding somewhere behind him. Pressure on his back, unable to turn, Felicius called, 'What's happening?'

Centurion Vitulus shouted in his ear, 'The general said you lot are a bunch of pansies and he wants some real soldiers to take over and get the job done!' Around him men groaned, spat and cursed the newcomers. Felicius just grinned.

'Well, the Fourth Cohort of Gauls are the finest fighting unit in this army, so it shouldn't be a surprise!'

Theo shot Felicius an inquisitive look, both men still leaning into their shields. 'Unless any man here wants to prove me wrong?'

The Batavi roared, an ear-splitting cry that seemed to give even the rain pause. Gods knew what it did to the Franks.

'Well, come on then, let's get it done!'

The Batavi centre surged forwards, eager to catch their comrades on the flanks. The day ran red, blood misted with the rain. The Batavi butchered every armed man in sight, leaving none alive.

* * *

The sun was setting, somewhere in the west, hiding behind a wall of thick cloud. The wind had receded, so too the rain. It seemed as though the clouds had run dry of spears and had paused to refill their armoury.

Felicius sat on a small wooden folding stool, a surgeon stitching his right arm. He had no memory of taking the wound, but such things were common enough. It was not until the battle rage subsided that a soldier noticed the cuts and bruises he had taken on the field. Felicius had seen men fight for hours with horrific cuts on their torso or leg, only to die in their sleep that night. He was in the command tent of General Theodosius, along with the other senior commanders of the army.

Theo had acquitted himself well in the battle and had a shiner of a black eye and numerous small cuts on his arms and legs to show for it. His smile lit up the darkening chamber. A whirlwind of energy, he buzzed from one man to the next, wine tumbling down his neck like a drain ditch catching water. Felicius smiled to look at him, cheeks flushed, eyes blazing. Theodosius had embraced his son warmly after the battle, in full view of the Batavi, who had chanted his name along with that of their favoured god, Hercules. It seemed they had chosen him to be their commander. If Maximus had the Heruli, the Batavi were to belong to Theo.

The bustle of the room silenced suddenly as the general entered. He still wore his mail and the same rain-soaked cloak he had been wearing all day, and mud splatters covered his legs, blood on his boots. 'Gentlemen, pray silence. We need to change our plans; this is taking too long.'

He walked over to a table set up in the middle of the tent, a map of Britannia unfurled on top. 'Now, we are here,' he said, placing his finger on the map, at a spot just south of Durovigutum. 'There is a mansio there, so I hope we can gain some further information when we reach it tomorrow.' He pointed to the town of Durovigutum.

'There is a squadron of archers based there, I think,' Felicius added, wincing as the surgeon finished the last of the stitches in his arm. 'Syrians, if I remember rightly.'

'Let us hope they are still there,' Theodosius mused. 'Now, depending on what intelligence we can garner at the mansio, I'm going to split our forces.'

There was a collective intake of breath, and men looked to one another in astonishment. 'Are you sure that is wise, sir?' Clementius cut in. The prefect had not had the easiest of relationships with the general since Theodosius had landed in Rutupiae. He had ridiculed Clementius for the state of repair in the fort, before laying into the readiness of his men. It was true the Second legion were far from the force they were in the glory days of the empire, but that could have been said for any number of the old legions that had been left to rot on the periphery of Rome's domain.

'Yes, thank you, Prefect, I am quite sure. We do not know what we are going to find upon reaching the northern territory, and I think it may be wise to have a force in the east and the west. That way we can scout more ground between us and flush this Valentinus out from the shadows.'

In the silence that followed, every man found a reason to avoid the general's eye. A brazier crackled in the corner of the tent. Felicius heard the wind howl outside, hammering blows on the tent's leather.

'How will you split the forces?' Maximus asked after a time.

'I will keep to the eastern side of the island and take the most northerly road from here. When we reach Durovigutum, Maximus, you and Clementius will await the arrival of the comes rei militaris Lupicinus and take the western road, circling north once you reach the west coast.'

'Lupicinus? Marcus Lupicinus?' Theo asked, eyebrow raised.

'Yes, one and the same. Word reached me this morning that the emperor has seen fit to dispatch the general to support me in our effort to reclaim these lands. Don't ask me why as I do not know myself.' Theodosius frowned, eyes hard. Felicius said nothing. He had no notion as to who this Lupicinus was, but it couldn't bode well for Theodosius if Emperor Valentinian had thought it wise to send another senior commander over to Britannia already.

'But Father, you have done nothing wrong, surely?'

Theodosius smiled, that wolf grin of his. 'Life in court is a game, my son, a game you will learn all too well one day. I admit it is a game I do not play too well. I am a soldier, an honest man. I speak my mind at all times. It does not always win me support amongst my peers.'

And that is why you were sent to this backwater in the first place, Felicius thought. He remembered his meeting with Jovinus, when he had asked the general if it would be him that led the rescue force to the island. The man had looked horrified at the very prospect. He remembered too the time he had spent with the western field army, short though it was. Senior commanders had spent their days jostling with each other for Valentinian's favour, each man spending their men's lives like coin as they sought to outshine their peers in the theatre of war.

'So Lupicinus has been sent here to spy on you?' Maximus said through a smile. Felicius wondered how much the general's nephew was enjoying this. The two men did not seem to have the best of relationships.

'I imagine so, yes, which is why I want him in the west. Any report the emperor hears of our progress here will come from me. We shall have three ships on the eastern coast, full of supplies and spare equipment, under the overall command of Captain Fidelis, who seems as though he will be a reliable man.'

Loyal would have been a more accurate word, Felicius thought. Loyal first to Theodosius, and then to

Rome. Felicius had no interest in the power games the high and mighty played. His only interest was reaching the north, defeating the enemy and finding his family. He thought he might kill any man that got in the way of that.

'Do not allow yourselves to become distracted, gentlemen,' Theodosius continued. 'We must stay true to our aim, which is to strike at the enemy with the speed and power of an arrow in full flight.'

They were dismissed shortly after, every man leaving the tent lost in thought. Felicius went off in search of wine, enough of the stuff to drown his sorrows in. He had been full of hope when his feet had landed back on the shores of the island he had come to know as home. This was the land on which he had met his wife, where his daughter had been born and he had first felt the melting of his heart as he held her in his arms.

How could imperial politics get in the way of doing what was right? It was something the prefect had never understood, though he had seen it happen often enough. When serving on the Rhine, he had been forced to watch and wait whilst an army of Germanic tribesmen grew from five hundred to over a thousand. All the while, the Roman forces stood and did nothing. That had been because General Jovinus had not been present on the field, and he had made it known he wanted the victory to be his, and his alone.

Victory the man had got, but at a heavy price. Had the enemy forces remained dispersed, it would have cost less in blood to put an end to their rebellion. Politics, a pox on it. He spat on the floor, as if to rid his body of the disgust.

At the rear of the marching camp, he found a cart full of wine. Taking two skins, he decided to walk the perimeter, despite the smell of rain in the air. He felt the need for solitude, before he drank himself into oblivion.

15

He read the letter for the third time, hoping to find different words, but his red-rimmed eyes scanned the same desolate message. His wife and daughter were missing, taken by the enemy.

A single tear trickled down his cheek, his head pounding all the harder. He had been awoken by the dawn trumpets, signalling the army to make ready to depart. Seemed he had not even made it back to his tent. He woke under a cart, rolled up in his cloak.

Vitulus had given his commander a questioning look as he had staggered back to the Fourth's place in the column, the men lined up, ready for the day's march. He had not even bothered to meet his friend's eye.

A silent march of four hours had brought them to Durovigutum, where they were met by the messenger Felicius had sent north to Sixtus. He had taken it to a private room in the mansio, closing the door to the cauldron of noise that was the army's officers in the main reception room. He sat there, propped up on the end of a reclining couch, his life crumbling faster than the parchment gripped in his white-knuckled hands.

How could this have happened? He raged in silence, furious with Victorinus. How could his friend have allowed them to be taken? How could he have been so stupid?

Forcing himself to breathe, he uncurled his fists, which took some effort, and winced at the pain in his palms where his nails had dug in through the parchment. He read it once more. Victorinus's wife Sarai and their boys were also missing. Halfhand was dead, Severus missing. He knew what a blow that would be to his old friend. He valued the brothership of the areani as much as anything else. They were his men, his responsibility, and Felicius knew he would run through hell to see them all safe. He took three more breaths, slow and deep. Tears ran like rivulets down his face, but he felt calmer, accepted what had happened.

It had been his choice to let his wife and daughter

retire to the farmhouse, rather than insisting they travel south with him. And would they have been any safer if they had? He could not remember the number of times he had needed to fight on that desperate march south. The world had seemed so different then; it had been like an open wound, raw and unpredictable. None of them had known the best course of action. His wife had still been reeling from the discovery of her father's body, an image of the governor, throat slit, the writing in blood on the wall. Valentia.

His anger returned, this time aimed at Valentinus, a man he had not even met. He was the wind through the trees, the smoke on the horizon. Somehow, they needed to trap him, force him into battle. Then they would grind him into dust. He read on, reading the words at the bottom of the page his heart had not let him see before. Victorinus had a hunch where the traitor was hiding. Felicius read the line again, and he stood suddenly, a fierce ball of energy burning brightly within him.

'Epiacum,' he whispered, picturing the fortress on the mountain pass, one of the most remote forts in the north. And then he was moving, crashing through the door, back into the reception room. A silence spread like blood on stone; heads turned towards him, mouths hung open, the words they were voicing receding into the air. 'Epiacum!' he shouted, his wits deserting him. His heart was racing, pounding, blood fizzing through his veins, making him feel dizzy. 'Epiacum! Valentinus is in Epiacum!'

And then he was tired, so tired he could have fallen and never risen again. He stumbled, crashing into a table, knocking a jug of wine to the floor. The sight of the wine brought back memories of the morning trumpets awakening him from his drunken slumber, and he felt his stomach turn.

'Felicius? Prefect Felicius? Are you quite well?' a voice said, and then he sprayed vomit down his front. *That's going to be a bitch to get out of my armour*, was the last thing he thought before the darkness took him.

* * *

'Tell me about Epiacum,' Theodosius said as they rode in the centre of the column. It was smaller now, and Felicius found himself missing the reassurance of having the Heruli and the Second Augusta packing out their ranks. They had, though, gained two hundred Syrian archers, who formed the rear guard, their blue cloaks sailing the light breeze. The Numerus Syrorum Saggitariorum had been serving in Britannia for over a hundred years, their unit having been renamed the century before. The men in the ranks still hailed from the far east and were known simply on the island as the Hamians.

'It is high up in the hills,' Felicius said, feeling much better in the bright dawn of the morning. The low hanging cloud had vanished with his hangover, and having slept most of the previous day and night, he was once more ready to lead the charge north. 'There is a mining settlement there, lead, I think. The fortress was built there to guard the miners.'

'Defences?'

'Standard stuff for the most part. It has walls and turrets, iron barred gates and defensive ditches running around the perimeter, up to seven on the north side if I remember correctly.'

'Artillery?'

'Not that I know of, Domine.'

Theodosius grunted. 'That will be one less thing to worry about, at least. Why more defensive ditches to the north?'

Felicius shrugged. 'In theory that is the only direction in which the fort should be attacked from. The only road leading to it comes from the north.'

'We can reach it if we go cross-country?'

Felicius paused, wracking his brain as he tried to remember the terrain. 'I think so. The terrain is hard, but passable. We'll have to leave the wagons behind though.'

The general considered this a moment. 'We can carry provisions for a few days, at least. We stay on the road until the last possible moment, then approach the fortress from the east. I will get word to Lupicinus that he needs to come up from the south and west, and your friend Victorinus can organise an attack from the north. If, *if*, we all reach Epiacum at the same time, we shall surround Valentinus, crush the bastard before he has a chance to get away.' He smashed a fist into his open palm, eyes blazing as he visioned the slaughter.

'Domine, do you know this Valentinus?' It was a question Felicius had been burning to ask. Jovinus had been reluctant to speak of what he knew, that had been clear. He wondered if he could garner more from the Spaniard now that they had marched and fought together.

Theodosius looked away from Felicius, his eyes scanning over the countryside. Across every horizon, fields coated in red moss rolled away uninterrupted. There was a small farmstead to the east, but that was the only indication the land around them was in-habited.

The silence stretched a while longer and Felicius

began to worry the old man would never speak again. But eventually, he did.

'Yes, Prefect. I know the man we are hunting.' He spoke with his eyes still on the horizon, though his mind seemed far away.

Felicius had been around people long enough to know when to speak and when to stay silent. He kept his mouth shut, knowing the answers he sought were coming.

'He is the emperor's cousin, or so he claims anyway.'

'Cousin?' Felicius nearly choked on the air. Could that really be true?

'Yes. Valentinian, Valentinus – you can see the similarity in their family names. Anyway, he was always prowling the shadows at court, whispering in listening ears how unfair it was that he had received nothing from either Valentinian or Valens. His two cousins ruled the world, and yet he was left with nothing.'

Felicius was still trying to get his breath back. He coughed as quietly as he could.

'He didn't have nothing, of course. He lived a life of privilege. He had honours and titles, albeit with very little actual responsibility. But he wanted more! More power, more money, more... everything,' Theodosius trailed off. His horse grew skittish beneath him as a fox scuttled across the road. He calmed it with quiet words and a soothing stroke of its neck. 'And that is when the problems began.'

'Problems?'

'At first it was money going missing. One of Valentinus's duties was to oversee the coin that came from Rome to be paid to the legions in Britannia and Gaul. On paper of course it would seem that all was as it should, but more and more of the regional governors began complaining they had not received the correct amounts, didn't have enough to pay their men.'

Felicius nodded, sudden understanding dawning. He had been present on more than one occasion when his father-in-law had sputtered and cursed as the pay wagons were unloaded and a chest or two had been missing. Twice that Felicius knew of, the governor had dipped into his own pockets, desperate to ensure the men on the Wall got the money they were owed. He wondered now if the man had ever been repaid.

'And then one day, in the presence of the emperor, he was accused of rape.'

'Gods below,' Felicius muttered, beginning to wish he hadn't asked.

'It was my daughter who accused him.'

'Fuck—'

Theodosius cut Felicius off. 'Yes, quite.' 'Now, my daughter could bring no proof, and of course the word of a young woman in court compared to that of a senator – the cousin of the emperor at that! – would not have held up. I was in two minds as to whether I believed her myself, if I'm being honest.'

Theodosius trailed off once more. Felicius risked a glance sideways and saw moisture in the general's eyes. He coughed once more, cursing himself for bringing Valentinus up.

'It was not until it became evident that she was with child that the perilous state of her situation became clear. I had to do something, had to act.' The fierceness was back in Theodosius's eyes, the conviction in his words iron. 'I went to the emperor. Gaining a private audience with his august majesty was not too difficult. I was a trusted general in his army, after all. He is a reasonable man, Valentinian. A good man. He has not gone mad with power or insisted people worship him as a god, as others have before him. He listened to what I had to say, even met with poor Aurelia and comforted her himself. She is a beauty, my Aurelia, no doubt about that. I've had many suitors after her hand in marriage, and only a few of them seeking it to gain advancement at court.

'But she is also principled, well brought up. I know there is no chance she would have given herself willingly to that cretin, not out of wedlock. Her mother and I decided it would be best if she returned to our estates in Hispania, to have the baby there, out of sight. Word soon spread, of course, that Aurelia was pregnant. I don't know if a slave or merchant with a loose tongue and an inclination to bag himself a few coins saw her and her swelling belly as she got in the carriage to take her west, but it spread like wildfire around court. And then, wouldn't you believe, within weeks, four more women came forwards and told their own stories. All well-bred, three of them married to well-to-do men. And guess what?' Theodosius finally turned his eyes to lock onto Felicius. The prefect saw no softness there, just fire and steel. 'They all had his children, little boys with the same pale skin and dark hair. The oldest must be fourteen or fifteen by now! He'd paid them off, even whisked the children away, all to "hide their mother's embarrassment", of course.' He hawked and spat, his hands shaking on the reins. Felicius's thoughts turned to the younger Theo, and how much he knew. His friend had mentioned nothing to him, but then he wouldn't have, would he?

'So he was exiled. The official story given to us at

court was that he had powerful friends in Rome, a brother in particular, a lawyer, who had done certain favours for the emperor during one of the many religious disputes the city seems to have these days. Unofficially, we all knew it was because he was kin to the emperor. Just the money alone would have been enough for me to see the man to the noose, but the rape? The lies? What sort of man does such a thing?'

Felicius had no words. He opened his mouth twice, only to blubber like a fish out of water. What was there to say? Nothing that would bring Aurelia's honour back, nothing that could rid her of the memories. But what happened to her child? Was this really the right time to ask? *Gods, I've dug myself a hole here.*

'She had the baby, Aurelia. He is named Marcus, a simple, common name. She had wanted to name the boy Theodosius, after myself and Theo, but I could not allow such a thing. We even found a match for her. Man by the name of Honorius, he is the son of a merchant back home, done very well for himself, the father, anyway. But he is a likeable young man, and he dotes on my Aurelia. He is bringing the boy up as his own, and making a damn fine job of it.' He nodded, as if he was convincing himself the words he spoke were true.

'So, you see, I'm sure, Prefect, just why I jumped at

the opportunity to come here and rid the world of this whoreson?'

Despite everything he had just heard, Felicius had to hide a small smile. He'd never heard the word whoreson used by anyone other than his centurions before. 'What are your orders from the emperor, sir? If I may be so bold.' It was a good question, he thought, especially as he was marching to war against this Valentinus. If there had been orders given for the traitor to be taken alive, then all of the senior officers should be aware.

'His imperial majesty did not mention his cousin by name when he gave me this assignment. He just told me I was to rid the island of every traitor I found, by any means necessary.'

Felicius nodded. It was good to have clarity. Once more he thought back to his meeting with Jovinus, his mind sifting through the events of the subsequent weeks as he tried to remember the man's words. 'Jovinus told me that he had been aware of this Valentia for some time, and that he had been receiving reports from Britannia on its progress. Were you aware of this?'

Theodosius spat again, ridding his mouth of the bitter taste this conversation had left on his tongue. 'No. Believe me, Prefect, if I had known what has been brewing up here these last few years, I would have been on a ship with an army in a heartbeat, emperor's permission or not! It was only when I met with Jovinus and he told me of the work he had done to clear the sea of pirates that I became aware.'

The wind picked up; more dark clouds lurked on the eastern horizon. Felicius shuddered at the prospect of another wet day. He'd only just dried his cloak out from the last downpour. 'Why would they keep it a secret? What is there to gain by allowing Valentinus to slowly build followers the way he has?'

Theodosius laughed, a sour sound that carried no joy. 'You really do know very little of the inner workings of the empire, and I'd wager you're a better man for it! Divide and conquer has always been the Roman way. I'm sure you are familiar with the term.'

'Of course.' Felicius nodded. 'We set one tribal chief off against another, fill one's pockets with gold, maybe even ship a few weapons to them. That way when our man wins, he is our man. Until we do the same thing with his next enemy and our man is then dead and buried. Repeat and repeat. We've been doing it since the days of the great Caesar.'

'Exactly. Play the petty barbarians off against one another, let them slaughter each other, let no one tribe get so strong they pose us a serious threat. But every now and then, one of them succeeds and gives us a bloody nose. Now, the powers that be have recently decided that this tactic could be used to subdue threats within the empire as well as those we face from without. So when Jovinus first got wind of this "Valentia", he decided he should employ a man to start his own little coup, and see if the two men would end up at war with each other, rather than us.'

'He failed to mention that to me,' Felicius said with a frown.

'Ha! I bet he did, lad! I haven't even got to the punchline yet. The man he employed in his devilish little act of make pretend treason was none other than the prefect of notaries, Secundus, stationed right here on this island.'

Felicius had to smile, despite himself. He could put the rest of the puzzle together himself. 'So Jovinus thought he was setting Secundus against Valentinus.'

'But?' Theodosius arched an eyebrow, amusement in his eyes now, the fury abated.

'But Secundus was already in the pay of Valentinus. He took Jovinus's money, added it to the haul Valentinus had already stolen when he was in charge of the soldiers' pay, and they ended up twice as rich as they were. All Secundus had to do was send a report back to Gaul once a month, stating that everything was under control and his new little faction was already taking men from Valentinus. I'm assuming no one bothered to send a man over here to check.'

'Got it in one! "Who guards the guards?" as the old saying goes. Secundus was in charge of the agentus in rebus; he was the spymaster! Why waste time and more money sending someone over to Britannia to spy on the spies of the island? Britannia has always been a backwater. To be honest, I'm not convinced it will stay part of the empire for too much longer.'

'No?'

'Think on it. You've fought on the Rhine and the Danube; you've seen first-hand the multitude of tribes that are fighting for land over there in Germania. More and more of the bastards are coming from the eastern plains, and they need land, and lots of it. We won't let them into Gaul or Pannonia, not if we can help it. But once they reach the northern shores of Germania and get a nose for sailing, where are they going to come?'

'Here?'

'Exactly. That wall we built along the north won't be much use when our enemies are all attacking from the east. No, my boy, our days on this island are numbered.'

'Then what is the point in all this?' Felicius said,

suddenly exasperated. He gestured to the marching column around them, the soldiers singing and laughing as they walked, the mules lugging carts of kit and provisions. It was a migration in itself.

'Pride, mainly. Valentinian won't want to be remembered as the man who lost an island; leave that to his successors. It is all a game, my young friend, all a game.' He trailed off. Once more his eyes roamed the horizon; once more his mind seemed to drift far away.

For the first time in his life, Felicius gave thanks that he was not from more noble stock. He didn't think he would be cut out for the cloak and dagger wars men of the imperial court fought in the shadows. Give him a battlefield any day, a sword in his hand, a man like Vitulus at his side. That was the life for him.

'I read your letter,' Theodosius said, his eyes snapping back to Felicius. 'The one your friend sent you. You were unconscious at the time, or might as well have been, anyway.'

Stunned, Felicius said nothing. Eventually, he managed to stammer out a reply. 'Why?'

The general shrugged. 'In my short experience working with you, you have come across as a sensible, well-mannered officer. Wanted to know what had made you lose the plot like that.'

'You could have just asked,' Felicius snapped. He

was shocked his superior would do something like that. A man's personal correspondence was just that – personal.

'I could have. But I wanted the truth, and all of it. I am sorry about your wife and daughter. We will get them back, you know that, don't you?'

'I will get to them, if it's the last thing I do,' Felicius said with conviction. He thought of what the general had just told him of Valentinus. Visions of his wife being raped flashed through his mind. His knuckles tightened on the reins, and his whole body seemed to tremble.

'Peace, Prefect,' Theodosius said in a soothing tone. 'They will not be harmed. Valentinus is many things; stupid is not one of them. They are political prisoners and will be treated with respect. He will know the time may come when he may need to use them as a bargaining chip. I need you to tell me more of your friend Victorinus.'

Felicius took two deep, calming breaths. He reasoned that the general was right. His family could indeed be used as a makeweight in some sort of deal, if it came to it. She was the daughter of the former governor of northern Britannia, after all. 'What do you need to know?'

'Can we trust him?'

'I would trust him with my life,' Felicius said without pause.

'You trusted him with your wife and daughter,' the general pointed out.

Felicius frowned. 'I don't think he can be held to blame for what happened. He has a small body of men, and they are living like outlaws in the forest. His family were taken too, as I'm sure you're aware from my letter. And it is my fault they were with him when they were taken. Sixtus did not have the men to protect them; he tried to tell me that. I asked him to do it anyway.'

Theodosius nodded. He pulled his cloak tighter around him as the wind blew stronger. It did not feel like a summer's day. 'I am. And you cannot blame yourself for the actions of another man. You left your family under the protection of your friend in good faith. I have asked around about this tribune from the areani. Men say he is a drunk, a disgrace. They say the areani as a whole are a bunch of outlaws, that men are sent to serve in their ranks as a form of punishment. Is any of this true?'

Felicius weighed his response in his mind, tipping mental scales one way then the other. 'All of it,' he said after a short pause. 'The areani is where units from Britannia used to send their men who were a liability, ones they just needed to be rid of but could have done without the hassle of all the paperwork for just kicking them out. Then, of course, the quantity of recruits began to dry up, units grew smaller and more desperate for manpower, and there were no more drunkards or troublemakers to send north of the Wall. When I left Vindolanda for the south, the areani numbered six men, and two of them were little more than boys.'

'And now they number two, if what I have read is correct.'

Felicius shrugged. 'The Caledonians are all south of the Wall. Don't suppose it matters much any more.'

'Yes, there is that.' Silence spread between the two men, a companiable silence. Felicius felt his respect for the general grow. It was not like any man of his rank would spend the time he had getting to know all the officers under his command. Felicius knew he was receiving no special treatment. Theodosius spent as much time as he could with each of the men who commanded the units that made up his army.

'Shall I go north, sir? Join up with Victorinus? Might be easier if I communicate with him directly, rather than us relying on messengers.'

Theodosius looked at Felicius a while, the old man riding easily, straight backed and at home in the saddle. 'So the two of you can conspire a plan to get your families back before the blood starts flowing, you mean?'

'No, sir—'

'Peace, Prefect.' Theodosius chuckled. 'The gods know I would be the same in your position.' His face screwed up a moment, lips pouted as he thought. 'Although I can see the merit in it. You and this Victorinus can scout around a little, come up with a plan for an attack from the north. You can then bring that back to me and I will have first-hand intelligence on the state of play, plus what your friend plans.' He mused a moment longer, a finger reaching to his face to stroke his lip. 'Do it. Take eight men with you, enough to knock a few heads together if you get in a scrap, few enough to travel quickly and hopefully unnoticed.'

'Thank you, Domine,' a relieved Felicius said with a nod. He had been thinking about his family when the idea struck him. Surely Victorinus had some clue by now as to where they were being held? 'I will leave Vitulus here in command of my men. He is most capable and won't let you down. With luck I'll be back with you in a week to ten days, and we can move forwards with our plans.'

'Can I go?' an optimistic voice said from behind them.

'Ah, of course. A daring mission to the north, half a chance everyone in it might get themselves killed. Where else would my son want to be?' Theodosius said with a warm smile. As father and son locked eyes, Felicius saw the love and respect the two men held for each other. It was touching, and before he knew it, he was smiling with them.

'I'll see him safe, Domine,' he said to the general, smiling over to Theo, who looked like a dog who'd just found a new stick, the best stick, and was wagging its tail with vigour.

'Prefect, there is no man I would trust more. When will you leave?'

'Within the hour, with your permission. I'll pick a tent party from amongst my men, load up with provisions and be on the road.'

Theodosius nodded. 'Ten days, Prefect, you have ten days, and then I expect to see you on the northern horizon. I shall get word to Lupicinus and Maximus, let them know where they should be heading. May the gods be with you both.' He reached out and cupped his son's face, much to Theo's embarrassment.

16

The rain seemed to seep right through him. It was that light drizzle, so fine yet so dense, as if the very air itself was pure moisture. He had given up with his sodden hood an hour or so ago. It weighed heavy on his head, the rain seeping right through. Seemed a pointless gesture to keep it up.

The darkness was absolute, thick clouds blocking all sign of the moon. At least the wind had abated, and now, after a good two hours of hard walking, he had warmed enough to stop his teeth from chattering. The world around him was silent, as if a blanket had been thrown over it. A great big wet one. There were no foxes scurrying across his path, no owl calls from the treeline to his right. Just the soft padding of his boots on the mud path, his heavy breath misting before him.

This was the third time he had snuck out from the camp under the cover of dark. He had been extra careful this time. He'd positioned his bunk right by the sentries on the western perimeter. It had just been a matter of patience. They had to patrol, was part of the job, and when finally, one went left and the other right, it had been the work of moments to scurry down the gentle incline, dark cloak making him invisible on this blackest of nights.

He knew he must have been followed the last time, when he had met with Cassius deep in the woodland back east. How else would Victorinus had known to abandon his plan of riding south and west? He must have sent a man to follow him. Maybe that man had even heard the whispered conversation he and Cassius had shared. Who knew. Not him, anyway.

The last few days had been the hardest of his life, and his young years had been made up of hard days. Wasn't easy being him, though others seemed to think it was. He'd moved more times than he could remember, had to change himself with every one. Reinvent how he spoke, how he walked, how he behaved. Wasn't easy being him.

Fact was he deserved a lot of credit. It had been he

who had put his life on the line after all, when they were north of the Wall and the first lick of flames had been spotted. The men he'd charged hadn't known he was in on the act, hadn't realised he was actually their ally. But they were just hands for hire, not true believers, true disciples of Valentia. Their deaths had been a sacrifice to a cause they never understood. Not that he wasted much time thinking about them. Them or any of the others who had joined them on the other side. None of that mattered, not in the grand scheme of things.

They were all just pawns in a game for the ultimate prize, a game which they could not afford to lose. This had been years in the planning, years of waiting and training. He'd rehearsed his part until he was blue in the face and he could dream of nothing else. But it had all been worth it, he supposed.

Not everything had gone to plan; even the best plans turned to shit when blades were drawn and blood spilled. Halfhand had told him that, and the truth of it had held strong as iron. Halfhand, now there was one part that had gone off script. He hadn't expected to like any of the men in the areani, hadn't expected to respect them. 'They're just a bunch of drunken losers,' he had been told. 'A flock of sheep. All you need to do is herd them in the right direction.'

Well, he'd tried that; turned out shepherding wasn't for him.

But the men he had been ordered to infiltrate had left a mark on him. He'd cried in his cloak when Cassius told him Halfhand was dead. Severus, too, had been a good man. Over twenty years he'd served the empire, manning the vessels on the Rhine frontier, sticking it to the tribes at every opportunity. Halfhand had done his time in the ranks, taking a wound of honour in the last civil war, not that he talked of it much. Both dead. Both would have made valuable assets to the cause.

Cassius revelled in the killing. He loved the deception, the sense of power that came with it. He seemed not to feel the weight of their task on his shoulders, but rather thrived on it. 'Should have seen Severus's face when I stuck him,' he'd bragged, as if it was the grandest thing anyone had ever done. Pastor had just felt sick.

He rounded a corner, rain-soaked cloak dragging him down. His knees began to ache, and he knew tomorrow would be a long day. He saw men up ahead, sitting on horseback, blocking the road. His heart beat faster.

The closest was unmistakably Cassius. His blond hair was bare. Even lank with the rain it was a shining light in the night. He saw white teeth as his friend grinned as he approached. 'Took your time, brother!' Cassius called. Loud, much too loud.

'Hush,' Pastor hissed, head spinning to check the road was clear behind him. It was, of course it was. He tried to control his breathing, to slow the throbbing tempo of his heart.

'Relax! There's no one there,' Cassius said with a casual gesture. 'Why is your arm still in a sling? No one to fool here, brother.'

Pastor looked down in confusion. He had become so used to wearing the thing, he hadn't thought to take it off. He did so now, tucking the sling inside his sodden cloak.

'Were you followed?' a man said, pushing his horse forwards. Pastor felt his heart miss a beat as he looked up into eyes darker than any night. The man was hooded, his mail glimmering beneath his dark cloak.

'No,' he said in a soft voice. An odd feeling, to look into the eyes of someone you worshipped, knowing they thought nothing of you. The hooded man was already looking beyond him, and Pastor felt his hopes sink like an anchor. He would never get what he desired from this man.

It had been a shock, riding with Victorinus into

the small farmstead in the middle of nowhere. He had been struggling with himself at that point, doubtful he had made the right decision to betray the men of the areani. But then he had seen Victorinus stoop and hug his son to him, a son the man had never mentioned before in his presence. How could a man so lost to the world as Victorinus manage to treat his child like that? When a man such as the one before him, a powerful man, with wealth and influence, could not even bring himself to meet his gaze.

Strange thing was, it didn't make him hate the man any more. If anything, it pushed a divide between Victorinus and him, made him even more determined to betray the tribune. He'd made the decision then to suggest kidnapping the family. Doubtless Cassius would have done it if he hadn't. That hadn't been the plan, not originally anyway. They were just meant to be given a scare, a warning to Victorinus to keep out of the way. Secundus had been all too eager to take care of it himself.

Speaking of that cretin, he was there now, slight frame covered in a skin of some animal or other. He looked down at Pastor, through his bulbous nose, and sneered. 'You look like a drowned rat, boy.'

Pastor tried to think of something sharp and witty

to reply with, but he came up short and his teeth began chattering again.

'I need news, boy,' the hooded man said, leaning down from the saddle. 'Where is this Victorinus and the Spanish horsemen?'

'Five miles or so to the north. They're heading for Epiacum.'

'They know where we are based?' The voice was an icy whisper.

'Victorinus has guessed. He knows. He knows that I am not one of them. He has said nothing yet but I know he will soon. He's leading me on, seems to be just waiting for the—'

'The right moment,' a voice said from behind him. And then all was chaos.

Men streamed from the night, howling, screaming, screeching in their blood joy. Blades flashed in pockets of moonlight and Pastor winced as a spear flashed past his face, whistling past him before burying itself in Secundus with a wet crunch. The man toppled from his mount, blood bubbling at his lips.

The clash of steel filled his ears now. He rushed beneath the nearest horse, only for the beast to grow skittish and rear up on its hind legs. Panic took hold and he rolled away to the right, shoulder crunching on the cobbled road. He screamed in pain, left arm cradling the right, rose and made for the trees on the side of the road. He never made it.

A bulky shadow with a glimmering axe blocked his path. Tall and broad, dark hair and a wicked grin. 'There you are, you little traitor,' Drost snarled, baring his teeth in a savage grin. He swung hard and fast with the axe, high to low, and Pastor danced out of the way, struggling to free his sword from its scabbard. Eventually, he bared the blade and parried Drost's next heavy blow, but he was young, slight, weak of wrist and lacked conviction. His sword spun from his hand, turning his wrist the wrong way, and his body flowed with the motion. Once more he crumpled to the cobbles, the drizzling rain cold on his face as he turned to see the big Caledonian standing over him.

So this is where my story ends.

Shame really, to have seen so little of life. If he'd have known he'd only have a handful of years, he thought he would have done more with them.

'Valentia!' was the scream in the darkness, somewhere over Pastor's right shoulder, and the ground shook to the beat of galloping horses. They streamed from the endless night, swords raised, horns sounding. Pastor grinned. Salvation had come.

He saw the hooded man fighting from horseback.

His sword was slick with blood as he hacked at a Spaniard who was struggling to control his mount. The first blow took the soldier on his shoulder, the next severed his neck. An already bloody night got a bit grimmer.

Pastor stumbled and cursed as he raced to be at the hooded man's side. Even now, in the midst of all this, he could think of nothing else than seeking the man's approval. Maybe he would save him, turn away a death blow and earn a place in the old bastard's heart. Maybe they would fight to victory together, would finally be seen for the man he had become, and a new chapter in their lives would begin.

Of course, none of that happened. Just as he reached the hooded man, the man whirled his bloody sword over his head. 'Retreat!' he bellowed, over and over again.

'Wait!' Pastor shouted, but his small voice was lost in the din of clashing metal and galloping hooves. His father's men turned their mounts back west and streamed into the night. There was an eerie silence when they had gone. Pastor was left on his knees, feeling as if he had just dunked his head underwater.

* * *

Victorinus hawked and spat blood on the road. He was panting like a dog, probably looked a bit like one, with his matted hair plastered across his face under his drooping hat. It had been a simple plan, but a good one. But even the best laid plans go to shit when the blood starts flying; Halfhand had told him that.

They'd followed Pastor, virtually packing up the whole camp shortly after he'd left, and kept their distance as they stalked the dark road. The lad hadn't a clue. A small part of Victorinus felt slightly ashamed at that. Had the boy learned nothing in the months he had spent with the areani?

Felix had brought fifty or so of his Spaniards with him for the attack. The rest were still on the road now, had obviously delayed their departure a little too long. A couple of hundred cavalry would have seen the job finished.

Still, Victorinus reasoned they had dealt their enemy a bloody nose at least. He had laid eyes upon Valentinus for the first time, not that he would be able to point the man out in a crowd. There was no moon to speak of, and thick rain clouds drizzled down on them from above. It was that fine rain, the one they all hated. Seemed like it worked its way into your skin and chilled your bones.

'Survivors,' he called to the Spanish horsemen.

'We need survivors. Check and see if any of the whoresons are still breathing.' He pulled his hat from his head and wiped his face with the bloodied cuff of his mail, then regretted it. Gods, he was tired. Too old for this shit. He thought for the thousandth time how different his life would have been if he had just allowed himself to be happy. To have stayed on his farm with Sarai and his boys, growing crops, tending the animals, and watching his children grow into young men. What a fine life it would have been.

'Got a survivor for you, Chief,' Drost said. Squinting into the darkness, Victorinus could make out a scruffy thing trapped under one of Drost's huge arms. Took him a moment to work out who it was, but when he did a slow smile spread across his face.

'Reckon that's a good start,' he said, and spat blood again. 'Keep a tight hold of him, we'll question him in the morning. Right now, I want to get out of this rain and get some sleep.'

* * *

The clouds retreated when faced with the rising sun. They left a bruising shade of purple above, a fitting colour, Victorinus thought. He'd slept for a couple of hours but was too wet to get comfortable. He knew his mail would need rubbing down and oiling, but couldn't bring himself to do it. Rising and shaking off his damp cloak, he walked the perimeter of their latest woodland camp, standing in a small clearing so the sun could kiss his skin. Small pleasures, he thought. He was well used to the life of living on the road, making whatever camp he could as he and his men rode from east to west in the wilderness north of the Wall.

But there had always been some security in that. Always knowing he could turn around at any time, head back south and pop in on his wife and children. Head down to Eboracum and have a few nights out on the town with Halfhand and Severus. Selfish, he told himself. All the time he could have been at home, he was deep in his cups in some tavern or whorehouse, throwing away his coin when it could have been used to buy timber to rebuild his barn or new livestock for the small community in the farm. That was what Publius would have done. Now there was a good man, a man to look up to.

He gave a small nod to Prefect Felicius, who was up and stretching by a smouldering fire. It had been a surprise to see his friend and a small party of men from the Fourth at their camp when they had returned in the darkness. Felicius said he had nearly been killed on the spot when he approached, such was the tension amongst the men left to guard the camp. Victorinus had only smiled. It was good to know that Felix's men were alert. They had agreed to delay swapping information until the morning. Both men were exhausted from either riding or fighting, and clear heads would be needed if they were to make any progress.

'How'd you sleep?' Victorinus asked as he approached.

'I think the damp has gotten into my bones; they feel rotten. You?'

'About the same,' Victorinus replied with a half-smile. 'Listen, brother, about your family...' He felt an urgent need to say something, to plead his case before his friend could unleash his inevitable fury.

'If you could have saved them from being captured you would have. Just like you would have saved your own. Do not worry on that front, Sixtus. I am saving my anger for this Valentinus; I feel none towards you.'

Victorinus nodded, feeling more relieved than he would have cared to admit. Halfhand was dead, Severus still missing, though he had all but given up hope the man was alive. Cassius and Pastor were traitors. He'd never been a man with many friends, but even by his standards, it seemed like he had reached a new low point. Might have ended him if Felicius had turned his back on him too.

'I think I know just the young man to ask about our families, what do you reckon?' There was an evil glint in Victorinus's eye as he spoke. He'd had enough of skulking around forest tracks. The first sighting of his enemy had sparked a flame deep within him, and it was burning bright.

'After you, Tribune.' Felicius smirked, offering a mock bow. 'You two.' The prefect turned to a couple of his men, sitting on logs and sharing water from a skin. 'Build this fire back up, make sure it's hot.'

* * *

'I don't know!' Pastor squealed for the third time, wincing as the burning iron hovered inches from his flesh.

'"I don't know" ain't going to cut it here, lad,' Victorinus said. He had expected to feel rage, to be shaking with barely contained anger, but now he was here, the traitor stripped and tied in front of him, he felt oddly calm. Detached was probably the better word, and full of regret. He had no business torturing young boys, wasn't something he had any experience in, wasn't something he ever wanted to do again. But his wife and boys were missing, somewhere out there in the great expanse of the north, and he wanted them back.

'I'm going to ask you one more time, and then Felicius here is going to burn the skin from your ball sack and use your acorns to play fetch with his dog.'

'Does he have a dog?' Drost asked, looking up from sharpening his axe, a slight frown on his face.

Victorinus turned to the Caledonian in despair. 'Not helpful,' he hissed. 'Now, where has Valentinus taken our families?'

'I swear, I swear by all the gods I don't know!' He was thrashing at his bonds now, his wrists and ankles seeping blood where the rough rope was digging through the skin. That was the least of his problems, though.

'Fine,' Victorinus said, opting to change tack. 'Where is he holding out? Is it Epiacum?'

'Yes,' the boy whimpered, nodding vigorously. 'That was always the plan, anyway. But I have been with you for months! It could have changed!'

'You would have been told if it had, though? Your secret little meetings with Cassius, he must have told you something?'

'No, nothing.' Pastor shook his head from side to side with such force Victorinus thought he might actually break his own neck. 'He said he wasn't allowed to tell me anything, in case—'

'In case this happened,' Felicius finished. He moved the knife closer to Pastor's groin and Victorinus got a whiff of simmering flesh. He was glad he'd skipped breakfast.

Cursing to himself, Victorinus rose to his feet and took a couple of steps away. Around them were a half circle of men. Drost sharpening his axe, ready to deliver the death blow himself once the time was right. Felix and a clutch of his men, each one now as devoted to their cause as Victorinus was. He took a couple of breaths to compose himself. The fire crackled and popped behind him; the wind rustled through the trees. He felt his anger subside.

'How many men does this Valentinus have?'

'I don't know!' Pastor screamed. 'I don't know anything! How could I? I've been with you for months!'

Victorinus cursed again. Annoyingly, it sounded reasonable enough. 'Why were you and Cassius sent to bed yourselves with me? Why am I important?'

It was something that had been nagging at him. He had a very small command, and most of the time he was north of the Wall. The senior commanders in northern Britain all thought him nothing more than a drunk – which to be fair, he was. He felt the itch then, the longing for a skin of wine. But he quashed it down. Last time he had fallen off the wagon he had achieved nothing. Just a string of burnt-out taverns, a few men dead. Hadn't got him anywhere though.

'It was Secundus who had the idea. Said you were dangerous, resourceful. He said you'd gotten yourself out of more scraps in the north than he could give you credit for. He said if anyone was going to stand in our way it was you.'

'I'm almost flattered,' Victorinus said, and he meant it. Of all the high society that had looked down on him over the years, no one had sneered more than Secundus, Prefect of Notaries.

'I'm insulted,' Felicius said. 'My boys are the best unit in the north. I wasn't invited to turn traitor.' This got a few chuckles from the half circle of men.

'But you are the son-in-law of the former governor. Valentinus knew he would not turn you.'

'So, what was the plan for me?'

'Drive you south, which we did. He knew if we surrounded Vindolanda with Caledonians then you'd see you had no choice. You did exactly what we thought you would do.'

'But I came back with an army! Bet your master didn't reckon on that, did he?'

'Actually, he did,' Pastor said, seemingly growing

into it now. 'How can we be victorious without a glo-rious victory?'

'So that's the plan, is it? Wait for the emperor to send an army and then beat it in the field? Show the local populace what this new "Valentia" can do for them and then Valentinus can set himself up as emperor?'

'Exactly!' Pastor yelled with a triumphant glee. 'First, we subdue the Caledonians and the Germans, win the support of the local people. Then we take the north, then the whole island! The people will support us in our fight against Rome. Before you know what's happening, we are marching on Gaul and finally my father—'

He stopped suddenly. There was a moment of si-lence, in which everyone except Pastor seemed to frown in confusion.

'Your father?' Victorinus said, snatching the knife from Felicius and holding it under the boy's eye. 'Say that again.'

'My father will finally get what he is owed,' Pastor whispered.

'Lupus Valentinus is your father?' Victorinus said, but he was more thinking out loud than he was talking to Pastor. 'And Cassius?'

'The same. Though we have different mothers. It is

a long story.'

'And one you will tell me one day, whether you want to or not. Is Severus dead?'

Pastor nodded, quivering eyes round like coins. Too frightened to speak.

Victorinus hunched back on his haunches. He had known the man was dead, but having it confirmed still hit him like a hammer blow. After a while, he rose and walked away from the fire and the quivering boy. Felicius followed soon after.

17

It took little time for Felicius to fill Victorinus in on what he had learnt.

'So Valentinus was raping women and paying them off?' Victorinus spat in disgust. He had frequented his fair share of whorehouses over the years and knew he wasn't one to preach. But paying for sex with someone willing to take the coin is one thing; to take it by force is something else entirely.

'And Theodosius said he was taking the children. All the ones he was aware of were boys.'

'Including the one my sister gave birth to.' A hooded figure spoke from behind them.

'Gods, lad, you're supposed to be staying out of

sight. Remember what we agreed on the road?' Felicius hissed.

The figure lowered the hood to reveal the features of a young man. He had a crop of dark hair and sun-kissed skin, not unlike Felix. His eyes were slanted, set slightly too far apart, giving him a lazy expression. 'Who are you?' Victorinus asked.

'I am Theodosius, son of the comes rei militaris Theodosius.'

'Well, here we go,' Felicius sighed.

'You are the general's son? Why are you here? And why does it need to be a secret?' Victorinus asked Felicius.

'Because if he gets himself killed it will be my fault! He's meant to be staying quiet and out of the way.'

'I have fought and killed!' Theo snapped. 'And am my own man. I want this Valentinus dead as much as you. He raped my sister! Brought shame upon my family. I would see him pay for his crimes.'

Victorinus rubbed his eyes. It was almost too much to take in. Gods, but the itch for wine was coming back with a fury. 'This Valentinus, the man we are fighting, raped and impregnated the daughter of the general Rome has sent to defeat him?'

'Yes, that's about it,' Felicius muttered. 'But that

doesn't mean you can put yourself in harm's way just so you can get your revenge,' he said to Theo.

'I promised you I would not. I am not my cousin, some hot-headed fool looking to get himself killed. But I want to fight, I want to prove myself. And I want to see Valentinus hung from the nearest tree. Nothing you can say to me will stop me fighting for that.'

'I like him already,' Victorinus said. He walked away from the group, back towards Pastor, who was sitting now, hands and feet still bound. Drost stood over him, axe sufficiently sharpened. He whirled it in circles in front of the youth, a wicked grin fixed to his face.

Victorinus lowered himself to a squat. Opening his water skin, he passed it to Pastor, who drank greedily. 'Who is your mother?' he asked when Pastor had quenched his thirst.

'Never knew her name,' the lad said with a shrug. 'She was a slave at court, used to do laundry and other chores for Valentinus in his rooms. All I was ever told was one night my father came home drunk, took my mother and had his way with her before she could so much as scream. And even if she had, who would have come to help? My father is a powerful man; my mother... she was nobody.'

He began to cry, softly at first. Before long, tears

ran like rivers down his face, his body sobbed and he hugged his knees in sorrow. 'My whole life I have been trained for this. Living in one place then the next. Learning how to speak like locals, integrating myself with the right people. My whole life, just to play a small part in the rise of someone else's. He doesn't love me, my father; he barely acknowledges that I am alive. Do you know how many times I can remember actually being alone with my father? Just once. Once, in my entire life. And only then it was so he could explain to me exactly what he needed me to do.

'We are nothing to him, his children. Pawns in his game, that is all. I swear if I could go back to the day in that tavern again, I would tell you everything.' He stopped. He couldn't speak any more, Victorinus could see that.

The tribune felt an overwhelming feeling of sadness. This was what Maurus would think when he grew up. He would think his father didn't love him, that his father never spent any time with him. Once again, he realised what a fool he had been. His hand went for the pouch at his belt. He cursed when he remembered it wasn't there. Amor. Despite all he had done for the boy, Maurus had given him the thing he loved most in the world without a moment's hesitation.

Was he any better than this Valentinus? Who was he to stand up to this man, this would-be emperor, and say that what he did was wrong? He too had made his son feel worthless; he too had mistreated a woman, if not in the same way. So many mistakes; not everyone got the opportunity to put them right.

'Pastor,' he began in a small voice, putting his hand on the young man's shoulder. 'Your father has taken my family. You remember them, yes? Sarai, my wife. Maurus and Silvius, my children.'

The boy nodded, wiping his running nose with his tied hands. 'I'm so sorry,' he whispered.

'If I don't get them back, then one day my son is going to say the same things about me as you have just said about your father. See, I'm no role model, no man to look up to. I've done horrible things with my life. Sarai and I, we had... we had another son.' His own tears were coming, and he struggled to hold them back, choking on the words. 'A beautiful little boy. But I was selfish, arrogant. I went north with my men for a few weeks one winter, and when our patrol finished, I went straight to Eboracum, got drunk, messed around, did whatever I wanted. Didn't give any thought to my poor wife, stuck indoors with two small children, all alone. And little Leo got sick, a cough at first. Then a fever, and then he stopped breathing.' It felt as though a lifetime's worth of emotion came flooding out of him. He slumped forwards, unable to support his own weight, gasping for air as the tears fell like spears from the sky to spatter on the mud beneath him.

'I need to make things right. I need to find my sons, to tell them how much they are loved. I need to kiss them, to see them play in the sun. Can you understand any of that?'

Pastor didn't speak at first, though he kept his eyes locked on Victorinus. The tribune thought he could see the boy thinking, and his mouth opened but no words came out. 'Yes,' Pastor said eventually. 'Yes, I understand. And yes, I will help you.'

* * *

Night fell as he approached Epiacum, riding south past the extensive defensive ditches. Seven rows had been re-dug since his last visit here, some months previous. His father had always had this fortress in mind as the place he would make his base, and it was easy to see why.

The only road lay to the north. An attack from any other direction would have to come from cross-country, and it was not good ground for marching, let alone fighting. There were tracks that led up to the gates on the southern, eastern and western walls, but they were little more than churned-up mud. The fort itself was built on a natural knoll in the hilly landscape, surrounded on all sides by defensive ditches. The high stone walls appeared impregnable as he approached the northern gate.

He paused, just out of bow shot, looked up into the purple sky, dotted with stars. He'd done things he wasn't proud of in his short life, things to please his father, things he thought would endear himself to the man who had remained so detached throughout his formative years.

He hadn't wanted to come to Britannia, but his father had said they had little choice. He had been happy, of sorts, back in northern Gaul, in a small but lavish villa, where he and his brothers were raised and educated by a small army of slaves. He hadn't known at the time the place was some big secret, hadn't known he and the other boys were being groomed for a purpose.

There was so much he wanted to do. If he were free, free to make his own choices and live the life he wanted, he thought he would go east, all the way to the Euphrates, cut back and wander the streets of Constantinople. The east was thriving, or so everyone seemed to say, just as the west was dying. But few things in life are fair; he'd learnt that, at least. And his life was not his own, or hadn't been. Didn't mean it couldn't be, though.

'Halt!' a voice called from the battlement. 'Identify yourself!'

'Valentia forever!' Pastor called, kicking his mount on, regardless of the warning. 'My name is Pastor Benedictus; I should be known to you. I am in the employ of Lupus Valentinus.' *I am his son*, he wanted to scream, but he knew that would win him no favours, least of all from his father.

'Do you have the mark?' the sentry called.

'I do, though if you could see it from up there in this light then you have better eyes than me!'

That got a few chuckles. Just what he was after. Every man who had committed themselves to the cause had the mark, top of the right arm where it could easily be hidden. Nothing fancy, just a V, same shape as the fires that had burned across northern Britannia, announcing their arrival.

He could hear the muffled conversation of the guards. No one would be permitted to enter the fortress after dark, that was standard practice. He hoped, though, that his name might allow them to make an exception. He had seen from the road the sprawling camp to the east, the picketed lines and neat rows of tents. Epiacum was only built to house around six hundred men; there must be more than three times that amount here now. Inside the walls would be the men his father trusted the most. Men who had been the first to commit, had maybe even done it without the promise of coin.

Outside would be the deserters, the men who had abandoned their stations on the Wall, or wherever Rome had placed them. They were here for the gold, promised an easy victory. Nothing would change for them, not really, that was what they would have been told. What difference did it make to the common soldier who their emperor was? As long as their pay came at the end of the month, did they really care what man they swore allegiance to at the start of every year?

And it wasn't as if usurpers and civil wars were new. Pastor reckoned there must have been at least three since the great Constantine died, and his own sons had been responsible for them. No, the common soldier didn't give a damn for the higher ups, the 'cream', as they were known. They just wanted their coin, a good woman, and competent officers – the last of which were increasingly hard to find.

No, Pastor did not want to be out in the tents, especially when Victorinus, Felicius and the field army arrived. He wanted to be behind those high stone walls, as close to his father as he could get.

A side gate opened, just a crack, hinges squealing in the silent night. Two men with spears levelled approached, and Pastor dismounted. Throwing back his cloak, he raised the sleeve of his tunic, showing the men the tattoo. 'Satisfied?' he said, trying to sound more confident than he felt.

One of the men nodded. 'We've been told to expect you. The chief thought you had been captured on the road the other night.'

'Was a close-run thing,' Pastor said, puffing out his cheeks. 'But I'm here now. Is Valentinus inside?'

'Aye, he's here.'

'Then take me to him.'

He walked his horse through the gate and tried not to flinch when it slammed shut behind him. A faceless soldier took the reins of his horse. Another called, gesturing that he should follow him. Pastor allowed himself a small smile. He was still alive, and despite the imminent danger that surrounded him, he felt more in control of his life than he ever had before.

It was time to go and see his father.

* * *

Victorinus watched from the shadows as Pastor entered the fortress. He tried to take in as much detail as he could, but it was hard to see in the darkness, even on a clear night such as this one. He scanned the battlements, eyes drawn to the towers on the corners. Was there artillery up there? He had seen a ballista used once, in a battle north of the Wall. It had devastated the Caledonian force as they charged towards the Roman defences, killing two or more men with every bolt. So much so the men had lost their nerve and retreated before coming into javelin range. *How will we breach those walls?* The thought grated at him. He had a couple of hundred men under his command, but Felix's cavalry was not trained to assault stone fortifications. Their home was the open plain, an enemy in disarray. In that scenario they were lethal, but horsemen were of no use when your enemy was behind ten feet of stone.

Movement behind him. He turned, fingers to his lips. He did not want to alert the enemy to his presence. It was Drost that emerged from the shadows. He dismounted and approached on foot. Victorinus saw the moment in the Caledonian's eyes when he laid eyes on the scale of the task facing them.

'What is it?' Victorinus asked.

'We have a problem, quite a big one.'

'Yes, I can see that.' Victorinus motioned to the fortress in the distance.

'No, not that, though that is a big problem. I went for a little ride west. Seems there's a horde of Caledonians coming this way, not sure if they are heading here or looking for a road back north. Either way they'll be on the road here by dawn.'

Victorinus cursed. They'd seen no foreigners, Scotti, Germani or Caledonian, for a few weeks. He had been starting to hope they'd all crept back to wherever they'd come from. It seemed not. 'How many?'

'Couple of thousand at least, though can't tell if they're all fighting men or not. Might be some women and children with them.'

Victorinus cursed again. 'Do you think they have been paid to fight with Valentinus? Or are they just on their way home after a summer raiding and killing?'

'Does this Valentinus even know of the army on its way here yet? How could he? He knows of us, of course, especially since you put every tavern his men drank at to the flame.'

'Yes, yes, not my finest work, I know.'

'Not having a go, Chief, I know you've been through a lot. Just saying, I'm not sure he knows what's coming to him. Why would he suddenly ask the tribes to fight alongside him? Doesn't seem like that has been his plan from the beginning. Like Pastor said, they were the distraction, giving Valentinus cover so he could gather an army and then force them from his new lands.'

'So they're on their way home? Then we simply let them pass, no?' Victorinus said with a scowl, not really seeing the problem.

Drost was silent a moment. Victorinus sensed his apprehension. The Caledonian licked his lips, fingers rubbing his cheeks. 'Spit it out, man!' Victorinus said. 'I haven't got all night.'

'Sorry, Chief,' Drost muttered. 'Thing is, the northerners, they're my tribe.'

That gave Victorinus pause. Never before had Drost spoken of where he had come from. He'd just turned up one day, asking to be part of the areani. Victorinus had asked him where had come from and why he was at the Wall all alone. He'd simply said his past was his business and no one else's. Victorinus had been desperate for men; he was always desperate for men. 'Does that change anything?' he asked the younger man.

'Possibly,' Drost said, fingers still rubbing his unshaved cheeks. 'What if there was a way I could get them to fight for us?'

18

Dawn crept slowly over the eastern horizon. It was nearly October now, and the first signs of autumn were clear in the chill air. Morning dew was heavy underfoot. Victorinus thought the grass had a certain crunch to it; not quite frost, not yet, but winter was making its first move, stretching its limbs, getting ready to reach out and take hold of the land.

'Are you sure about this?' he said to Drost. The two men stood in the shadow of the treeline, on the northern edge of the east-to-west road. A mile or so further east was a crossroads, and there the Caledonians would find the way north, and home.

'Sure as I'll ever be,' Drost said, though his voice shook with nerves. He had his axe ready, gripped loosely in a sweating palm. 'We need the manpower if we're going to get your family back.'

Victorinus reached out and cuffed Drost behind the head. It was the most affection he'd ever shown the man. 'I'll do it, if you want. There's nothing for you in this war, nothing for you to gain by staying and fighting. Not looking like you're going to be getting paid any time soon!'

'It has to be me,' Drost said, his eyes fixed on the approaching column on the road. 'I never told you how much you and the others have come to mean to me. I had nothing when I found you. No friends, no family, nothing to live for. You've given me that, Chief. You, Halfhand, Severus, even the two lads, or so I thought.' He drifted off, cuffing the air with a palm. 'What I'm trying to say is that you're my family now. We've lost two brothers because of this already, wouldn't be right for you to lose your wife and sons too. Same for your friend Felicius. Men say he is a good man.'

'He is,' Victorinus agreed. He looked to the road. The column was closer now; he could make out each individual face of the foremost men. 'I'm coming with you,' he said. Felix and the Spanish horsemen were further in the trees, ready and mounted, out of sight, if they were needed. Though Victorinus knew if the time came for them to charge then he and Drost would already be dead.

Drost nodded, licked his lips and hefted his axe. 'You think Pastor will play his part?'

'Yes.' Victorinus didn't hesitate. 'The boy is a lost soul. I think he just wanted his father to love him, was desperate to win his affection.' Once more, he reached for the pouch at his waist and cursed when he found it missing. Amor. His horse was back with Felix and his men. The beast had become so much more than just a horse to him in the last weeks and months. It was as if it was now the last remaining link he had to his family. He hoped it would not be harmed if Felix ordered his men to charge. He reached up and lowered the brim of his hat, rubbed his hands over unshaven cheeks, couldn't even remember the last time he'd bothered to shave. Shaving involved looking in mirrors, and mirrors were too honest for him to bear. 'Come on then, let's get this done.'

They walked from the treeline, the morning sun caressing their skin with a warm embrace. They wore tattered tunics over rusting armour, were both un-kempt and probably stunk like a stable, but they gave the column of armed men pause all the same.

Victorinus heard Drost breathing shallow and fast, could almost feel the drumming beat of his pulse through the ground. 'Breathe deep, lad,' he said quietly. 'Slowly, calm yourself. Fights like this are won by the man who stays in control, not the man who lets his emotions guide him.' Drost said nothing; he maintained the same wide-eyed expression, tongue darting out between dry lips. Victorinus knew the feeling well, had experienced it himself enough before a battle or skirmish. The dryness in your throat, the sudden and urgent need to piss. The clamminess of your palms, the tightness in your bowels that made you feel like you were strapped to a rock that had been plunged into the ocean.

Drost was feeling all of this now, and hating every second.

'You there, on the road!' a voice called from the column. 'Who are you?'

Victorinus said nothing. There was a time to take command, a time to take the initiative and grasp it by the horns. And there was a time to step back, edge into the shadows and watch someone else shine. This was that time.

'I am Drost, son of Bredei, who was the rightful ruler of the Vacomagi tribe. My father was murdered in his sleep, his wife, my mother, taken to another man's bed. By the laws of the tribes, I come to challenge the man responsible to single combat to the death.'

There was a collective intake of breath. 'Gods below, man. Did you not think you should have filled me in on any of this before we marched out of those trees?'

Drost just shrugged. Seemed there was some colour back in his face now. 'I told you it had to be me.'

'You said you had to fight someone. Maybe elaborating that you need to fight someone because they stole your birth right would have given me a bit more perspective!'

Drost said nothing. Victorinus blew out his cheeks and chuckled. 'Explains what you were doing at the Wall, I suppose,' he said, thinking back to his first meeting with the young Caledonian.

Drost shrugged again, hefting his trusty axe in one hand. 'Everyone's got a past. Like I told you, I don't have a family any more.'

'Aye, you do, lad. They're in here.' He leant into Drost, tapped him on his chest, right over his heart. 'Fight for them now.'

There was a cacophony growing in the ranks of the Vacomagi. Men jostled and shouted in their mother tongue. Victorinus picked out the odd word here and there. It seemed they were deciding if Drost indeed had the right to demand single combat. By the nodding of heads and beating of chests, he reckoned that on the whole, the men of the tribe agreed. After a while, a man stepped forwards. He was short and broad, a fine mat of dark hair atop his head with a beard to match. His eyes were dark green, glinting in the glow of dawn.

'Been a while, Drost, son of Bredei,' he said with a nod, speaking in Latin, before adding a few more words in the northern tongue.

'Murderer,' Drost spat when he had finished speaking. 'This pig thinks he can pay me off with gold and cattle,' he said to Victorinus.

'This the cur that killed your old man?'

'Aye! Oengus. He was my father's best friend, or so the poor bastard thought. Killed him in his sleep, then come the dawn told everyone he was chief now, and sent me packing.'

'Why didn't you fight him then?'

Drost smiled a small smile. 'Too scared.'

'Nothing wrong with a bit of fear, lad. Keeps you on your toes. Just don't let it rule you. Remember, controlling your emotions is key. Don't let him wind you up.'

There was more shouting amongst the men of the

Vacomagi, Oengus trying to calm them, arms raised high as he clambered for attention.

'What's happening?' Victorinus asked.

'They are calling him a coward for offering the gold. They are telling him he should fight.'

Victorinus nodded. 'And if you fight and you win, will the men here follow you into battle against Valentinus?'

'One thing at a time, Chief.'

'If you win, guess it'll be me calling you Chief.' Both men smiled, and Victorinus felt his friend's confidence rise a little. 'You can beat him. You'll have a better reach. Let him do the moving, make him tire. Ignore anything he says to you. He'll just be trying to distract you.'

'Aye. Thanks.'

The cacophony of voices rose to a crescendo before a calm of sorts emerged, with Oengus reluctantly grabbing a sword and shield and turning back to Drost. 'It would seem you have your way, foreigner,' he spat, hefting the round shield in his left hand.

Drost stepped forwards, no shield, just an axe. It was single headed, looked like nothing more than a wood cutter from a distance, though Victorinus knew he was as deadly with that as any soldier with a sword. A circle grew around the two men, as if it had been arranged beforehand. Victorinus kept himself at Drost's back, wary eyes on the crowd around him. He thought of all the things that could go wrong. If Drost was bested in the circle, how long before the Caledonian warriors turned on him? He wasn't known to this tribe, hadn't even known Drost was from the Vacomagi, a tribe based far in the distant north, well out of the range the areani were charged with scouting.

Men were chanting now, words Victorinus could not understand, and shields were being passed forwards from those on the outer edge, until every man, Victorinus included, was holding a round shield, boxing in the combatants. Another stepped into the circle, an older man with a long grey beard and dark, lank hair. He wore just a stained robe, nothing on his feet, his bare legs tanned dark by the summer sun. He spoke to both men, individually at first then both together. Victorinus wanted to ask what was going on but the only person who would have understood was Drost. The old man stopped speaking and a sudden hush fell upon the gathering.

'Keep control of your emotions!' Victorinus was surprised to find himself shouting. His heart was suddenly racing. His mouth was dry and raw adrenalin coursed through his veins. Maybe he should have been following his own advice. 'Make him move, let him tire. That's how you win.'

And then they began. Oengus lunged with his sword, a clumsy strike that Drost batted away with the blade of his axe, before stepping back out of range. Oengus stalked after, seemingly in no rush. He was snarling and spitting, shouting at Drost, whose face remained as impassive as stone. Oengus lunged again, sword licking out from right to left, low to high. Drost didn't even bother with his own weapon this time, just ducked away and took another step back.

'Three paces from the shields!' Victorinus called, and he was pleased to see the younger man change his direction and begin to side step. All was mayhem behind the shields now. Men thumped Victorinus in the back as they jumped and scrambled to get a better view. He was sure bets were being taken, money or livestock put down as collateral as men sought to get one over on their friends – that was what would have been happening were it Romans around the circle, anyway.

Drost was still circling, his axe held low in his right hand. His posture was almost lazy, inviting his opponent into making wild swings with his longsword, then he'd dance out the way before the blade got too close. Victorinus found himself nodding, then shouting and cheering as Drost dodged another swipe from the longer blade.

'This is how you do it! This is how you win!' He'd seen many boxing matches, fought outside taverns in Eboracum. They were all won by the fighter that kept his distance, who edged into the bout and relied on his brain rather than his fists. This was the same, far as he could see, just with steel instead of boxing gloves.

Oengus lunged once more and seemed to over-reach. Momentarily off balance, he was unable to withdraw his right arm quickly enough, and at once Drost pounced. Changing the grip on his axe mid-swing, he brought the blade up and slammed it down with all his might, crunching it down onto Oengus's elbow, the blade burying itself in bone and sinew, before Drost wrenched it free with a savage cry of victory.

Stunned, Oengus staggered back, sword clanging to the ground, a look of horror on his face. From the elbow down, his arm was in ruins. Blood pumped from the open wound. His fingers were lifeless, unmoving, and it looked for all the world that the fight was over.

But Oengus recovered his anger before regaining his senses. He let go of his shield and pulled a knife from his belt. The crowd went wild, mad on the bright blood in the morning air and, to a man, whooped for joy as their chief made one last reckless charge for victory. Stepping forwards, his useless right arm dragging behind him, he lunged and swiped with the dagger, the blade moving so fast Victorinus could barely keep it in his sights.

Drost could though, and he was a man in control. He dodged and ducked, sidestepped and parried, his face still a picture of concentration. Oengus's burst of adrenalin lasted for a short while longer, before he collapsed to one knee, blood still pumping from the grievous wound in his arm. He had lost too much blood, exerted too much energy, and now he was done.

Victorinus cheered and threw his shield to the ground. Moving into the circle, he embraced the victor, holding Drost's hand high in the air for everyone to see. 'Knew you could do it!' he said, slapping the Caledonian on the back. 'Now finish the whoreson!'

Drost did not, however. The greybeard approached once more, his dirty feet squelching in Oengus's blood. He spoke to Drost in low tones, a calming hand reaching out and firmly grasping the younger man's shoulder. The people around them were chanting now. 'Drost! Drost! Drost!' Oengus was still on his knees, his lifeblood spilling in pools around him.

They talked for a while longer, the greybeard and Drost, both men gesturing to Oengus as they did. Victorinus wondered what was happening, and for a moment thought the old man might actually be trying to persuade Drost to spare the other's life. But if he was, he spoke words Drost chose to ignore.

Approaching Oengus, he knelt down in the mud, reached down and grabbed hold of Oengus's knife, then helped ease his opponent down, so he was lying flat on his back. Drost held the knife to the side of Oengus's torso, fingers counting the ribs. The two men nodded to one another. And then Oengus died, the knife driving through his ribcage to pierce his heart.

'Drost! Drost! Drost!' the men of the Vacomagi screamed until their voices were hoarse. Victorinus allowed himself a small smile, then walked back towards the treeline. His friend was in no danger now.

* * *

The sky was clear again that night. The stars twinkled and the moon cast the land in a blue shade. Victorinus sat around a fire with Felicius, Felix and the new chief of the Vacomagi. The four men didn't speak much, not at first, just shared a skin of wine, breathed in the night air, and enjoyed the fact they were all still alive to experience it.

Victorinus lounged on the ground, plucking lazily at the grass around him, twirling it through his fingers before letting it fall back down. He passed the wine skin on without drinking when it came his way. He had no further need for that. The voice in his head seemed to have subsided, for now at least. Felicius sat on a fallen log, grinding a whetstone up and down his sword. He seemed lost in thought, his face set in a frown. Felix looked the most relaxed Victorinus had seen him since they had met. He had earlier proclaimed their victory was now guaranteed, and he was eager to begin the attack on Valentinus. Drost looked exhausted; he was droopy eyed and his skin still deathly pale. He still held the knife that had formerly belonged to Oengus.

'Won't be many more nights like this now,' Felicius said, gazing up at the stars. 'Winter is on the way, grows closer with every passing day.'

Victorinus nodded. The trees were starting to look more orange than green, and the mornings were getting colder, even if the evenings were not. 'Let's hope we're not still camping in the woods when it arrives.'

'I don't know, I've spent many a winter in a

marching camp, huddled by the brazier in my small tent. It's not so bad.'

'Ever done that in northern Britannia though?' Victorinus said, eyebrow raised.

They all laughed. 'No! No, that is true,' Felicius conceded. 'We shall have to get this war won by the end of October, then we can all winter in Epiacum.'

'How long until October?' Drost asked, still staring at the knife.

'Five days,' Felix said, before taking a swig from the wine. 'So how are we going to do it?'

'Do what?' Drost replied.

'Take Epiacum, of course.'

'I've put some thought into that,' Felicius said, eyes suddenly bursting with life. 'Theodosius marches north with just over a thousand men. Lupicinus marches from the southwest with eight hundred or so. How many do we have here in the north now?'

'Nearly two and a half thousand, mostly men of the Vacomagi, thanks to their new chief.' Victorinus gave Drost a salute. The men of the Vacomagi had agreed to fight with Rome against Valentinus. It seemed they were one of the few tribes that had raided south who had not been paid upfront by the usurper, and it had rankled with the senior men in the tribe that their former chief had agreed without receiving payment, when other tribes had been paid a small fortune.

That, coupled with the fact some of the older heads amongst them still remembered Drost's father fondly, and claimed the man's fate had never sat well with them. Drost said he hadn't asked too many questions. Without the men of the tribe, they could not hope to take Epiacum.

'So, all together that's around four thousand men. And we think Valentinus has what, two thousand?'

'Far as we know,' Victorinus agreed.

'And most of those men are camped to the east of Epiacum, not within the fortress itself.'

'Aye.' Victorinus nodded. 'There a punchline coming?'

'How many of those two thousand men are really invested in this Valentia nonsense? How many do you think really give a shit?'

'None of them, they are there for the coin,' Felix said with certainty, and Victorinus thought out of the four of them, he would know best. His own commander had gone over to the rebels for the coin, after all, leaving most of his unit behind when they refused to follow him.

'So I'm thinking, I ride back to Theodosius tomorrow, I tell him we should attack the camp first.

Lupicinus and Maximus coming from the southwest attack the western wall as a distraction. And then you and your men from the north attack the north gate.'

'If Pastor sticks to his word,' Drost cut in. 'Otherwise, we shall be dying at the north gate.'

'He will,' Victorinus said. 'He won't betray us again, not now.'

'It doesn't matter if Pastor does or doesn't. What matters is we draw Valentinus's eye, don't let him focus on what's happening to the east. If we can turn just some of the men in that camp, then it's over for him.'

'Agreed,' Felix said. 'I'd sure like the chance to stick it to Porcius.' He was referring to his former prefect, who had defected to Valentinus early on in the summer.

'You'll get your chance, you've earned it. So, we have the skeleton of a plan, and I like it. Let's leave the rest of the details for now. Plans all go to shit when battle is joined and the blood starts flowing anyway.'

'Halfhand,' Drost said with a sad smile. 'I still miss him. Severus too.'

'Me too, lad. Me too. They were good men, deserved better. And you know what, we're going to win this for them. For Halfhand, for Severus. And we are going to get our families back safe and sound,' he added, turning to Felicius. 'No would-be emperor is going to stop me spending the rest of my days telling my boys how much their father loves them.'

He rose with a start, suddenly assaulted by tears desperate to break free from his eyes. He walked over to the horses, stabled together in a makeshift pen. Amor was on the side, head drooping over the wooden fence. The gelding's ears pricked as he approached, and he smiled through his tears to see it. He leant in and kissed Amor on the nose, rubbing the beast's flank as he did. 'Are you ready to go to war? One last time, Amor.'

19

OCTOBER, AD 367

'Ready spears!' Theodosius called from his place in the centre of the line. Felicius hefted his with his men, wincing at the pain it caused in his shoulder. How many times had he done this over the years? Time and time again on the training field, launching the javelin at a wicker target. The targets were slightly different now, but the javelin wasn't any lighter.

'Loose!' came the call from the general, repeated by Felicius and the other officers, and then he was stepping and grunting with his men, his javelin intertwining with hundreds of others as it whistled through the air, arcing down and crashing into the enemy.

The enemy. He hadn't given much thought to the

fact that his enemy were Roman soldiers, just like him. They too had awoken that morning and pulled on their mail. They had strapped on their helmets, the same helmets his own men wore. Belted their swords and hefted their shields, the same swords and shields his own men had.

Except the enemy each had a giant V on theirs, blazed in gold against a blue background. Except the enemy had accepted a traitor's coin to abandon their posts and allow large bands of barbarians to ravage the land it was their duty to protect. These men were not Romans.

He snarled as the javelins rained death on the enemy soldiers. He didn't know which unit it was he was fighting, for they had abandoned any of their old insignia. But he could tell they were scared, caught unawares, and unprepared for war. So far so good.

He and Theo had ridden back to Theodosius, finding him on the road, a day's march from Epiacum, and outlined the plan they had agreed with Victorinus. The general had seemed to rise in stature as well as spirits upon hearing a whole tribe of Caledonian warriors was going to fight on their side. 'Like rats deserting a burning barn!' he had exclaimed when Felicius said the men camped to the east of Epiacum might surrender.

There was just one element to their plan that remained unknown. There had been time only to send a messenger to Lupicinus and Maximus, not to wait for a reply. They had no notion of their position, or who or what they had encountered on their march up the western side of the island. Theodosius had been resolute when questioned if they would still push on with their assault. 'Of course!' he had roared. 'With or without my nephew, Epiacum shall be ours!'

And so here they were.

The javelins hit with a wet smack, and blood spurted into the morning air. It was cold, the men's breath misting as they charged. 'Formation!' Felicius called, sword free in his palm now. 'Keep the line!' he bellowed, knowing how easy it was for a soldier to allow his bloodlust to get the better of him and charge ahead of the rest. Those were always the first men to die.

They came down the gentle incline from Epiacum's east, the grass up to their knees, red moss under their boots. Felicius cursed as he staggered, left leg burning, Vitulus leaning in with his shield from his right to stop him falling. The Fourth Cohort were in the centre of the advance; the Syrian archers held the rear, Theodosius choosing to save their arrows for now. Theo and his Batavi were on the right, the Iovii on the left.

The camp opened up before them as they advanced, the early morning sun on their backs. There were cookpots and fires abandoned by the poorly dug defensive ditches Theodosius's army had been simply able to step over. Spears lay where their owners had left them, the odd sword or helmet too. The sentries had seemingly been more concerned with preparing breakfast than watching out for an attack, and Felicius felt a nagging doubt in the back of his mind.

Surely it would not be this easy?

But the enemy were still trying to rally. Horns blared across the plain; men ran between the tent lines, some without armour, some just wearing loin cloths. But they all had swords and shields, most wore helmets, and slowly they were beginning to form a battle line.

'Sound the charge! Hit them now! Don't let them recover!' Theodosius boomed over the cacophony of battle, and at once his trumpeters added their own high shrill blasts of noise to those already sounding, and Felicius pointed his sword at the enemy, just fifteen paces away now, and screamed at them to charge.

The ground was still uneven underfoot and made harder as they had to step and hop over the enemy dead, bleeding out with javelins sticking from them. But the Fourth Cohort held together well, shields interlocking as they passed the blockage of the dead and dying, and hit home with a mighty crash.

Felicius punched his shield at the first man he came across, knocking him flat on his back. Stabbing down as he stepped over the fallen man, he lifted his shield over his head and used the bronze rim to smash a helmeted head, swiping right with his now bloodied blade. 'ROMA VICTRIX!' he bellowed, swiping left with his sword this time and biting deep into another man's arm.

'ROMA VICTRIX!' his men chanted back to him, Vitulus to his left struggling to keep pace with his commander.

Before he knew it, Felicius was into the enemy's fourth rank, a trail of wounded left behind him. His men had lost their cohesion. There was no longer a man on both his shoulders. He could sense it, without needing to turn his head, but he didn't let it slow him down. The enemy were in disarray, leaderless, scared, unmotivated, and he was going to finish them off.

Panting, left thigh burning, he more staggered than leapt into his next victim, bowling the man over and smashing him with the flat of his shield. He took two more steps then his left leg caught on something unseen, and he pitched over on his front, landing with a thud and trapping his shield arm beneath him. He rolled right and raised the shield, a flash of something bright against the blue sky and a thud on the shield, an axe head poking through. 'Shit,' he murmured, shaking the linden board to loosen itself from the axe blade, but it was stuck fast. He swiped blindly with his sword, felt it bite into a leather boot, and the pressure on his shield faded. He rolled right once more, something hot next to him, a cooking fire spluttering, indifferent to the carnage going on all around. Felicius could not stop himself rolling into it, sending a cooking pot and embers flying into the air.

He staggered, battle drunk, to his feet, dropping his shield to beat out the fire growing up his right arm. 'Shit, shit!' A blur of movement in his peripheral vision and blinding pain down his side. The sword that had struck him moved back, ready for the killing blow, a grinning man at the end of it. Felicius moved his left arm round to take the next blow on his shield but then remembered he'd dropped the thing in panic. The sword came at him from high and he leapt at his attacker, getting inside the swing before it could take his life. He crashed into his assailant, lowering his head at the last moment so the man got a face full of iron. His world went white for a moment, but then the colours came back and red was the first thing he saw. His assailant had blood oozing down his face and his nose was flattened. He spat out a tooth and raised his sword once more, screaming a wordless battle cry.

It was the last sound he ever made. A javelin flew over Felicius's shoulder and took the man high in the chest. He was propelled back into a tent and was soon lost in the collapsing leather.

'Don't wait for us, sir,' a voice said. 'You just go off on your own!' Vitulus said, a casual grin fixed to his face, as if he were enjoying nothing more than a late summer stroll.

'I had it in hand!' Felicius spat, still feeling off balance.

'Oh, aye sir, I saw that. Clever little diversion, rolling through the fire and dropping your shield like that.'

'Oh, just piss off!'

'You're welcome!'

More men from the Fourth were at his side. One handed him back his shield, and Felicius gritted at the pain in his side. He ran a hand down his flank and to his relief found his mail had held. 'Forward, men!' he called as he took an unsteady step on his agonising left leg, groaning at the effort it took to keep moving forwards. How long had they been fighting? Surely only a matter of moments?

They were well into the camp now, surrounded by tents and panicking men. The enemy were fleeing back towards Epiacum, but Felicius doubted Valentinus would be opening his gates to let anyone in any time soon. He grinned at that thought, a savage grin that promised nothing but more blood and death. Movement ahead of them, a soldier in a crested helmet rallying every man he could. As Felicius watched, he got them into a Boar's Snout formation and at once they began to charge. 'Shields! Shields! Close formation, form up!' he bellowed to his men, thanking the gods he had invested the hours of training in them he had as they responded in a heartbeat.

The wedge came at them, crested helm at its point, and Felicius growled as they came within five paces, raised his shield and left his sword low, sending it snaking out in the instant before the officer crashed into him. They collided with a snap and a bang, Felicius's sword burying itself in his attacker's groin. The man was suspended in mid-air, his face a picture of shock and agony, and then he slid down Felicius's shield, lifeblood puddling in the grass.

* * *

Felicius raised his bloody sword, ready to confront his next opponent, but a soldier wearing just a tunic, bearing no shield and holding only a javelin, dropped the weapon and raised his hands as he saw his commander fall. Felicius let him be. More and more men began to copy the first, laying down their weapons and throwing themselves to their knees. He smiled to himself; it was over.

Lowering his sword and shield, he breathed hard, adrenalin oozing out of him faster than blood from a gaping wound. 'Get the men back into lines,' he called to Vitulus, who stood panting just a few paces from him. He took the time to take in his surroundings. They were not good tents, the ones the enemy had been housed in. In the two closest to him he could make out holes on the tops and sides; another was drooping in from the top, without enough wooden supports to hold it up within. He wondered once more what these men were fighting for. Rome had many faults; allowing her men to fight without pay and poor equipment was occasionally one of these, but surely if you were going to revolt against the empire you would do it for something greater? Otherwise, what was the point?

'The men are back in formation, sir,' Vitulus said with a nod.

'Pick twenty men to start collecting weapons from those who have surrendered. The rest are to stay in formation, but can eat and drink if they have supplies on them.' They had been ordered to march with just battle gear and water skins, but Felicius knew from experience it was only a green recruit that didn't stuff a snack or two into a pouch at their belt. Not all battles were as short as this one. He himself had a hard biscuit pocketed away at his waist.

He was contemplating the biscuit when he heard the first crack, somewhere in the distance. A pregnant pause of silence, a moment of bewilderment, as one man looked to another, a frown upon every face. The men of the Fourth had stopped disarming the rebels, paused mid-snack. And then the carnage began.

The first ball of fire smashed to the right of the Fourth, tearing apart a section of the Batavi, who were in the process of getting back into formation. Then another hit, not ten feet from where Felicius stood. He was thrown from his feet, the ground seeming to explode as the flaming rock flattened two men before bouncing off the turf to hunt for more.

'Catapults!' Felicius roared. 'Get back, back! Away from the walls!'

His men didn't need telling twice. At a run they retreated, all thought of disarming and rounding up the rebel army forgotten. They skirted tent pegs and jumped flaming cooking fires, shedding shields and helmets and swords, anything that could slow them down. More flaming rocks rained death all around them. The air was alive with the crack and whistle of the catapults, rich with the stench of burning flesh.

The sound of hoofbeats to the north, a lot of them, and Felicius could make out the Spanish horse streaming from the treeline, Felix at their head, the dragon banner flying high and proud in his wake. Theodosius himself rode to meet them. The two men had a brief exchange and then the general was riding into the midst of the Fourth, searching for the crest of Felicius's helm. 'Prefect, get your men formed back up this instant! We cannot allow the enemy to re-group, not when we are so close to victory! The cavalry will harry their flanks, and this time the Syrians will give your boys a rally or two before you close on them.'

'But the catapults, sir?' Felicius had a hard time making himself heard over the cacophony of falling boulders and panicked men. 'They will tear our men to pieces!'

'We must rely on your friend Victorinus to deal

with them. Now to your station, Prefect.' And with that, the general was gone.

Felicius looked to the north, hoping Victorinus was up in the treeline somewhere, watching him, or maybe he had already engaged and was right now attacking the north gate. Wherever he was, Theodosius and his men were delivering on their part of the plan; it was up to his old friend to do his now.

* * *

'Shortest battle I've ever seen, I reckon,' Drost muttered.

'How many exactly have you seen?'

Drost shrugged. 'More than I had a year ago, and that's a fact.'

'Aye, suppose that's true enough,' Victorinus conceded. 'But you're right, weren't much metal in those rebels. Seems like we're off to a good start. Our turn now, I guess.' They had watched on as the army of Theodosius had attacked with the dawn, tearing their way through the enemy camp. Seemed it was all but over now.

He rose from the brush that had been concealing them. They walked back from the treeline, and under the canopy it was as if the sun had not risen at all.

Mist swirled around the waiting men of the Vacomagi as they muttered to each other in their strange tongue. 'Time to get them ready, oh mighty Chief,' he said to Drost with a grin.

'They'll do their part. Most of these men have waited their whole lives to shed Roman blood.'

'Those bastards down there aren't Roman,' Victorinus muttered. He walked over to the left flank of the waiting tribe, where Felix and his Spanish horse stood idle. 'Don't reckon your lads will be needed after all,' he said, taking the decurion's hand in greeting.

Felix smiled; no man ever truly wanted to take their chances in battle. 'I am grateful for it, Tribune. We will move out of the trees onto the eastern plain as agreed though, just in case anything unexpected happens.' The Spanish horse had been ready to charge down from the north and join with Theo's Batavi should the first engagement of the day not go as planned. The impressive defensive ditches that surrounded Epiacum had not been extended to the military camp on the plain, and it would have been a simple charge for the experienced cavalry unit.

'Wait until we are engaged, there'll be less eyes on you then.'

'We shall. Good luck, my friend. May your gods be with you.'

'And you, brother.' He made to walk away, then checked himself. 'Keep an eye on my horse, will you?'

Felix smiled. 'Nothing shall happen to Amor whilst you are gone, my friend.'

Victorinus nodded, not knowing whether to feel embarrassed or not. Felix, though, was a horseman born. He understood well the bond a man could make with his mount. With that thought, Victorinus was off to war.

The first wave of Vacomagi were split down into ten-man teams. Each team was responsible for one ladder, hastily constructed in the last two days out of the strongest trees they could find to tear down. If he was going to be more honest with himself than he was actually prepared to be right now, he wasn't even sure they were long enough to reach the top of the walls, but it was too late now either way.

He made sure he was standing front and centre of the men who would attack first. These were not his men – he meant nothing to them and could not even communicate with most of them – but he was damned if he wasn't going to be on that first charge. This was for more than any empire or noble cause. This was for his family. He could see the walls through the trees; they were in there somewhere, Sarai and his boys. He was coming to get them back.

Drost shouted out some commands, completely inaudible to Victorinus, but he sensed the men around him tense. He felt the familiar need to piss, the tightening of his bowels, the sudden dryness of his throat. This was how it felt to be alive. The man next to him offered him an open wine skin, and every part of his body yearned for just one sip, but he shook his head resolutely. Never again would he allow himself to be so reliant on that damned stuff. It was the wine that had led him here, as much as Valentinus and his cursed rebellion. He would stay away from now on; that was one promise he would not allow himself to break.

Drost roared and pointed his axe at the fortress and his men moved off as one, Victorinus snarling as he joined the charge. It was two hundred paces from their place of concealment to the walls, using the road to avoid the ditches, and he hoped Drost had been clear that each man should run in silence. There was not much hope of reaching the walls undetected, but pure curiosity would have most of the defenders charged with manning the northern gate and the walls looking east. It would do the attackers no favours to advertise their attack.

They covered the first hundred paces in a flash, Victorinus with his eyes fixed on the battlements, seeking out movement, finding none. He found himself grinning. Could they do it? Could they be up the ladders and on the walls before the defenders knew they were even there? His hopes were dashed before they had covered another fifty. The team to his right dropped their ladder and the men stopped for an inquest into whose fault it had been. There was shouting and gesturing. Fists were raised; even a sword or two. Victorinus cursed and ran into the midst of the argument, hefting the front of the ladder and dragging it a few paces forwards. 'Well, come on then, you curs!' he turned and called, not knowing or caring if they understood a word he said. The ten men just stared at him for a second or two, before one stepped forward and grabbed the back. The rest soon followed suit.

Twenty paces behind the rest now, Victorinus could only watch in horror as arrows soared over the battlements and rained hell on the Vacomagi, who were helpless, encumbered with their ladders as they were. 'Come on!' he roared to the ten behind him. 'Forward!'

Drost's men were dying. Arrows fell like rain from the sky and took their lives as they heaved their ladders up against the walls. The first one hit the top of the battlement with a roar of approval and relief from the Vacomagi beneath, but as the first brave man took his first steps up the rungs, two pairs of arms appeared at the top of the ladder and heaved it to the side, sending it tumbling to the ground where it cracked apart, splinters flying through the air.

There was an alarm sounding from the top of the gate. A great brazier was lit, and Victorinus imagined mailed men running through the streets of the fortress, ready to aid the defenders. 'Come on!' he urged again, upping the pace until his team were finally beneath the walls. 'Get it up!' he yelled, heaving with the others as they raised their ladder to the battlement, just to the left of the gate. 'Go! Go!' he urged the first two men, and up they scrambled, swords bare in their palms. Victorinus looked wildly around for Drost, fearing he would see his friend cut down on the cobbles, an arrow through his chest. But the big Briton was halfway up a ladder the other side of the gate, his axe gripped tightly, moving with surprising speed for a man his size and build.

'I'll be damned if I'm going to let him beat me to the top!' he shouted to no one in particular, and he pushed the next man in line to the ladder out the way before taking the rungs two at a time, half expecting to be cut down at any moment.

Up and up he went, his feet growing heavier with

every step, breath coming harder and faster. His mail weighed him down and chafed at his shoulders. His shield, hung on his back, caught on the back of his feet with every step, and he could feel the blood trickling to his soles before he was halfway up.

But he was still alive, untouched by arrows. Above him, the first man onto the ladder clambered over the battlements, only to come hurtling straight back down, screaming a wordless cry as he fell. The second man fared better, and Victorinus could hear the clashing of blades as he struggled up the last few rungs. Reaching the top, he more fell than jumped over the wall, landing on his back with a thud that drove the last wheezes of breath from his lungs. 'Fuck this,' he muttered as he staggered back to his feet, snatching up his fallen sword and swivelling his head around for someone to kill.

There seemed to be no one in close proximity so he ran to the nearest brazier, picked up the longest bit of timber he could find, set it on fire and ran until he was standing over the gate, and he waved the flaming torch from side to side. Almost immediately, the second wave of Vacomagi streamed from the treeline, screaming their war cry as they did.

The gate. Pastor. Victorinus threw the torch over the gate and turned around just in time to see a spear flash past his face. He cursed and ducked left. Bringing up his sword, he caught the spear as it was pulled back and used his leftward momentum to drag it sideways with him, knocking his assailant off balance. The two men took a moment to recover and circled each other. The spearman was young and tall, thin as a twig, bright eyes quivering under his helmet. Victorinus knew he had him, knew the lad would have no stomach for the fight. He feinted right then darted left, bringing his sword across his body until his right arm was fully stretched across himself. Then with all the force he could muster, he forced it back in a savage blow, the blade smashing into the spearman's helmet, driving the man clean off his feet. It was a simple job to stab down on his chest, blood already bubbling on the young man's lips as Victorinus wrenched the sword free.

The entire first wave of the Vacomagi had made it onto the battlements now, those who had survived the climb anyway, and it was so crowded it was a wonder anyone found any space to swing their weapons. 'Drost! Drost!' Victorinus called to the big Briton, who seemed to have had his fill of killing already. Blood dripped down his face. His axe blade was red to the hilt and he seemed to have brain matter dripping down his front. 'The gate! We need to open the gate!'

'No need to worry on that part, sir!'

Victorinus looked down, onto the cobbled courtyard. The gate was open, Pastor stood in the puddle of
light that seeped through, a bloodied sword in his
hand, two corpses at his feet. They didn't speak, just
exchanged a nod, before the youth was scampering off
into the fortress. Victorinus felt a wave of relief wash
over him. *Keep my family safe.*

Drost ordered a party of men down the nearest
stairs; the rest cleared the last of the enemy from the
battlements. Victorinus opened the water skin he carried tied around his neck, drank deeply and thanked
the gods he was still alive. He tried to look to the east
but could see nothing over the walls, which were
oddly deserted. An icy tinge of terror ran up his spine,
freezing him to the spot. Why was there no one on the
eastern walls? Surely Valentinus would have men
manning all the walls and gates at all times? Especially the gate that led out into the camp that housed
most of his army?

Below him, on the cobbles of the fortress, the reinforcements had arrived and fifteen hundred or more
Vacomagi burst through, charging the neatly formed
unit of soldiers emerging from deeper within the fort
with their finely painted blue shields, shattering their
lines before their officers could get them to rally.

Victorinus barely noticed though. He was still stood up on the parapet, looking towards the eastern wall. Why was there no one there? An ear-splitting crack thundered from somewhere within the fort. A flaming boulder hurtled up towards the sky from behind the rooftops, and Victorinus suddenly had his answer. 'Catapults! They have catapults!'

Two more catapults launched their missiles into the air and Victorinus watched the boulders arc and fall until they disappeared behind the eastern wall. He thought for a moment, trying to keep calm. Felicius was the other side of that wall, the general Theodosius and his army with him. But Felicius was no fool, he was certain Theodosius wouldn't be either, and there was nothing he could do to help them apart from taking the machines out.

He bundled down the wooden steps from the battlement to the cobbles, pushing through a throng of bloodied and wounded tribesmen until he found Drost. 'They have siege weapons; we have to take them out before they obliterate the field army.'

Drost nodded. 'Then lead the way.'

The relief force sent to retake the northern gate was wiped out. Twenty of Drost's tribesmen walked amongst the wounded, dispatching them without thought or care as the rest of the tribe rallied and reorganised. Drost was giving orders whilst Victorinus tried to control the thumping of his heart, growing ever more impatient with every resounding beat. It seemed leading a band of tribesmen was not the same as leading a unit of Roman military. In the army every man knew their place, knew who their superiors were and obeyed their orders without hesitation – mostly anyway. It seemed among the Caledonian tribes this was not quite the way. Drost was their chief now, and therefore their leader. But just because he gave an order, it didn't necessarily mean it would be obeyed. Men were clamouring to speak over him, seemingly offering their opinion or venting their frustrations. Drost, for his part, seemed to be handling the situation well, listening to each man in turn and replying in a calm and soothing voice to those whose objections were more aggressively put forward.

'What's the holdup?' Victorinus called, unable to stay silent any longer. 'Men are dying out there.'

Drost pulled himself away from his men. 'They say they have done their part, and that they should be taking what they can carry from the fort and going home.'

'What?' Victorinus spluttered. He could feel his face going red with rage. 'The battle is not yet won!

We have taken one gate! The enemy still hold the rest of the fort!'

'That's what I'm telling them, sir, just give me a moment.'

'Give you a moment? You're their fucking chief, aren't you? Tell the bastards!'

'It... it isn't that simple, sir. I'm the first man in the tribe, yes. But the tribe is a democracy. Each man is entitled to his say on big decisions. Remember Oengus did not want to fight me, but the men of the tribe forced him into it? Same situation here.'

The big Briton turned back to his men and once more spoke to them in his own tongue, leaving Victorinus to stand alone and grow angrier. It was farcical, standing there doing nothing whilst his friends were dying, their lives snatched by flying boulders, launched just a few paces away from where he stood. 'Fuck this,' he growled to himself, and he snatched up the shield he had relieved from his back and jogged off between the two nearest buildings, leaving the squabbling Vacomagi to their democracy.

He moved down the via principalis at a run, armour chafing at his shoulders and hips. The shield in his left hand may as well have been made of the lead taken from the mine the fort was built to guard, it was so heavy. His breath came in ragged gasps and as he passed the last row of barrack blocks, he came to a stop in front of the principia, the headquarters of the fort. He stopped, eyeing the open entrance to the courtyard of the principia. There was no movement, nothing. He turned back the way he had come; again, there was nothing. Once more he felt the icy tinge of fear sneak up his back, taking hold of him in a firm grip and not letting go. Where was everyone?

To his left was the praetorium, the commander's house. It was in there Valentinus would have been living, and there he assumed his family had been held hostage. He felt an almost overwhelming urge to run there, to burst down the doors and kill everyone he crossed until he found Sarai and his boys. He was about to give in to the urge, to begin his charge, even if it meant his death, when a voice called out and stopped him in his tracks.

'Well, if it isn't everyone's favourite alcoholic! Was starting to think you'd lost your bottle completely and had decided to sit the rest of this one out.' Cassius stepped out of the principia. His long blond hair shone in the golden light of the sun. His pale skin had darkened throughout the summer, giving the youth a healthy complexion that sat well on him. He was wearing mail, a blue cloak over the top. A cavalry helmet hung in his left hand, a naked blade in his right.

'You,' Victorinus breathed. He'd liked Cassius, truth be told. The boy had always been loud and arrogant, rash and carefree. But his smile and good humour had picked Victorinus up when he'd been feeling low, and the gods knew he felt low often enough to need that kind of man around him. Pastor's betrayal he blamed himself for. Since the first time he'd met the lad, he'd thought there was something off with him, something he had been holding back. But with Cassius there had been none of that. The bright blue-eyed boy had appeared to be everything he was in fact not. Innocent, grateful, honest.

'Me,' Cassius beamed. 'Not on your own, are you? Where are the famed warriors of the miles areani? Finest unit in the north! Isn't that what you told me when you recruited me? No one better? Where are they all now, Sixtus?'

'Only my friends get to call me Sixtus,' Victorinus said, sweat-soaked hand tightening on the grip of his sword.

'Friends, yes. Not got too many of them left now, have you? Pastor is on the side of the righteous with me. Drost seems to be leading his own band of merry warriors – oh yes, I saw your little assault on the northern gate. Very impressive. I'd always wondered just what it was Drost was running away from. Glad he's managed to reconcile with his people, even if only for a few short days before we kill him. But anyway, friends. Halfhand, Severus, sadly no longer with us. That must have hurt, especially Halfhand, I mean, that guy was practically your right-hand man. Which was fortunate, as that was the only hand he had left!'

'Shut your mouth, you little cunt,' Victorinus growled. 'Was it you that killed Severus?'

'I did,' Cassius said, grinning from ear to ear. 'You want to know how he died? How he screamed at the end?'

'Where are my family?' Victorinus said, not wanting to know how his friend suffered. He was angry enough as it was.

'Ah, yes. Family. Is there anything in life more important to a man than his wife and children? Anything a decent man cherishes more?'

The catapults cracked once more. Three boulders flew over their heads, soared across the eastern wall, and were lost to sight. Cassius watched them go, a half-smile plastered on his smooth face. Victorinus didn't turn his head, didn't so much as flinch.

'Where are they?' he said again, keeping his voice low, battling to keep his emotions in check. The man who lets his emotions get the better of him is the man that ends up dead. That was what he'd told Drost; something along those lines anyway. He reckoned it was about time he started taking his own advice.

'They're safe. For now, anyway. Felicius's too, in case you were wondering. You won't live to see any of them, though.'

'You going to kill me, are you?' He took a step forward, his hobnailed boots grating on the cobbles beneath.

'Reckon I could. And if I don't, someone else will. My father has ordered your death, so one way or another, it will happen.'

Victorinus allowed himself a small smile. 'Valentinus really is scared of me, isn't he? Wonder what I've done to put the shits up him so bad.'

Cassius laughed. 'My father fears no one. Not you, not that army out there on the plain. You have been a bit of a pain though. All those men you killed, the taverns you burned. I must admit I don't think my father bargained on Rome getting a relief force here so quickly. Guess we have you and Felicius to thank for that. Still, everything is going to plan.'

'We're in your fort, boy. I don't think that was part of Daddy's plan, was it?'

'What, this place?' Cassius gestured around him.

'You really think we were planning on holding out here? This fort barely holds five hundred men, though it has served its purpose. This could have been a lot different for you, you know.'

Victorinus felt a slight shift in the air behind him. He felt, rather than heard, the slow footfall of a man creeping up behind him. He kept his eyes fixed on Cassius, and the young man put on a show of pretence for a while, but eventually his growing excitement betrayed him, and his eyes kept flickering from Victorinus to the space over the tribune's left shoulder. He may as well have told Victorinus where the attack was coming from.

'Oh yeah, why's that then?' he said, happy to keep Cassius thinking he was falling into his trap. He began to pace slowly to his right, careful to keep his eyes on Cassius the whole time and not give the game away.

'You could have taken the coin and joined us, just like most of the others did. You know we have every senior commander that was stationed on the Wall, most of their men and all.'

'Traitors,' Victorinus spat.

'Turns out most men would rather be alive and a traitor than loyal and dead. Dead like Halfhand, dead like Severus. I didn't tell you how Severus died, did I?'

Deep breaths. *The man who lets his emotions control*

him is the man that loses the fight. 'I'd wager he died a lot better than you're going to.'

Cassius laughed once more, his bright blue eyes shimmering, taunting. 'You know I could do this all day, but unfortunately, I have somewhere else to be. And you, Victorinus, have to die. Don't worry, I'll make sure your wife doesn't get lonely.'

'You fucking—'

Victorinus stepped forwards to attack Cassius, but at the same time he felt a grate on the cobbles behind him. He turned, half ducking as he did, and felt the rush of wind as a blade passed inches over his helmet. He took two quick steps backwards, nearly lost his footing, and regained himself just in time to send another blow ringing off the boss of his shield.

He had no time to get a good look at his attacker, and the sound of Cassius's boots as he ran off around the corner grated at him. *The man who lets his emotions control him is the man that loses the fight.* Balls to that. He'd never been a great one for giving out advice anyway.

He roared as he sprang forward. Shield out, sword raised, he crashed into his attacker, knocking the man clean off his feet. He saw a flash of pink skin under a grey helmet before it was all covered with a blue cloak. Still screaming an incoherent war cry, he stabbed down with his sword and felt it break through mail. The man screamed, and Victorinus wrenched the blade free and made to stab down once more. But before he did, he felt a burning pain rush up his body from his right leg. Looking down, he saw a knife sticking out from his right boot, at the top of his foot where it joined with the leg. 'Bastard!' he bellowed. Letting his shield drop, he gripped his sword in both hands and drove it down with all the force and anger he could muster.

His assailant raised his hands and wailed in terror, but the sword split an open palm like it was made of rotting wood and buried itself in the man's chest.

Victorinus was still standing in the deserted clearing, oddly quiet in the lulls between the catapults loosing their boulders. His sword dropped to the floor, and he wasn't far behind it. His right foot was a ball of fire. Shards of pain shot up his leg and as the adrenalin sapped out of his body, he wanted nothing more than to curl into a ball and cry.

'Leave you alone for five minutes.' Drost flashed him a smile as he knelt down. The men of the Vacomagi were streaming from the north, past the stricken Victorinus and right towards the catapults.

'Cassius,' Victorinus hissed through clenched teeth. 'He went that way, towards the artillery.'

'Let us deal with that, my friend. Can you walk?'

'Nope.'

'Then we shall find you a cart. Stay put. I'll get a couple of my men to assist you.'

'Not like I'm going anywhere,' Victorinus muttered as Drost moved off. He heard a roar and a clash of iron out on the eastern plain. Suddenly alert again, he wanted nothing more than to run to the eastern wall, climb the battlements and see what was going on. 'Damn this foot to hell,' he cursed. 'Never would have happened to me ten years ago.' He'd heard it said before that age was a blessing. It gave you knowledge and wisdom denied to the young. He supposed that was true enough, but just then he'd have paid his weight in silver to have been as agile as he had been in his youth. Just one more reason to stay off the wine.

Two men appeared from the principia with a small cart. There were no mounts available so they were pulling it along with all their might. 'Leave that!' he called to them, knowing there was little chance of him being understood. 'Get me up on that wall!' He had to see what was happening. Had to see how his friends were faring.

20

Lupus Valentinus allowed himself a small smile. The late summer sun was warm on his face, the land around him almost picturesque. Long grass swayed in the light breeze, the imposing mountains looming in the distance. If he had been allowed to pick somewhere to begin his new order, northern Britannia would not have been his first choice. But such choices were often denied to men who had the ambition and tenacity to change the course of the world. You simply had to roll with what you had. It was a beautiful country, though, if a hard one.

His mare snorted and stirred beneath him, and he reached down a hand and rubbed her flank, hushing her with a soothing tone. Around him, the army he had assembled marched in good order, and he felt himself grow with pride at the sight. They were just five hundred, for the moment, marching south away from Epiacum. He had never intended to hold the small fort, but it had served its purpose, for him anyway. It was one of the more isolated forts in the province, with just one main road coming from the north. But there were small tracks and paths through the hills and mountains to the south and west, and he was confident he and his men would be able to march away in good order without being spotted, in part due to the unusual design of the fort.

Coming out the south gate, they had been all but invisible to the army under the general Theodosius in the east. The fort had been built on a natural knoll on the land, and therefore was not the standard rectangular shape Rome had always built her defences. The southern gate was situated more to the southwest than the south, and once the attack on the northern gate had begun, it had been the work of moments to give the order for the catapults to begin shooting and get his men ready to march and set off before they got caught up in the action. He had, of course, had to sacrifice a small unit of men once a runner had brought the message that the northern gate had fallen sooner than expected. But the centurion he had given the order to had saluted and gathered his men as if they had been ordered to do nothing but a routine marching drill through the hills, rather than a short sprint to certain death.

Such power, he thought to himself. That was the mark of greatness, he had always thought, when you can order a man to certain death and have that order followed without question or hesitation. That was the foundation Rome had laid on her path to greatness. Caesar, Augustus, Hadrian, Aurelius, Constantine. These great names from the distant past, these titans, gods, that had shaped the world anew, made it their own and been immortalised at their deaths. Those who had succeeded them had failed to live up to their example. Constantine thought he had built a new dynasty, but his sons saw that run to ruin. Diocletian before him thought he had recast the Roman world in a way that would last a thousand years, but it was Constantine himself who cast that vision to the flames.

And so, his cousins had come to the twin thrones. Valentinian in the west and Valens in the east. What fools they were. Valens at least seemed to be making a fair job of it; the east was thriving, or so people said. Coin flowed like water through Constantinople and the law of Rome was iron in her provinces. The same could not be said for the west. Valentinian was sickly, seemingly on his deathbed every time he turned in for the night. Those at court had become so concerned about the man he had been forced to elevate his young son to the position of Augustus, joint ruler of the Roman west. A wry grin fixed Valentinus's face at the thought. If his cousin were to give in to his many ailments, his path to glory would be all the more certain. Whilst Valentinian lived, there was a figurehead for the generals of the west to rally around, a sense of honour and legitimacy in what they did. If he was he to die though, would the great Jovinus, Theodosius and their ilk fight for the boy? Valentinus doubted it.

He had considered waiting to make his move until his cousin finally crossed into the Elysian fields and the boy Gratian sat on the western throne. But everything was in place. He had stolen himself enough coin for three rebellions whilst in his position of master of the treasury – frankly the whole enterprise had been far too easy, demonstrating to him the need for change. Valentia would be everything Rome was not. Efficient, ruthless, fair. Already he had won the support of the peoples of northern Britannia, providing a safe haven and protection to those who flocked to him when the barbarians ravaged their land and stole their women and children.

Needless to say, he had not mentioned the fact it

had been he who had invited the barbarians to come and raid. He hadn't even needed to pay some of them; they were just happy for a chance to raid Roman lands without the fear of repercussions. He had not, however, bargained on the fact Rome would organise a relief force so quickly. He had thought seeing to the deaths of Nectaridus and Fullofaudes early on in the rebellion would slow down any response from Rome. However, it seemed an enterprising officer from Vindolanda had force-marched his men south and made a crossing to Bononia in Gaul. That coupled with the fact Valentinian had made the very uncharacteristic decision to send Jovinus from his side and have the general personally clear the Narrow Sea of Germani pirates had nearly caught him unprepared.

War was unpredictable if it was anything, though, and Valentinus felt he had reacted to the changing situation around him well. He had more men in the west, occupying the fortress in Maglona. Fifteen hundred infantry and four hundred cavalry awaited him there. Men who followed him not for the gold in his treasury, but for the ideals he stood and fought for. The soldiers camped on the fields outside Epiacum were not true believers, not men to live to see the world rebuilt anew. They too had served a purpose. He smiled once more. He hadn't even paid them yet, had told their officers the coin would come once victory had been achieved. They would die fighting for a cause that hadn't paid them so much as a slither of bronze. Yet another reason why he was the man to recast the empire, lead it into a new dawn.

His fine mood soured a touch as he turned to look behind him and saw Pastor, riding in his yellow cloak. Valentinus had sired many children, mostly sons, but not all, as many whispered. Pastor was perhaps the most disappointing of the lot. He was quiet, thoughtful, quick to challenge and desperately needy. He had hoped the children would be raised to be both loyal and independent. Cassius was a fine example of this. Pastor, though, craved his father's attention. The boy reminded him of a dog, ever hoping to please its master. But to the master, the dog was never anything more than a dog. Sure, it would be mourned at its death, but only for a brief time, then the master would move on. Valentinus had been sure Pastor would die when he had ordered the lad to infiltrate the miles areani. Truth was, he couldn't find a better use for him. Cassius, of course, had bedded himself in with the drunken fools well and had been sure to steer their clueless leader into the right place when the first fires were lit north of the Wall. Thousands of the barbarians had migrated south without them having the slightest clue! Oh, what he would have done to have been able to see that tribune's face when he realised.

He grinned, still looking at Pastor. The boy looked up, saw his father grinning and smiled back. Valentinus cursed. The last thing he needed was the boy thinking he wanted to talk to him. Life had been hectic for the last few days, organising the defence of Epiacum and the timing of their exit. Ensuring there were sufficient mounts and supplies, equipment and weapons for the soldiery. He was looking forward to a few days' solace on the road. After all, there was no one left in the west to oppose him.

To give Pastor credit though, it had been he who'd returned with a bloodied blade to report the north gate had fallen sooner than expected, and he had volunteered himself to look after the hostages, and even now he kept his mount close to the wagon that caged them. Inside were the families of the drunken tribune Victorinus of the areani, and the wife and daughter of the prefect Felicius, the man who had managed to get himself over to Gaul and raise the alarm. He had not intended to steal Felicius's wife; that had just been a happy coincidence. Victorinus, though, had proved himself to be more of a pain than first thought. Secundus, who had foolishly gotten himself killed when they were attacked at night by Victorinus and his men, had said the man was a drunken fool, but also that he was stubborn, resourceful and loyal to Rome. He had so far proven himself to be a worthy opponent.

Valentinus had to grudgingly admit the man had won some respect from him. Not only had he enlisted the support of a whole wing of Spanish horse, but he also now seemed to have one of the Caledonian tribes fighting for him. It was reassuring to have the man's family. Either they would have to be hanged to set an example or used as a bargaining chip in the unlikely circumstance he found himself in a tight spot.

There is no one left to oppose me now. The general Theodosius had just a couple of thousand men; there would be no more reinforcements this late in the year. Storm season would soon be upon them, and only a fool entrusted the sea with ships full of armed men when the weather could not be relied on. Even the great Caesar had lost a portion of his army trying to cross from Gaul to Britannia too late in the year. And if it could happen to Caesar, it could definitely happen to Valentinian.

Valentinus was just cresting a ridge when he got the first sense that everything was not well. There was a commotion ahead of him, a rider galloping hard back down the line. 'Report,' he snapped as the rider reined his mount in alongside him.

'Body of men in the distance, sir,' the rider said with a salute.

'And? Whose bloody men are they?'

'We don't know, sir. Too far out to make out their banners yet.'

Cursing, Valentinus kicked his mare into a gallop and rode to the head of the column. Atop the ridge he could see for miles, the country a great sweeping valley before him. Sure enough, in the distance, a dust cloud swirled and he could make out the outline of marching men. Banners hung in the air above them, but try as he might, he could not make them out. 'Get a rider out immediately. I need to know who they are,' he said to the nearest man with a crested helmet, not caring of their rank.

As the rider went off, Valentinus could do nothing but wait. He had the column halt and gave the order for every man to be ready to fight. It was a tense time, with slaves bustling up and down the column, bringing the men food and water, rubbing down the horses and clearing the wagons to the flanks where they wouldn't be in the way. 'Who are they?' Valentinus muttered to himself. There was no force in the west left to oppose him. The forces in Maglona were fiercely loyal; had he not spent enough time with them to be sure of that? Theodosius was behind him to the east, and all other units that had not sworn him an oath had fled south. So who was this? His fingers twitched on the reins. His back suddenly became appallingly itchy, and as he shifted in the saddle the first beads of sweat trickled down his head. *There is no one left to oppose me.* He tried to control his breathing, bring his heart rate back down.

He felt a presence at his shoulder. Already irritated, he turned to see Pastor there, a small smile dancing on his lips. 'What do you want, boy?'

'Think I know who they are,' Pastor said.

'Well?' Valentinus raged, his good humour from mere minutes ago gone with the wind. His back itched again; palms were clammy.

'They're Germans.'

Valentinus blinked at the boy, then laughed. It made some sense. Letting the raiders loose in Britannia was never going to be without risk; it was inevitable some would have gotten carried away and roamed far from their ships. 'How lost are they?' he joked. 'They must have walked the width of the island. I said they could take back with them whatever they could carry, but this lot will need an extra ship to get all their loot home!' He roared with laughter at his own joke, the nerves and frustration easing out of him. He breathed deep; all was well.

'Oh no, you misunderstand,' Pastor said, that small smile still playing on his face. 'They're not your Germans.' He turned and looked back east, where Epiacum still loomed in the distance. 'They're his,' he said, and thrust out a finger to point at another dust cloud, making steady progress towards them.

Speechlessness was not something Valentinus was overly accustomed to. He turned frantically from east to west, his neck burning, cheeks flushed. 'What is happening?' he whispered, his body seemingly going numb.

'Those men over there' – Pastor pointed to the west – 'are the other half of Theodosius's army. The men behind us are the half he allowed you to see. I'd imagine by now the army you have at Maglona has been disbanded, the men either renewing their allegiance to Rome or running for the hills.'

'But... no.' Valentinus could taste bile at the back of his throat. Everything he had built, the years of plotting and scheming, it was all falling apart in front of his face.

'It was me that told them you would be coming this way, in case you were wondering. You know all I ever wanted from you was a bit of respect. The odd bit of attention, just a little chat here and there. Just wanted you to ask how I was feeling, how I was getting on, you know, things like that, simple things a father should do.'

'How?' Valentinus breathed, still looking from one army to the next.

'But you weren't interested, weren't interested in any of us. Why have all these children if you have no intention of raising them? All those women you raped, why did you do it? Was it just the desperate need for power, to feel as if you controlled someone else? Even if just for a few minutes? I'm glad now, glad you never bothered. You sending me to join the areani was the best thing you could have ever done for me, you know that? I saw first-hand what it was to be a family. Those men who fought against you weren't tied by blood like we are, but by all the gods they were brothers. They knew each other inside out, and each one of them would die to see the others live. Two of them did, in fact. Your favourite Cassius saw to one of them, though he shall be getting his soon enough, if he still breathes, that is.

'And as for those women and children you've been keeping in the wagons, they've got husbands and fathers out there who will do anything, anything to see them safe. What would you have done if it were me kidnapped, Father? Would you have even lifted a hair to see me brought safely home? I very much doubt it.

I'm just another means to an end for you, aren't I? Another tool you can use to manipulate your enemies. Well, I'm done playing your games.'

Pastor walked over to the wagon and opened the back door, ushering out the prisoners inside. Valentinus watched dumbfounded as he directed the blinking prisoners towards the closing army in the east. 'What have you done?' he roared eventually, shock giving way to anger.

'Not about what I've done,' Pastor said, turning back to his father and shrugging. 'It's about what you did. All this is about you and your bruised ego after all.' With that he turned and walked away, following the small huddle of women and children making their way back to the east.

'No. No!' Valentinus raged. Freeing his sword from his scabbard, he kicked his mare into a charge and raced at Pastor. He was blinded by rage, momentarily indifferent to the twin armies marching to crush his dreams. He wanted nothing more than to kill, to kill and kill until he'd worn his bloody rage thin.

He was just raising his sword, Pastor looking up at him, still the annoying half-smile fixed to his face, when there was a flash of movement on the peripheral of his vision, and the next thing he knew he was thrown from his mount, blinding pain tearing through the right side of his body. He landed awkwardly, mail thumping on the grass and digging into his skin, making his bones rattle. He rolled and bumped, sucking in half gasps of air, until eventually he was still, flat out on his back, his body a tattered ruin, pain everywhere. So much pain.

When his vision had cleared, he blinked and squinted up into the sunlight, seeing his son, Pastor, standing over him. The lad had his sword drawn, the point digging into his neck. 'It's over, Father,' he said in a small voice. 'Your rebellion is over. Valentia is no more.'

'You... have... betrayed... me?' he managed to wheeze out through shallow breaths. It felt as though his lungs were on fire, that there was gravel lodged in his throat and weighted manacles strapping his limbs to the ground.

'No, Father, it was you who betrayed me. All I ever wanted was a father, someone to look up to, to teach me the ways of the world. A mother would have been nice too, you know, though the gods alone know what you did with her once you were finished with her. Never even knew her name. Doubt you did either.' Pastor shrugged once more, his bright, round eyes oddly devoid of emotion.

Valentinus saw the change in his son for the first

time, cursed himself for not noticing it sooner. He'd thought the boy seemed different when he had returned to Epiacum in the middle of the night. Valentinus had just assumed he was scared; he'd been through a bit, after all. He'd never shown any affection towards his children, even the ones he considered his favourites. Love made you weak, so he reckoned, anyway. It gave you something to be fearful of, and in the high-power games of imperial politics, there was no place for fear.

Slowly, painfully, he rose to a sitting position, silently cursing his mail. Why did he even wear it? Wasn't like he did any actual fighting himself. He'd never been much use with a sword, truth be told. It was his speed of thought rather than his speed with a blade that had seen his rise, though maybe some skill with the latter would do him some good now. He looked up and around. The soldiers from the east were upon them, banners swaying proudly in the breeze. He saw the captive woman, Sarai, sobbing as she threw herself into the arms of a blood-coated soldier, limping heavily, favouring his left foot. The soldier wore a wide-brimmed hat and a heavy yellow cloak. He was unshaven, a haggard look to his ageing face. So, this was Victorinus, ready to play the part of husband and father after all. Secundus had told him

Victorinus cared little for the woman and two boys he had all but abandoned on a small farmstead in the middle of nowhere. War had a way of changing people though; seemed this man had learnt his lesson. He struggled to his feet, eyes still on the man who now hugged two small boys tight to his chest, openly weeping as he did.

Valentinus felt bile rise in his throat. How could he have been bested by such a man?

21

Felicius was so overcome with relief he could have sunk to the floor. Ahead of him, the remaining men still loyal to Valentinus lowered their weapons and raised their hands. Over the ridge the surrendering men stood on, he could make out a dust cloud swirling towards them. Maximus, Clementius and Lupicinus had come, bringing with them the men of the Heruli and the Second Legion. There would be a time to discover what those men had gone through, what they had learnt and who they had fought. But that time was not now.

He could make out Pastor on the ridge top, sword drawn, point digging into the neck of a stricken man. The man was draped in purple, glimmering mail beneath. He wore his blond hair loose so it sat in curls at his shoulders, a neatly trimmed beard over his pale-as-snow face. Valentinus, then; the resemblance to Cassius was remarkable. They had captured the boy as they marched around the southern wall of Epiacum, Felix and his Spaniards quickly running the boy down. *So, this is victory*, he thought to himself as he tried and failed to command his shaking hands to sheath his bloodied sword. Felt like he'd been fighting every day of his life; in truth, he couldn't really remember how long this rebellion had been going on for. How long had it been since he'd stood on the walls of Vindolanda and seen the black smoke on the horizon? The endless bodies of the northern tribes appearing in the distance.

In all his years in the military he didn't think he'd ever had a year quite like the last. He'd fought in the east, in the blistering heat against armoured horsemen who seemed invincible as they'd charged. He'd fought on the Rhine against the barbarians from across the river, matched himself against the fur-clad warriors and found himself their equal. Maybe it was just that time and distance made those memories seem less than what they were. Surely he had felt this exhaustion, this relief before? If he had, he could not remember.

'Father!' a small voice squealed in delight. Snapping his eyes back into focus, Felicius saw a small, dark-haired girl running towards him, arms open. Her face was mud streaked, and she seemed a great deal skinnier than when he'd last set eyes on her, back on the crossroads on a glorious summer's day, just a few months ago. A lifetime ago.

He knelt in the mud, rivers running from his eyes so he could barely see. She fell into his arms, and he buried his head in her neck and breathed in her scent, savouring every moment. When he opened his eyes, he became aware of a presence over his daughter's shoulder, a shadow, dark against the pale light of the autumn sun. As he looked up, his eyes locked with those of his wife, and they stayed there a long moment, neither speaking, each just drinking in the view.

'I'm so sorry,' she said at last, almost falling into him, 'I should have told you from the first.'

Felicius moved his daughter into his left arm, embraced his wife with his right and kissed her cheek. 'Tell me what, Lucia?' he said through a choked breath. He'd half thought he'd never see his two girls again, and his head swam in the waves of emotion that rocked him.

'About all this. My father, he knew. He was warned of what was to come, but he ignored it, said it would all wash over, that God would protect us. I knew the moment we found his body that... that it would come to this.' Lucia sobbed into his shoulder, and Felicius found himself smiling, despite everything.

'Your father's faith blinded him at times, but it was that faith, that calmness, that made men love him, follow him. Do not blame yourself, and do not blame him. Your father was a good man, much better than many others who have held his position. You should be proud to be his daughter, as I am proud that you are my wife.'

They stayed there, in that embrace, the three of them. Around them, Theodosius's men disarmed the last remnants of the army of Valentia, and the Germani warriors raised their spears and swords to the air, hooting and yelling their victory cry. The rebellion was at an end, and peace had been restored to this most remote province of the empire.

* * *

Dawn broke pink against the purple sky. Tribune Sixtus Victorinus was up to see it, and he kissed his fingers and raised them to greet the rising sun. He'd never been one for religion or gods, had always kept his mouth shut when some argument or other broke out as to which god prayers should be delivered to. But his father had always rose early and kissed his fingers the way Victorinus had just done and greeted Sol Invictus, lord of the sun. 'Immortal sun, vanisher of the dark, I salute you,' he whispered, just the way his father had. He had more cause than usual to be grateful that bright morning. Closing his eyes, he relived the first moment Sarai had run to him. The scent of her hair, the beaming smile of his son. All he had done, all he had fought for, had been for that. It had been worth every new scar he had acquired on the way.

'So, you've lost the wine and found religion, have you?' Sarai asked, leaning on a tent pole, wearing nothing but a blanket wrapped around her.

Victorinus smiled. 'Would it be the worst thing?'

She shrugged. 'I guess not. I remember your father doing that, saluting Sol every morning.'

'He was a better man than I,' Victorinus said quietly, almost to himself.

'You're still a work in progress.' Sarai moved forwards and allowed herself to be encased in an embrace. They kissed, long and slow. The first sounds of the camp awakening came as they drew apart. A trumpet blared for the changing of the watch; cooking fires were banked high, the smell of woodsmoke drifting on the breeze. Men called to each other, shared jokes and boasts, each one just happy to be alive to see the sun rise. The previous day had been a bloody one.

There were over a thousand Roman soldiers being held prisoner in the centre of the camp, their arms and armour taken, senior officers being held separately, awaiting their execution. The general Theodosius had been entirely without mercy when handing out punishment to the rebellious men. The common soldiery were to be split up across the empire, used to make up numbers in understrength units as far off as Thracia. For some of them that would be a punishment almost as unbearable as death. The units of Roman Britannia were mostly made up of local men, and they would have wives and children they may never see again, without having the chance to even say goodbye.

Victorinus sympathised with those. They had no real notion of what it was they had gotten themselves into. They would have been promised coin, a better life, and they wouldn't have asked too many questions. Soldiers were like flocks of sheep; it only took one or two to latch on to something new, the others blindly following the leaders.

It was the leaders that Victorinus felt nothing for.

Fifty men in all had watched on in solemn silence the day before as the gallows on which their lives would end were built. It was incredible what the engineers could build in such a little time, and Victorinus could see the vast wooden structure as it emerged from the shadows. A huge platform, six holes carved from the wood, six lengths of rope swaying in the morning breeze. Those fifty men would not live to see that sun set again. He could not begin to imagine what they were feeling this morning.

'Stay here with the boys,' he said, hearing the two youths awake now in the tent. 'I will go and find us breakfast.'

He was happy but sombre as he made his way through the camp. The army had bedded down in the tents the traitorous army of Valentia had been housed in the day before. The men had been too exhausted to build any defensive works, and the enemy was thoroughly beaten. None had escaped to carry on the fight; the men of Valentia were either dead or held captive. Theodosius had been just as remorseful with those who had lost their lives in the struggle the day before. Giant pyres had been built overnight, as far to the east of the sleeping army as was possible. Carts had carried the bodies over the plain, and before long the corpse fires would be lit and they would all wish they still had the sharp stench of woodsmoke in their nostrils. A burning body was not a pretty smell. Victorinus dreaded to discover what stench hundreds would make.

Finding the cooking fires, he smiled and made small talk with a soldier as he took five bowls of steaming porridge, balanced on a flat piece of wood. Leaving, he did not go immediately back to his tent and waiting family, but diverted to the centre of the camp, where the prisoners were being held.

Lupus Valentinus had not been given the privacy of a tent to spend his last night in. He was in a cage, previously used to house livestock, in open display of the passing soldiers. Propped up against the bars, he was covered in excrement and rotting vegetables. Victorinus nodded at the two guards barring the entrance, before stating his rank and demanding entrance. The prisoner looked up as he stooped into the cage.

'Sixtus Victorinus, I believe,' Valentinus said, his voice crackling like burning parchment.

'Aye.' Victorinus fought down the natural urge to salute, before sitting opposite the man and offering him a bowl. 'It's hot,' he said.

'Do you know I find my appetite rather diminished this morning.' Valentinus managed a smile. 'Some water would be appreciated though.'

Victorinus passed over a skin, and the rebel drank greedily. 'Ah, the sweet taste of fresh water. It's the little things you take for granted, isn't it?'

'Think you've been taking a few more liberties than that.'

'Well, what is life without a little gamble? I hear you're quite the gambler yourself, Tribune.'

'Aye, I was.' Victorinus adjusted his hat, feeling uncomfortable now, alone with this man. He tried to remember what impulse had driven him to come here. He looked away from the prisoner and found his eyes locking with Pastor. The youth was watching them both from twenty feet away, perched on a log beside a fire.

'He's been watching me all night,' Valentinus said.

'Wants to make sure you don't find a way to wriggle out of this cage, I don't doubt.'

'Yes, I dare say he does.' Valentinus winced as he sat up, rubbing at a sore point on his back. 'What is to be his fate?'

'Pastor's?' Victorinus frowned.

'Yes. Is he to swing from a noose with me? Would be a cruel thing, to let the treacherous boy live after all he has done to you.'

Victorinus scoffed. 'Gods, what a whoreson you are. The boy will live, and live well. I will see to that. Far as I can see, all he has done is what you made him do. With the right guidance and care, he will grow into a fine man.'

'From what I hear, Tribune, you are hardly the role-model type. I saw you hugging those boys of yours yesterday. I'm surprised they even knew who you were.'

Victorinus was still looking to Pastor, who in turn made a show of not noticing. 'Seems we've all made mistakes, traitor. Difference between us is I get a second chance at putting mine right. You'll be dead by sunset.'

'Yes. Yes, you're probably right.' Valentinus tilted his head as if considering that. 'When are they going to do it?'

Victorinus shrugged. 'Whenever the general is ready, I guess. You should try and eat your porridge, say your last prayers to whatever god it is you pray to.'

'He was asked to spare the others, you know. He declined, Theodosius. Though his son begged him to reconsider.'

'Aye, I know. Theo is a good man, though his father has his orders.'

'His ambition burns as bright as mine, you know.

Just you wait and see. Even if his time is passed he will do whatever he can to see his son advance.'

'Then he is a better father than you. I will arrange for Cassius to be brought to you before the executions. You can say your farewells to him if you wish.'

Victorinus rose and left the cage picking up the plank of wood with the four remaining bowls of porridge.

'I am sorry my son killed your friends,' Valentinus called as Victorinus moved off.

The tribune turned, a tear forming in the corner of his eye. 'You aren't sorry for a damned thing. Don't blame your sins on your son. You have much blood on your hands, much to answer for when you cross the river into the land of the dead. As I said, emperor of nothing, say your prayers.' And with that, he turned away.

* * *

It was late afternoon when the hangings began. The prisoners that were to be shipped across the known world were forced to watch as their commanders were dragged up the wooden stairs to the platform, nooses tied around their necks. They were not given the opportunity to speak, to repent their many sins or rage their defiance. Six by six they were raised to the platform; six by six their corpses were cut down. And so it went on.

Valentinus and Cassius were the last to die. The former at least managed it with a trace of dignity, his face set in a determined frown as he stood stoically as the rope was tightened around his neck. Cassius trembled and cried, shaking his head and begging for mercy. Victorinus found he had none for the boy. He'd expected to feel himself soften as the youth was dragged onto the platform, but the boy had killed Severus, as well as playing his part in Halfhand's demise.

They were pushed together, and they fell together, before dying together. And that was that. Victorinus gave a nod of approval, before adjusting his hat and turning away. He pushed through the crowd, avoiding all eye contact until there was open ground before him. 'Tribune!' a voice called, and Victorinus turned to see young Theo making his way towards him.

'Well met,' Victorinus said, extending a hand as the younger man approached.

'Has my father spoken to you yet?'

'Briefly, this morning, but only to ask after the wellbeing of my family. Why?'

'My cousin Maximus is to be given a temporary

command on the island, organising the remaining loyal forces and hunting down the last of the deserters. He says the west is full of them. You are to be appointed to his staff.'

Victorinus frowned. 'But I am in the areani. Who will operate north of the Wall?'

Theo laughed. 'My friend, we are in chaos south of the Wall! And besides, your man Drost has signed a treaty with Rome and has agreed to communicate any suspicious goings on in the far north. We need you here, Tribune. Your skills will be valuable.'

'So be it. Then I shall go and enjoy what time with my family I have. I bid you good day, Theo.'

He turned and walked away, through the celebrating soldiers getting drunker by the moment. He reached the edge of the tents and paused, a smile spreading across his face. Sarai was sat by a low-banked fire, Felicius and Lucia to one side of her, Drost and Pastor the other. His two boys ran around the small group with Marcelina, the children whooping with joy. Pastor was the first to see him, and he rose and approached, something clutched in his hand.

'This, I believe, is yours.' He held out a small leather pouch, worn and tattered.

Victorinus smiled all the wider. He took it and

rubbed his fingers across the leather. Reaching in, he pulled out a small wooden horse. 'I thought this lost,' he whispered.

'My brother had it. Gods knows how he found it, but that was ever like Cassius.' Pastor hesitated a moment. 'They are gone now?'

'Aye, lad, I'm sorry.' He reached out a hand and clasped the boy's shoulder.

Pastor cleared his throat and squared his shoulders. 'Don't be sorry. They got what they deserved. It is I who should be sorry, for everything I did, for what could have happened to your family—'

'They are fine, and you had no choice in any of what you did. You were wise enough to see things for yourself in the end, and brave enough to act on it when you did. That's good enough for me. I have been given a position on Maximus's staff, to help clear the island of the last of the deserters and rebels. Don't know what rank yet, don't know what I'll be doing. But I'd be grateful if you came along with me.'

There were tears in Pastor's eyes, tears of shame and relief, all at once. 'I'd be honoured to serve under you once more, sir.'

'Good lad. Your first job is to get your old commander some food, think you can manage that?'

Pastor grinned. 'Reckon I can, just about.' He saluted and walked away.

'Leaving me already, are you?' Sarai stood in the last red light of the day. Her skin was dark and smooth, her eyes dazzled. Victorinus thought he'd never seen anyone so beautiful. 'Aye, being given a new command, or so it would seem. But it won't be like before though, I'll be back as soon as I can.'

'Man has got to feed his family, I suppose.' She tilted her neck, kissed him long and deep. The children squealed as they ran around them, and quick as lightning, Victorinus reached down and scooped Maurus up, engulfing him in a bear hug. The boy laughed and winced at the rough touch of his father's beard as he kissed his cheek. 'Got something for you,' he whispered in his son's ear, before producing the horse.

'Amor!' Maurus said in delight, snatching the wooden horse from his father and hugging it tight.

'Promised you I'd bring it back, didn't I?'

'She kept you safe,' Maurus beamed.

'She sure did, lad. She sure did.'

He put the boy down and he went back to his games, chasing his younger brother around the fire. Victorinus looked from his friends to his wife, then finally down at his children. He'd had to lose a lot to remember what he'd had in the first place. Had to fall apart in order to put himself back together. But he'd faced his demons and won; even saved an empire in the process. He hugged his wife tight and raised two fingers to the setting sun.

He smiled; the worst days of his life were behind him.

* * *

MORE FROM ADAM LOFTHOUSE

Another book from Adam Lofthouse, *Raven*, is available to order now here:
https://mybook.to/RavenBackAd

HISTORICAL NOTE

Not much is known about the *barbarica conspiratio*, or barbarian conspiracy, that took place in Britain in the year AD 367. What is known is that for a period of time, Britain was almost completely cut off from the rest of the Western Empire, the island in disarray. Ammianus Marcellinus, the Roman historian who was in the east at the time, gives it a mere paragraph in his *The Late Roman Empire*, which perhaps shows that even those alive at the time had little idea of exactly what happened.

The historian Ian Hughes, in his book *Imperial Brothers*, which covers the reigns of both Valentinian and Valens, goes into a bit more detail, but again, he had little material to work with. We do know that

Fullofaudes and Nectaridus, two senior military officials in Britain, were killed early on, and that the famed magister militum Flavius Valerius Jovinus (note that in the book I have dropped the 'Flavius' from Jovinus's name, due to the amount of characters based on real people bearing the first name Flavius!) was first called upon to raise an army and sail to Britain to subdue the island. We know too that he never made it, possibly due to the activity of the Alamanni on the Rhine frontier. So the comes rei militaris Flavius Theodosius was sent in his place.

As to the why, that was left entirely to my imagination. Why had tribesmen from across the Wall and sea suddenly decided to attack the provinces of Britain at the same time? Valentia is a word that crops up from time to time when researching the later Roman empire. No one seems to be entirely sure as to exactly what it is, though. Whilst researching for *Eagle and the Flame*, I came across a senator named Lupus Valentinus who had been spared punishment for a grievous crime thanks to a brother in Rome, who Valentinian held in high esteem. Putting Valentinus and the barbarian conspiracy together sent my imagination swirling, and I had the bones for my story.

Rebellions were all too commonplace by the fourth century, and the people of Rome would have become all too accustomed to civil wars and periods of rapid change. What if Valentia had been part of one of them? Once the idea was in my head, it seemed too good to pass up. I had my antagonist; I had his ambitions and knew what drove him. What I needed was my hero.

The *miles areani*, the scouting unit that our favourite drunken Victorinus is a tribune of, are mentioned in various sources, both primary and secondary. As to the role they performed, it seems to differ from source to source! I stuck with them being a scouting unit, though I know of other novelists who have used them in a different capacity. I wanted to begin the story with a small core of characters, and follow their journey through an ever-changing political landscape. I do hope I've pulled it off!

There are, of course, certain key characters in the novel that spawn from my imagination, Victorinus and Felicius first amongst them. But Jovinus, Theodosius the elder and younger and Maximus were all real and all will play a huge part in the next twenty years or so of history. The Roman empire had gone through continuous change up to this point in the fourth century, and let me tell you, it's not about to stop. Victorinus and Felicius will be back, for once more civil war is in the air, and our two heroes must pick their side...

Eagle and the Flame is my fifth novel, and in many ways has been the hardest to write. As much as this novel is about change in the Roman world, whilst writing this my own life was turned upside down (and then there was Covid, and lockdowns, and the world seemingly becoming a stranger place to live). The words you have read are not the original ones that formed the core of the book, for I ripped up a draft and started again not once but twice whilst writing this. I started in the first person, writing from Victorinus's perspective, then decided I didn't like it and changed. Then I decided I still didn't like it, threw the pages on the flames and begun once more. I was certain there was a story in here waiting to be told, I just had to find the words to flesh it out. I think I've just about nailed it, and I certainly hope you do too!

I'd like to finish up by giving a huge thanks to the team at Boldwood Books. In particular my editor Vic Britton, whose keen eyes (and sharp knives) trimmed the fat from the story and made it a much more coherent read. (We won't talk about the number of historical characters in the book named 'Flavius', I fear that war is not yet over!) Also to Jennifer Davies who copy edited the manuscript, and unknowingly gave me a lesson in capitalisation and highlighted my lack of education with spelling and grammar. I owe you one! Thanks to Jacqueline Beard MBE who proofread the manuscript, finding yet more typos and a couple of continuity errors that had completely bypassed me. The book is so much better for all your input.

This book is dedicated to Jo Randall-Kattner, my aunt, who we sadly lost earlier this year. She was warm and bright, made time for everyone, and was always a vocal supporter of my work. The sun lost some of its glow when she left us. If you have enjoyed the story then a little review on Amazon or Goodreads would mean the world to me. Reviews sell books! And nothing makes me happier than a reader telling me they've enjoyed what I've written.

So once more, thank you for taking the time to read. Victorinus and Felicius will be back before you know it. Until the next time.

Adam Lofthouse

ABOUT THE AUTHOR

Adam Lofthouse has for many years held a passion for the ancient world. As a teenager he picked up *Gates of Rome* by Conn Iggulden, and has been obsessed with all things Rome ever since. After ten years of immersing himself in stories of the Roman world, he decided to have a go at writing one for himself. He lives in Kent, UK.

Sign up to Adam Lofthouse's mailing list for news, competitions and updates on future books.

Follow Adam on social media here:

ALSO BY ADAM LOFTHOUSE

Enemy of the Empire

Raven

Outlaw: Nemesis of Rome

Shadow of Rome

Eagle and the Flame

WARRIOR CHRONICLES

WELCOME TO THE CLAN ✕

THE HOME OF
BESTSELLING HISTORICAL
ADVENTURE FICTION!

WARNING:
MAY CONTAIN VIKINGS!

SIGN UP TO OUR
NEWSLETTER

BIT.LY/WARRIORCHRONICLES

Boldw♦♦d

Boldwood Books is an award-winning fiction publishing company seeking out the best stories from around the world.

Find out more at www.boldwoodbooks.com

Join our reader community for brilliant books, competitions and offers!

Follow us
@BoldwoodBooks
@TheBoldBookClub

Sign up to our weekly deals newsletter

https://bit.ly/BoldwoodBNewsletter